ELVIS
AND THE
UNDERDOGS
SECRETS, SECRET SERVICE, AND ROOM SERVICE

Also by Jenny Lee

Elvis and the Underdogs

ELVIS
AND THE
UNDERDOGS

SECRETS, SECRET SERVICE, AND ROOM SERVICE

Jenny Lee

illustrations by Kelly Light

BALZER + BRAY
An Imprint of HarperCollins*Publishers*

Elvis and the Underdogs: Secrets, Secret Service, and Room Service
Text copyright © 2014 by Jenny Lee
Illustrations copyright © 2014 by Kelly Light

Library of Congress Cataloging-in-Publication Data
Lee, Jenny, date
  Secrets, Secret Service, and room service / Jenny Lee ; illustrations
by Kelly Light. — First edition.
    pages cm. — (Elvis and the underdogs)
  Summary: A sickly ten-year-old boy and his talking therapy dog
find adventure in the White House.
  ISBN 978-0-06-223556-5 (hardback)
  [1. Service dogs—Fiction. 2. Dogs—Fiction. 3. Human-animal
communication—Fiction. 4. Sick—Fiction. 5. White House
(Washington, D.C.)—Fiction. 6. Presidents—Fiction.] I. Light, Kelly,
date, illustrator. II. Title.
PZ7.L512533Se 2014   2013043070
[Fic]—dc23   CIP
                                                              AC

Typography by Alicia Mikles
14 15 16 17 18 CG/RRDH   10 9 8 7 6 5 4 3 2 1
❖
First Edition

For my mom, Haekyong Lee.

Thanks for a happy childhood

and making me hot breakfast every morning.

ELVIS
AND THE
UNDERDOGS
SECRETS, SECRET SERVICE, AND ROOM SERVICE

1

This story starts with me superglued to a window-seat cushion on a sunny Saturday in March. I know that sounds pretty crazy, but the way things work in my life, it's not that weird. Allow me to introduce myself: I'm Benjamin Wendell Barnsworth, but no one calls me that unless I'm in trouble. Most people just call me Benji. I'm the smallest kid in my fourth-grade class, but it doesn't bother me. Have you ever heard the expression "small kid, big personality"? No? Well, that's not surprising, because I just made it up. Sounds good, though, right? Now back to our regularly scheduled story.

One of my favorite places in our whole house is the window seat. I love it. It's right underneath a huge bay window that overlooks our front yard. In the afternoon, the sun pours in and makes me warm and cozy. I just lean my head back and pretty soon it's snooze city. This time, when I woke up from my nap, I couldn't move my legs. It totally freaked me out until I realized it wasn't actually my legs I couldn't move—it was my pants. But even that was a problem, since my legs happened to be in those very pants.

Upon further investigation, I discovered I couldn't move my pants because they were superglued to the window-seat cushion! It didn't take a genius to figure out my twin brothers, Brick and Brett, were to blame. How did I know it was them? Let's just say this wasn't the first time I woke up and found myself superglued to the window seat.

"Brrrrrreeeeeeeet! Brrrrrriiiiiiiick! Get down here now!" I screamed.

"We're busy!! Why don't you come up here???" they yelled back, cracking themselves up.

"Ha! Ha! Very funny. You got me! Good one! You two better come down and help me remove my butt from this thing before Mom comes home, or all three of our butts are gonna be in huge trouble."

Normally, I don't get in trouble when the twins pull a stunt like this. My mom is loud and crazy, but she's fair. This was different. Ruining the seat cushion would end badly for everyone involved. Long silly story short, the twins had already ruined the other side of the cushion when they superglued me the first time and had to cut me out of my pants. We had used the oldest trick in the book when you mess up a cushion. You flip it over! *Ta-done!*

So this time around it's not like we could just flip the cushion over. What were my brothers thinking? Did they think it was a magic three-sided cushion? Oh right, I keep forgetting. The twins never think!

Sometimes, as crazy as it sounds, I do wish I could be more like my brothers, because I have the opposite problem. I always think too much. In fact, sitting on the window seat is my favorite thinking place. And lately I've been sitting there a lot, because I really miss my dog Elvis. I know this might sound weird—that I can't forget this giant black Newfoundland dog who I only had for three days, and who technically wasn't even mine to begin with—but I can't help it. Those three days with Elvis changed my life forever. So I sit here and think about him and look out the window, past our front yard, all the way down the street. If I squint my eyes real hard, sometimes I can almost picture a tiny black speck way, way in the distance, and I imagine what it would be like if the speck got bigger and bigger and suddenly there was Elvis running up the street back home to me.

So there I was, literally stuck in my thinking-and-missing-Elvis spot, when my mom came home from the grocery store.

"Hey, Benji, baby, come help me with the groceries," she called out.

Uh-oh! How was I going to help her when I couldn't stand up?

"Sure thing, Mom. But uh, you see, funny story . . ." Oh boy, big brain of mine, don't fail me now. "I would, but I super miss Elvis and I'm so sad . . . it's like I'm paralyzed, and I can't move."

I wasn't exactly lying to my mom. I just wasn't telling her the whole truth. And it was by far the smartest thing I could have come up with. Here's the thing about my mom: She loves to share feelings. Her feelings, my feelings, my dad's feelings, the across-the-street neighbor's feelings, even total strangers' feelings. If you have feelings you'd like to share, my mother is the best listener ever. She says keeping your feelings bottled up, especially the sad or bad ones, gives you wrinkles. And since I don't want to be a wrinkly ten-year-old, and when I share I usually get a snack, I'm pretty happy to open up to my mom on a regular basis.

My mom put a bag of groceries on the floor and bellowed for my brothers to unload the car. Then she pulled an ottoman over and sat next to me. The twins came down the stairs like they were running for a touchdown on the football field. They aren't the brightest, but even they knew my mom coming home wasn't a good thing. Without saying a word, they barreled out the front door to get the groceries. Or maybe they were running away, leaving me to deal with this sticky situation. (Sticky, get it?)

"Tell me everything. What's wrong, Benji?" my mom asked, putting her hand on my knee.

"I really, really miss Elvis, and sometimes I sit here and hope he's going to come back to me. I know that's never gonna happen, but I can't help it. And I thought it'd get better because it's been so long, but lately it seems worse."

I took a deep breath. Sure, I was praying my mother wouldn't realize I was superglued to the cushion, but what I said was actually 100 percent true, and it felt good to get it off my chest. My mom didn't seem the least bit surprised by what I said. I could tell because I'm pretty good at reading the furrows in her forehead. Different ones pop up depending on whether she's worried, mad, hungry-cranky, or regular-cranky.

"Benj, honey, it's totally and completely normal for you to miss Elvis. He was a very special dog. And even though you only had him for a few days, he was your first dog. And everyone always remembers the firsts the most. Like I remember your first step, your first word, your first haircut, and your first loose tooth."

"The first time I ended up in the hospital emergency room?"

"Well, that's one of the firsts I actually try to forget. But all the good firsts in your life are really important, and you'll remember them your entire life."

My mom was not kidding about remembering all my firsts, because she's what you would call a power scrapbooker, meaning you better watch out when she's doing it, because she's got a hot glue gun and she's not afraid to use it—on everything.

"Hey, where were you when you had your first banana split? Do you remember?" she asked.

"With you," I answered immediately. Did I remember? Did I remember? Of course I remembered. I remembered like it was yesterday. We were down the Jersey Shore on vacation, and I was about four years old. My brothers were out on the beach doing the normal fun stuff you do when you're on vacation, while I was covered from head to toe in pink medicated lotion because I'd had an allergic reaction to the motel sheets and had a horrible red rash pretty much everywhere.

Since I couldn't be out in the sun, my mom and I were stuck in our beachside motel room together watching television, and then the television just died on us. Like there was this crackling sound, it went briefly to static, and then it just went black. My mom started laughing and said, "When it rains, it pours, doesn't it, Benji, baby?"

I didn't know what she was talking about, because it wasn't raining. In fact, it was a perfectly sunny day out. Then she said it was time for the two of us to make our own vacation fun. She put one of my dad's huge flowery Hawaiian shirts on me, and she rubbed pink lotion all over her own arms and face so I wouldn't feel like I was the only one who looked funny.

Together we finally left that boring motel room and walked straight to the ice cream shop on the board-walk. It had this cool green mermaid statue holding up an ice cream like she was the fishy underwater version of the Statue of Liberty. Everyone stared at us like we were crazy. Well, they looked more at my mom, but everyone always looks at her because she has really big blond, curly hair.

"Two banana splits, please!" she said when it was time to order.

The waiter immediately explained that their banana splits were huge, so it'd be better if we shared one. And without missing a beat, she told him we were aliens from the planet Calamine, researching desserts on Earth, and our planet had a strict policy against sharing when it came to desserts. In fact, they had a policy against moderation in general.

That banana split was the most beautiful thing I had ever seen. The vanilla scoop was on the left, followed by the chocolate scoop, then the strawberry scoop on the end. There was hot fudge, caramel, and strawberry sauce, at least two inches of whipped cream, and chocolate sprinkles. It was my first banana split. And yes, I will remember it forever.

"Oh, I get it now," I said, licking my lips at the memory. "So you're saying since Elvis was my first dog, he's extra special, and that's why I miss him so much?"

"Exactly. And that's okay. And that's why you still feel sad."

My mom was right. I only had Elvis for three days, but he was my very first dog. Now I had Ripley. He's the dog I was supposed to get in the first place, but due to a mix-up, I got Elvis instead. Ripley is a yellow Lab, and he's the complete opposite of Elvis, meaning that he's only sixty pounds instead of two hundred, he's yellow instead of black, and his fur is short and coarse instead of long and silky. Elvis has this lion mane around his chest, but I never told him that, because it would have gone to his head, like he was King of the Jungle. Trust me, Elvis already has a big enough opinion of himself.

Ripley is really sweet, and he always listens to me. Sometimes I think he can tell what I'm thinking before I even say it. Like how I sometimes forget to turn my bedroom light off, and right as I'm about to get up out of the bed to do it, Ripley just bounds across my room and jumps up on the wall and flips the light switch off for me. Elvis never listened to me, always had an opinion about everything, constantly ordered me around, and once threw me out of a window at school. But the biggest difference between Ripley and Elvis is that Elvis can talk.

Yes, talk.

I know, I know, everyone has that reaction at first. Dogs don't talk in real life. Dogs only talk in comic strips, cartoons, television, and movies. I get that, you get that, but the way I see it, no one ever told that to Elvis—not that it would have mattered anyway, because I doubt he would have listened. Because he did talk, at least to me. I'm the only boy I've ever heard of who can talk to a dog. It might be because I had a seizure at school and passed out, which is why I needed to get a specially trained therapy dog like Elvis in the first place and why I got Ripley after him. A therapy dog can help me if I ever have a seizure again or another medical crisis. I figure maybe when I fell down and hit my head on the very hard hallway floor of my school, it caused my brain to be able to understand this one particular dog.

"Benji, earth to Benji, come in. Are you feeling better now?" My mom shook my leg, and for a second I got worried she'd realize I was superglued.

I nodded my head yes and gave her a smile. It was true. I did suddenly feel better talking about Elvis. "I do. Thanks, Mom. Hey, can I ask you one more thing?"

"Anything."

"Do you think it hurts Ripley's feelings that I still write letters to Elvis and that I miss him so much?" At the mention of his name, Ripley, who was lying below me on the floor, lifted his head. My mom petted him and shook her head.

"I think Ripley understands and is totally fine with it. He knows it doesn't mean you love him any less. Now, show me some love, okay?" And with that she leaned forward and gave me one of her big mama bear hugs. It was such a great hug that I temporarily forgot about my other situation, but I remembered it soon enough, because as she hugged me, she stood up. And when she stood up, she lifted me up along with the window-seat cushion. Uh-oh!

Right then the twins walked back in the door with the last of the groceries. They took one look at me getting hugged with the cushion stuck to my butt, dropped the bags on the floor, and ran back out the door.

"Whaaaaaaaat diiiiiid you twoooooo dooooooooo?!!!" my mom yelled, and since I was still in her arms, it was really, really loud.

My mom ripped me off the cushion, and I took some of the fabric with me on my pants. Then she had the same thought we did the first time this happened. She flipped the window-seat cushion over, which was when she saw the other messed-up side. And then there was even more yelling.

As punishment, she made the twins skip their pickup basketball game with their friends, which really bummed them out, because they live and breathe sports. They might not think, but they do know how to move, and they pretty much do it constantly.

But that wasn't the only punishment my mother

gave out. It got worse. Much, much worse. She also said we now had to do one of our least favorite things in the world, which is to go to Macy's and watch her shop for a new seat cushion. All three of us begged and pleaded, but to no avail.

"If one of you complains for even a second more, I'll make you pay for this cushion!" she said.

That shut us up immediately. Twenty minutes later I had on a new pair of pants, and I climbed into our SUV with Ripley and my brothers, and we silently headed to the mall. As my mom drove, I looked out the window, and even though I was petting Ripley, I found myself thinking of Elvis again.

Here's another thing you should know about Elvis. He prefers to be called by his full name: Parker Elvis Pembroke IV, and it's probably what they call him where he lives now. But I never called him that, mainly because I knew it bugged him, but also because to me he really seemed more like an Elvis.

I didn't even realize this until the Secret Service showed up at my house to take him back, but Elvis's initials spell out the word "pep." That just makes me laugh, because Elvis is the least peppy dog I know. If I had to describe Elvis in one word, I think grumpy-know-it-all-cranky-pants would probably be it.

You're probably wondering why I just threw the words "Secret Service" in there. Here's what happened. Elvis ended up at my house by accident. After he was born and trained at a farm in Tennessee, he was supposed to go live in the White House as the dog of the president of the United States! But instead there was a mix-up, and a giant crate of Elvis was delivered to my house on Fernbrook Lane in Pennsylvania. Eventually, they all figured out the mix-up, and after a few days the Secret Service showed up with Ripley, who was supposed to be my original therapy dog. What could I do? The president wanted his dog. I had to give Elvis back.

I write letters to Elvis at the White House, but I don't tell anyone except my mom, and that's only because I don't have a choice. She supplies the stamps. She also tracked down Agent Daniels, the lead Secret Service guy who picked up Elvis from our house. He thought she was joking when she asked him to read my letters, but once you hear my mom's does-it-sound-like-I'm-joking? voice, you can tell immediately she's not. So he tried to blackmail her for her award-winning red velvet volcano cake recipe, which is the cake she served him when he came for Elvis. Lucky for us, Agent Daniels was thinking about my mom's cake as much as

I was thinking about Elvis.

My mom refused to give up her recipe (she got it from her mother, who made her promise to pass it down to only one person in her life), but she promised she'd FedEx Agent Daniels one cake every month if he read Elvis my letters.

Agent Daniels emailed my mom to say he's become quite the popular guy at work because he shares at least half of her cake with the other Secret Service agents. He said every time the cake arrives at the White House, Elvis drops whatever he's doing and takes off running. I like to think it's not because he smells the cake, but because he's waiting for the letters from me that come with it. But it's probably not true. If me and a cake were drowning in a lake at the same time, I'm not sure Elvis would know which to save first. I can even hear his voice: "Benjamin, I have at least a few minutes to save you. A cake goes soggy very quickly indeed."

The funny thing is that Elvis can't even have any of the cake because there's chocolate in it, but my mom always throws in one cupcake that's the same recipe but without the chocolate just for him. So now I've written Elvis one letter a week for the three months, two weeks, and two days that he's been gone.

"Hey, Mom, did you get stamps today? But if you

didn't, that's fine too," I called out from the back of the SUV.

I hadn't mailed my latest letter yet because I was waiting for my mom to get some new cool stamps. I always like the special-edition stamps that the post office puts out. If you're going to have your letter inspected carefully because it's going to the White House, you might as well make sure it has a good-looking stamp on it.

"I did." She sighed. I could tell she was still upset about the cushion.

"Did they have some cool ones?"

"They did." She looked straight ahead, not even glancing in her rearview mirror at me. She turned to my brother who was sitting next to her in the passenger seat. "Brick, go into my purse and don't touch anything except the little paper envelope that has the stamps in it. Pull them out and hand them to Benji."

"Yes, Mom." Brick reached into my mom's purse and handed me the stamps. "Hey, Mom, can I have some gum?"

"What do you say?"

"May I have some gum, please?" Brick asked again, using his best good-boy voice.

"No, you may not," my mom replied, using her best

don't-pretend-to-be-a-good-boy-when-you're-not-one voice.

Whoa, withholding a stick of gum meant she was really mad. I almost felt sorry for Brick. Almost.

Normally when we get to the mall, my mom lets the twins walk around by themselves, and I tag along with them. But today she meant business. She made us all go to the dreaded, super-boring home section of Macy's. When we got off the elevator, she stopped so suddenly, Brett almost ran into her. Brick grabbed him and pulled him back just in time. I was not so lucky. I smashed right into Brick, and let me tell you this—I'm pretty sure the shirt he was wearing hadn't been washed in this decade. Ugh.

Mom turned to us and said, "Now, I should make you come pick out the new fabric, but I'm not. Mainly because I actually enjoy picking out fabric, and having you three hovering around me will make it less fun for me."

"Can we go upstairs and walk around?" Brick asked.

"No, you may not. You have to stay close by. And I shouldn't even have to say this to you boys, because you weren't raised in a cave, barn, or galaxy far, far away. But no horseplaying around inside the store. You break it, I buy it, you get no allowance. Got it?"

"Yes, Mom," the twins answered. She turned and walked away, leaving us in her chilly wake.

Barely thirty seconds passed before Brick and Brett started tossing their lacrosse ball around. It's like my brothers are actually wild animals, and no matter how much they want to listen to my mom, their bodies just take over, and suddenly they're doing exactly what she asked them not to. But in defense of their stupidity, let me just say my brothers aren't just good at sports, they're excellent at them. So they rarely miss. I thought about reminding them how mad Mom was and how she wouldn't even give Brick a stick of gum, but then I decided to mind my own business.

Ripley and I cruised around the baking section, looking for cool-shaped cookie cutters. I only saw the basic ones we already had at home: stars, moons, Christmas trees, candy canes, animals. Why do they always make the same old boring cookie cutter shapes? Why not make giraffes, ostriches, or kangaroos? Why don't they get the chance to be a cookie too? I dug around the cookie cutters, hopeful I'd find something new. Every now and then I'd hear *thwoooop!* That is the sound a lacrosse ball makes as it whizzes by at fifty miles an hour a mere six inches over my head. Ripley, of course, started barking.

"Oh, Ripley, thanks for looking out for me, but just ignore it. That's what I do."

What happened next, well, it's one of those things that are hard to explain. But here's what I recall. It started with a little old lady wearing a very bright yellow raincoat. She walked up to me in the baking section, and when I first saw her I thought, Why is she wearing a raincoat when it's not raining out?

The raincoat lady told me she was looking for a new, extra-long cookie sheet. I nodded politely. *Thwoooop!* The twins had adjusted the height of the ball to now be six inches above the lady's head. I assumed she couldn't hear well, because she didn't even look up. She stared at me. I stared back.

"Well?" she asked.

"Well what, ma'am?" I responded, not knowing how else to answer her question that wasn't even a question because it was just a word.

"Young man, can you help me find an extra-long

cookie sheet or not?"

"Sure. . . ."

I looked on the display table and saw a few stacks of baking sheets and picked one up. I read the label and sure enough, it said it was extra long. Well, it didn't say it in those words exactly, but it did say it had two extra bonus inches. I handed it over to the old lady with a smile.

"Are you sure this is extra long?"

"Well, I don't work here, but the sticker on the front seems to say it is."

"Hold it up and let's compare."

I reached for and picked up a cookie sheet off the display table. "Okay, I'll hold up mine and you hold up yours," I said.

And then I lifted the cookie sheet over my head at the exact time Brick hurled the lacrosse ball toward Brett and *WHAMMO!* That ball hit the center of the cookie sheet with such force, I'm surprised my arms are still attached to my body.

Now, I'm not sure you've ever heard the sound of a lacrosse ball going a zillion miles an hour hitting a metal cookie sheet. It's a sound that can only be described as ridiculously, incredibly loud. Kind of like a *THWACK!* and a *CLANK!* combined, which would make it a

THWANK!! Now, even more surprising than the loud noise was the fact that somehow I managed to keep my grip on the cookie sheet. The force of the ball on the cookie sheet and me holding on made me stumble backward a few feet right into a very tall display of fancy ice cube trays. So if you're wondering what happens when a fifty-pound kid holding up a cookie sheet gets hit with a lacrosse ball and slams into an eight-foot-tall display of assorted ice cube trays, well, the only thing that comes to mind is a bowling ball hitting bowling pins and getting a strike.

Ice cube trays flew everywhere. There was a loud crash. Ripley went nuts barking and barking. The little old lady in the yellow raincoat started screaming. And of course, my mom heard the commotion and came running, screaming, "Bennnnnnnjiiiiiii!" How she knew I was in the center of the commotion, I don't know. When I asked her about it later, she said it's "mama bear intuition." She says she can just feel when one of her cubs is in danger.

It's also true that my mom is used to me being the center of commotions. When it comes to me and trouble, I somehow always seem to attract it. It's been that way my whole life. I don't start the trouble. It finds me.

So imagine a huge pile of pastel-colored ice cube

trays and me splayed out in the center of them, still clutching the cookie sheet, with Ripley barking like crazy. I sat up, and when my mom saw me, her eyes bugged out so much, it kind of freaked me out. She had that wild-eyed look like there was an ax murderer standing behind me. I even turned around just to make sure there wasn't.

"Benji, you're bleeding!" she said, putting her hand on my face.

I looked down at my shirt, and sure enough, lots of blood. Then I touched my face and looked at my hand. Lots of blood. Then I made a super-quick inventory check to make sure I still had my tongue. I stuck it out. Phew. It was still there. But all I could taste was blood.

The blood could have come from any number of places, so I kept investigating. But before I could find it, my mom pulled me up off the floor, ran over to a display of kitchen towels, and pressed one to my face, wiping the blood off my chin.

"You're okay, you're okay, you're okay," she said, kissing my forehead over and over again. Then she looked at my brothers, who were finally standing still, their heads down. "Don't just stand there, you two! We have to take Benji to the emergency room. We're leaving . . . now!"

The next part was funny, but I wasn't really in a laughing mood. It was one of those things you see and you think in your head, This would be funny if I was watching it on TV, but when it's happening to you, no one is laughing.

Brett and Brick started playing rock, paper, scissors in the parking lot to see who would ride in the front seat. And they both threw rock, which meant they had to play again. Then they both threw paper, which meant they had to throw again, and they were about to do it again when my mom yelled so loud, I'm sure if a plane was flying overhead they would have heard her.

"WHAT ON EARTH ARE YOU DOING? ARE YOU REALLY PLAYING ROCK, PAPER, SCISSORS WHEN I'M HOLDING YOUR BABY BROTHER, WHO COULD VERY WELL BE BLEEDING TO DEATH?!" Before I could freak out, she leaned in and whispered, "You're totally fine and you're not going to die, but these two have it coming."

"BOTH OF YOU GET IN THE BACKSEAT RIGHT NOW! AND YOU SHOULD BE HAPPY I DON'T TIE YOU BOTH UP TOP LIKE A CHRISTMAS TREE THE WAY YOU TWO HAVE BEEN BEHAVING. DON'T THINK I DON'T KNOW THAT THIS IS YOUR FAULT."

The twins scrambled into the very back seat. My

23

mom buckled me into the seat behind her. Ripley jumped in next to me, and off we went. For the first two minutes it was totally silent. Then Brick leaned forward.

"Hey, Mom," he called out from the backseat. "Now can I have a piece of gum?"

3

The next thing you know, I was sitting on a chair at my second home, the hospital emergency room. Unfortunately, I'm at the hospital way more often than the average kid. And this visit was breaking a pretty good run for me, because I hadn't been to the hospital for six whole weeks. You see, I was born super premature, so I spent the first few months of my life in the hospital, and ever since then I've been one of their best customers, because you name it, I've probably had it, sprained it, fallen off it, or had an allergic reaction to it. But today, lucky for me, Dino, my favorite nurse, was on duty. Dino gave me VIP status years ago.

He automatically gets paged if he's on duty and I'm in the hospital. Dino is a senior nurse because he's been working here for more than twelve years, so he knows everyone and everyone knows him. Though he's hard not to know, because he's also crazy tall and crazy big. He has a deep voice that always makes me think of a giant bullfrog, if a bullfrog was the size of a football field.

Dino pulled back the curtain, picked me up like I weighed nothing, and set me on a gurney. He cleaned off my face and then put this magnifying contraption thingie on his head so he could get a good look at my lip, which was completely busted and still bleeding.

As Dino bent over me, my mom bent over him. I knew she was bothering him, because he had that expression on his face. Kind of like he just opened a Go-Gurt tube and started to suck on it, but the yogurt had gone bad.

My mom and Dino respect each other, but they aren't exactly friends. She drives Dino batty because she can be a little melodramatic. Dino says the hospital has enough real drama as it is, so it doesn't need all the extra-whipped crazy cream she adds with her oversize personality and her healthy set of lungs. Dino likes to keep calm, hang mellow, stay loose. When he gets excited, people get nervous because he's huge, so he's learned to be steady as she goes. Plus, Dino's mom is apparently a lot like my mom.

"Mrs. Barnsworth, please. You're so close I can tell what you had for lunch."

I cracked up despite the fact that Dino was still holding my lip.

"Oh really, Dino? Then tell me—I'd love to hear it. What did I have for lunch?" my mom asked, crossing her arms.

When Dino rolls his eyes it's funny enough, but when Dino rolls his eyes while wearing magnifying goggles, it's super funny. I laughed even harder.

"Little dude, stop squirming."

"Thorry."

Dino released my lip, sat back, and almost bumped heads with my mom. He let the whole guess-my-lunch challenge go.

"Here's what I think happened," he said, flipping up his goggles. "I think Benji bit his upper lip when everything went down, and then he busted up his lower lip when he hit the floor or got too up close and personal with a flying ice cube tray. So it was kind of a one-two punch, a feat that only our little man Benji could manage while also taking down the kitchen section of our local department store. By the look of your shirt and this towel, a nosebleed may be in there too."

"Yeah, I bet my nose felt left out and was all, like, 'Hey, I'm the one who usually bleeds the most around here. Who said you two lips could bust open and bleed like that? I'll show you how to bleed.' And then the nose joined in and really made a mess. All together now, let's bleeeeeeeed!"

"Benji, that's not funny. And it's gross."

"Sorry, Mom."

Dino winked at me to show me he thought it was funny and said, "Okay, I guess it's time to decide whether I should superglue your lip."

"Superglue?! Superglue is what got me into this mess to begin with! You can't be serious!" Ripley popped up and stood close to the gurney to calm me down.

"Oh, I'm serious," said Dino.

"But—but—but if you superglue my lips shut, how will I talk? How will I get them apart?" I asked in horror.

Dino and my mom just started laughing, and Dino said, "No one said anything about supergluing your lips together. What I meant was whether I should superglue your bottom lip together where you managed to bust it wide open. It'd hurt less than stitches."

"Stitches?! Who said anything about stitches?! Do I need stitches?! I hate stitches! Oh no, anything but stitches!" I tried to leap off the gurney and make a run for it, but Dino was too fast for me and his hand was too big, because he basically stopped me from going anywhere by holding a mere two fingers against my chest.

"Yo, Benji, no stitches. I promise. I shouldn't have even brought it up. Totally my bad. Really." Dino looked over at my mom for help, but she just stood there with her arms crossed, being all smug and waiting for Dino to finally admit that he needed her help. Dino, of course, refused and plowed on. "These days it's easier to use glue to seal up wounds as opposed to . . . well, that other thing I won't mention, so I'm thinking that's what we should do with your bottom lip. Since you've already lost a lot of blood, I think we need to keep the rest inside your body, if possible. How does that sound?"

"Sounds good to me." I nodded. "But you're doing the supergluing, right? I kind of have a tendency to glue myself to things whenever I try to use it. Isn't that right, Mom?"

My mom smiled. "Yes, Benji, you supergluing yourself to the banister of the stairs is one of my favorite memories. Okay, I'm going to check on the twins and make sure they know I know this whole fiasco is their fault by giving them my best you-better-be-nervous face. Be right back." And she exited the curtained area.

Then I heard the snap of Dino putting on some new rubber gloves. He sat on a stool and took my bottom lip in between his thumb and his first finger to hold it still. I was very impressed with Dino's supergluing skills. He was done in, like, two seconds, and his hand didn't even shake.

"Okay, all done. But let's let it dry, so sit still."

I nodded.

"Okay, now let's be still in that way where you actually don't move."

I was about to nod again, but then I realized he was making a joke. So this time I did as I was told.

"Hey, so I haven't seen you in a while, B. I feel like you've grown an inch, or is it that you just have bed head?"

"Half an inch is bed head and probably half an inch is actual height. I stopped drinking coffee. I heard it stunts your growth." I spoke without moving. It's harder than you think.

"What? You used to— Awww, you got me. You had me there for a second." Dino finally released my lip.

"Hey, you know, I've been seeing a lot of the First Dog."

First dog? Was Dino a mind reader? How did he know my mom and I were just talking about that very topic this morning? *Déjà weird.*

"Yeah, Mom says it's natural to miss Elvis this much, because he was my first dog and that means he holds a special place in my heart. I mean, life. In my life."

"Little man, I meant First Dog, like in the First Dog of the country, not as in your first dog. But I guess that's the same thing. Anyway, I see him all the time on the news."

"Oh right, yes. Of course. I knew you meant that. Hey, do you think he ever thinks about us?"

"Highly doubtful."

Dino is not a man who minces words.

"Really? Not even a little?"

"I don't know, B. Think about his life right now. He lives in the White House. He gets to hang out with Secret Service agents. He gets to poop and chase squirrels on the South Lawn. And they probably feed him the best of the best there. For a dog, he's got a pretty sweet life. Every time I see him on television, he's got a different collar on. He's always sitting behind the president during his speeches. Apparently, lots of people make him collars and send them to the White House.

Usually with flags and stuff. Can you imagine having time to sew tiny flags on a dog collar for kicks?"

It was hard for me to swallow the thought that Elvis wasn't thinking about me at all, but Dino was probably right. Elvis had a way cooler life now, and he was probably so busy that he didn't have much time to think about boring old busted-lip me.

"Well, maybe he doesn't have time to miss me, like, every second, but I bet he thinks about me from time to time. You know, like when the president is busy doing president-y stuff." Surely he thinks about me when he hears the letters I send him? What if he doesn't even care? Just the thought of that made my stomach hurt, and I felt terrible.

"Whoa, whoa, what's happening here?" asked Dino. "You're looking a little green, kid. Do you need a throw-up basin?"

I shook my head no, and then I shook my head yes. Dino quickly handed me a bedpan, but nothing happened. "What about that night at the morgue with Elvis?" I asked. "I mean, that was pretty exciting, wasn't it? Elvis has to remember that night."

"Sure was. That was a fun night. I regret deleting all those pictures. If I had known Elvis was the president's dog, I would have kept them."

32

The night Dino, Elvis, and I snuck down to the morgue was probably one of the most exciting nights of my entire life. But I guess it probably wasn't for Elvis. He'd probably had about fifty nights as exciting as the morgue since he went to live at the White House. I sighed. "Well, at least I'll always have my morgue memory."

"Morgue? What's this about the morgue?" My mom popped her head back in. "What memory do you have about a morgue? Benji? Dino? Someone answer me, please."

Luckily, I changed the subject effectively, because I leaned over and puked. Ripley barely got out of the way in time. My mom's shoes? Not so lucky.

"Hey, B?"

I looked up at Dino. He was smiling down at me. Remember the guy has worked in the emergency room for the last twelve years. A little puke doesn't even faze him.

"Yeah, D?"

"I'm really glad I gave you that bedpan to throw up in."

I smiled weakly. "Oh, I guess I forgot."

Dino ran his giant gloved hands around the top of my head. He turned to my mom. "Did he bump his head when he wiped out?"

My mom shook her head. "I don't know. I didn't see it happen."

Dino looked squarely at me. "I feel a slight bump right above your hairline. Did you hit your head when you crashed into the ice cube tower?"

"Maybe? Why?" I ran my own fingers along my head and felt the bump he was talking about. "You know, this might not be a new bump. It could be an old bump I've always had. Mom, what do you think, new bump or old bump?"

"I honestly don't know, Benji," my mom said, feeling the bump. "Is it bad if it's a new bump?"

"Not necessarily. But I want to know if it's an old bump or a new bump, because if it's a new bump, we have to rule out a concussion."

"You think I have a concussion?" I asked. I had one before, and let me tell you . . . concussions are not fun.

"No, I don't think you have a concussion. But I have to make sure, or Dr. Helen will have my butt on a platter."

"Hey, I've got an idea," I said. "Maybe we should make a bump map of my head. You know, so the next time I bump my head and end up here, we'll know immediately if it's a new bump or an old bump that's posing as a new bump."

My mom looked at me. It was hard to tell whether she thought I was the smartest of her three kids or just the weirdest.

"Benji, that's a brilliant idea. So when we get home I'll shave your head, and use tracing paper to do a chalk rubbing of all your bumps, and . . ."

"Shave my head? Who said anything about—" I stopped. My mom was clearly pulling a fast one.

She smiled and winked at me. "Gotcha!"

4

I wish I could say that Dino's revelation about Elvis didn't bum me out, but it did. I know he didn't mean to hurt my feelings, and he'd feel terrible if he even knew I was so upset about it. Dino is always looking out for me. He moved me to a private room while we waited to hear from Dr. Helen, and he told my mom he'd check in on me while she took the twins home, changed her shoes, and picked up takeout for dinner. He even brought me a grape ice pop for my lip. But what he said about Elvis not really missing me when I missed him like gangbusters made my chest hurt in a way that I knew had nothing to do with my big wipe-out at Macy's.

Before I met Elvis, if I was in a bad mood, I'd hang

out alone in my room and read books to get my mind off things. The truth is, I used to be kind of a loner before Elvis, and I didn't have any real friends. It's not that I didn't have any friends because I'm super weird (I'm the normal kid amount of weird), or I smell (I don't), or I look funny (I'm no Prince Charming, but I'm perfectly average-looking except for my height, and weight, and the size of my ears), or I'm boring (if anything I'm the opposite of boring and have been told I'm oozing with personality). I just missed a lot of school because I was sick a lot, and I kept a low profile because I didn't like trouble from our school bully, Billy Thompson. And, well, it's hard to make friends when you feel like you're so different from regular kids. So I didn't put myself out there very often.

Then Elvis came, and he taught me something really important. Everyone needs their own pack. Elvis explained that having a pack is one of the most important things in life. Dogs and humans are social beings, and we need to feel connected to others.

Your pack is your group of friends, your peeps, your comrades, your go-to's, your brothers from another mother, your sisters from a different mister, your buddies, your buds, your pals, your boys, you get the picture. And these days my pack consists of two really close friends. There's Alexander Chang-Cohen, who is half Korean and half Jewish and has this amazing ability called total recall, where he remembers every single thing he reads and experiences every single day. It makes him very useful and a little weird, but that's why we're such good friends. We both used to feel so different from everyone else. Now we still feel different, but we do it together.

The third person in our pack is Taisy McDonald. She's the tallest girl in fourth grade, and the best athlete in our entire town and possibly our whole state too. She almost made it to the Olympics as a gymnast, but after years of competing and practicing, she had to stop because she grew too tall. Both of her parents are world-famous athletes. Her dad is an ex-NFL football player who has two Super Bowl rings, and her mother is Swedish and has a few Olympic medals. Now, the Taisy most people know is popular, crazy competitive, and a total tomboy jock. But she's actually super girlie too, meaning she always smells good, she talks a lot about clothes and shoes and accessories, and when you get a note from her at school, you can bet it'll have the craziest curlicue handwriting you've ever seen with pictures of hearts and daisies.

Taisy doesn't show this side to everyone, because she says society expects athletes to be a certain way. Then she likes to explain how women are complicated creatures. It's kind of like she's two different people, but the cool thing is that I get to see both sides of her, which is how I know we're real friends.

Now sure, it's great having friends to eat ice cream with, see movies with, and even be bored with. But I was also learning that having friends made it harder to sulk and be sad about things. Before I had a pack, the only one who noticed I was mopey was my mom. Now I had Taisy, and she knew immediately if something was bothering me. I mean, I had been alone in my hospital room for only a few minutes before Taisy sent me this text:

I CANNOT BELIEVE THAT (picture of a little sheep) ARE IN THE (picture of building next to a picture of an ambulance) AND (a little sheep) DIDN'T (picture of telephone) ME AND (a little computer with arms and legs) IMMEDIATELY. I HAD TO FIND OUT FROM MY UNCLE (picture of dinosaur)?!!! (Entire row of little yellow frowny faces)

Here are the things you need to know about that text: The little sheep pictures don't mean sheep. Each one is supposed to be a female sheep, otherwise known as a ewe, which Taisy uses instead of typing the letter

39

U like the rest of the free world. The building is the hospital, and the computer with arms and legs is the emoji picture Taisy uses to refer to Alexander Chang-Cohen because he's so smart and his brain has so much information we call him the human computer. And the UNCLE followed by an emoji dinosaur means Uncle Dino. Oh, did I not mention that? It turns out that Taisy is Dino's niece. And that's a complete coincidence.

I wasn't sure what to reply, so I went with short and sweet.

Sorry!

I received a text right back that she and Alexander Chang-Cohen were coming to the hospital to check on me. I wasn't exactly in the mood for company, but I didn't really have a choice. When it comes to my pack of three, what Taisy says goes.

So less than an hour later Alexander Chang-Cohen, Taisy, and I were all sitting around my hospital room, eating take-out fried chicken. Okay, they were eating fried chicken, and because of my busted lips I was just eating the mashed mac and potatoes cheese (which is what I call the yummy goop that you get when you mix, you guessed it, mac and cheese and mashed potatoes). While we ate, I told them the crazy story of how I ended up in the emergency room, and Alexander Chang-Cohen immediately said the probability of the ball hitting the cookie sheet was extremely low because the timing had to be just right.

"Yes, but the probability of it happening to Benji is very high," Taisy said. She looked right at me. I got a little distracted by the sparkle of her rhinestone barrette. "You're absolutely, positively the most accident-prone person I know, and I mean that as a compliment."

"I'm the most accident-prone person I know too," I joked.

"I can think of someone more accident-prone," Alexander said. "Wile E. Coyote."

Taisy and I cracked up, and Alexander smiled. He isn't the best joke teller, so he feels extra proud when we find him funny.

"Hey, you three, a little less laughing and a little more eating, okay?" Taisy's dad popped his head into the room from the hallway, where he had been standing talking to my mom.

"You don't have to check up on us, Daddy," Taisy said as she rolled her eyes. Taisy and her dad are really close, but he's a little too intense. He might be Dino's half brother, but Mr. McDonald has a completely different personality. Let's just say Mr. McDonald didn't win two Super Bowl rings by keeping calm, hanging mellow, and staying loose.

"I'm not checking up, I'm just saying good-bye. I'm taking off, and Alexander's mom said she'd pick you up in two hours."

"Two hours? That's, like, seven thirty. Remember, it's Saturday night, so I get a one-hour-later bedtime."

"I didn't forget," said Mr. McDonald. "I thought you and I could watch some tape of your archery practice from earlier. You know, review technique. I'll make popcorn."

"Daddy, c'mon, you pinkie promised you wouldn't get all crazy about archery!"

"Watching tape isn't crazy. It's just being smart. It's getting the most out of practice."

Taisy's eyebrow went up. Watching these two go back and forth was like a tennis match. Now the ball was back in Taisy's court.

"Dad, don't make me tell Mom on you."

And game, set, match to Taisy. Mr. McDonald shook his head and sighed. Taisy ran over and hugged him.

"I love you, Dad, but you have to go now."

"I love you too, champ." Mr. McDonald leaned down and gave Taisy a kiss on top of her head. Taisy playfully pushed her dad toward the doorway, and he walked out into the hallway, only to pop his head back in a moment later. "What if I let you make a caramel apple? Then can we watch the tape?"

"Sold!" Alexander Chang-Cohen shouted, raising his hand.

"Alexander!" Taisy warned.

Alexander put his hand down. "Sorry, but you know how carried away I get about caramel apples."

"Daddy. I'm texting Mom a pineapple and some frowny-face emojis right now." (Whenever Taisy texts about her dad, she uses a tiny picture of a pineapple, meaning he's prickly and tough on the outside, but supersweet on the inside.)

He put his hands over his head and said, "Please don't tattle-emoji on me! I'm going. I'm going!" And then he left.

"Hey, Alexander," I asked when the door closed behind Mr. McDonald. "Did you bring your laptop?"

Asking Alexander Chang-Cohen if he has his laptop is like asking a fish if it can breathe under water. He pulled it out, logged on to the hospital Wi-Fi network, and then put it on the tray table in front of me so I didn't have to get up. I immediately Googled "Elvis first dog" and clicked the "Images" button. An entire page of Elvis pictures filled the screen.

"Scooch over, Benj. Alexander needs to fit up here too," Taisy said, jumping onto my bed. "I need your opinions on my new signatures. Will you vote on which ones you like best? You stay in the middle, Benji. Knowing your luck, you'll scooch too far and fall off the other side of the bed. Alexander, sit on the other side of Benji, and we'll be his human guardrails."

Ripley whined. I guess he could tell I was a little agitated. Frankly, I didn't want to look at different versions of Taisy's signature while being squished by my friends. What I really wanted to do was keep searching for Elvis online.

"So what do you guys think?" Taisy asked, holding up her samples. "Do you like when I add that extra curlicue on my *y*, or is it too much?"

Sometimes when Taisy talks about things like clothes and cute signatures, I feel like she's an alien. I mean, there's just no way we can both be made up of the same stuff. I wondered if Alexander Chang-Cohen felt the same way. Maybe he did, because he didn't answer her question either. But then she nudged him.

"I don't think it's too much. I like it. My favorite is the one where you make a little vine of roses with the tail of your *y*, but that seems impractical when it comes to your everyday signature."

"I wonder if you can have more than one signature that you use regularly," I said.

"That's a good question. Benji, why don't you Google it?"

"I will in a second. But first I want to look for videos of Elvis. Dino said he sees him on TV all the time, so they must have videos online, right?" Taisy and Alexander Chang-Cohen didn't look surprised at all when I brought up Elvis, so I kept going. "Dino thinks Elvis's life is so exciting he probably never thinks of me at all, which is probably true but still sort of hurts my feelings. So I thought if I could see videos of Elvis, I'd be able to look at him and know if he seems the same, or if by chance maybe he looks a little sad because he misses me too. I know it's silly."

Taisy reached over and placed her hand on my arm, and I stopped talking.

"Benj, it's not silly at all. And what does Uncle Dino know about how Elvis feels anyway? He knows nothing about dogs. Trust me, I'd never let him babysit Princess Daisy."

Princess Daisy is Taisy's dog, and she's about as different from Elvis as you can get. She's small, off-white, and very ladylike. When Elvis and Princess Daisy met, I suddenly understood the whole opposites-attract thing, because it was like puppy love at first sight. Elvis got all silly over her immediately. Taisy thought it was super-cute, but I just thought it was weird.

"Alexander, who do you think is right? Dino or Taisy?"

"I don't know. I mean, I don't have enough data to make an informed opinion." Alexander Chang-Cohen looked a little nervous.

"What does your gut tell you?"

"I'm not sure, because right now it's a little full from dinner. So it's saying, Why did you have to eat that last chicken leg?"

"Alexander, stop avoiding the question."

"Obviously, I'm not a dog, but I know that if I was away, I'd miss you, even if I was somewhere exciting like on the moon. I don't know if where you are matters as much as that you're not with your friends. Does that make sense?"

"Awwww, that's so sweet." Taisy reached her long arms around me so she could do a group hug sort of thing, which was kind of awkward but nice too. "Benji, you knew Elvis best. What do you think?"

"I wish I could say he looks sad and like he misses me," I said, leaning forward to look closely at the pictures on the screen. "But he seems happy in these pictures. Then again, it's hard to tell for sure."

"Well, then, forget the pictures. We should do a search for personal videos that people took and uploaded," Alexander said, taking over his laptop. "You never know. Maybe there's some dog nut out there who's really into filming the First Dog."

And just like that, Alexander found it. The video of Elvis that changed everything.

I hit play over and over again. Elvis stood calmly behind the president while he gave a speech on the White House lawn. Then, suddenly, Elvis turned his head, staring directly into the camera. Next he moved his tail around, like there was a fly bothering him. Or worse, a bee.

"Why is Elvis doing that with his tail? Did he always move his tail like that?" Alexander Chang-Cohen pointed to the screen.

"I don't really remember seeing him ever do that. Maybe there's a fly or a bee he's trying to get rid of?" I said, but it just didn't seem like something Elvis would do.

Taisy leaned in to get a better look. She smelled like grapefruit—not the sour yellow kind, but the pink kind with sugar on top. Taisy has a very big collection of fruity lip glosses and lotions.

"I don't think he's trying to swat a fly. Then he'd swish his tail more, like the way a horse does," said Taisy. "It looks like he's doing that thing where he's tapping his foot because he's nervous, except it's not his foot, it's his tail. Rewind that part where he starts doing that thing with his tail again."

So I did, and the three of us stared at the screen. And we noticed that he wasn't moving his tail at all in the beginning. But as soon as he looked away from the president and right at the camera, he nodded his head just a tiny bit, and then he started tapping his tail against the ground. *Thump, thump, thump, thump, thump, thump.*

"Whatever he's doing, it doesn't look random. It looks like he's doing it on purpose, as if he's trying to say something, like he's using a . . . ," Alexander said.

And then all three of us said it at once, like lightning hit us at the same time: "Code!"

Now that we'd said it, it looked exactly like that. I was just relieved Alexander Chang-Cohen noticed it first, because I know how crazy it is to think a dog is using his tail to tap out a secret code. Alexander Chang-Cohen is a lot of things, but he's not crazy. In fact, he's one of the smartest kids I know. So I knew he was right.

"It's Morse code! It has to be. Start it over, Benji, and I'll try to decipher it. Taisy, hand me some paper and one of your glitter pens."

Taisy and Alexander Chang-Cohen moved the laptop toward the end of my bed and leaned across it. Taisy wrote down the dots and the dashes that she felt Elvis was doing, and as she did, Alexander Chang-Cohen converted them to letters. I tried to remain calm, because the excitement of it all was making me warm, which is usually an indicator that I'll get dizzy and faint. Ripley knew immediately, so he got up and whined for me to pet him. There's something calming about having a dog nearby, especially a dog as highly trained as Ripley. Ripley knew I was overexcited before I did.

After petting Ripley's head a few times, I calmed down and looked over at the piece of paper that Alexander Chang-Cohen and Taisy were working on. So far the letters they had were *B, E, N, J, C, O, M*. Benjcom? What's a benjcom? Then Alexander wrote down the letter *E* under the one dot that was the next letter, and I realized it didn't say "Benjcom," it said "Benj come"! It was true. Elvis was actually thumping his tail in code! And it was to me! The secret coded message was to me!

Suddenly I felt warm and everything went fuzzy. Just as I was about to faint, Ripley put his front legs up on the bed and licked my face. I blinked a few times, taking a few deep breaths. As the room came back into focus, Dino came in.

"What's going on? Benji, are you okay?" he asked. I guess I still had a funny expression on my face.

"I'm fine, Dino. False alarm. I thought I was going to faint for a second."

I guess it's Dino's job not to take the word of a ten-year-old patient. He immediately took my temperature and checked my blood pressure. He also checked my new bump that may be an old bump, and it seemed the same too. Only when he was positive I was fine did he turn around to greet his favorite niece, Taisy.

"Taisybell, how goes it?" He held out his hand for a high five. She ignored it and threw her arms around his waist instead. He lifted her up off the ground like she weighed nothing. She squealed with delight.

"How's my favorite uncle?"

"I'm all good. I'd be done with my day soon if I didn't have to hang around to find out what we're doing with little man B, though."

I immediately felt bad. "Dino, you don't have to stay on my account. You should—"

"Little man, stop. I'm just teasing. I've got time. Relax. Your BP is a little high, so the name of the game is to keep calm. I'll be back at the end of my shift to check in on you, okay? Bye, Taisybell. Alexander, you make sure these two behave themselves, okay?"

"Yes sir, Mr. Taisy's uncle."

As Dino walked toward the door, I called out to him. "Hey, Dino." He turned around in the doorway, and I couldn't help thinking he was almost as big as a door himself. "Thanks for texting Taisybell and telling her I was here. It's nice to have some company."

"No sweat. I always know what's good for my patients." He smiled and then he was gone. After a few seconds, Taisy walked over to the doorway and peeked out, just to make sure the coast was really clear.

Taisy and Alexander looked at me, their eyes big with wonder. "Now what?" Taisy asked.

"I mean, this is incredible, absolutely crazy incredible! Well, technically I guess not that incredible, because it's actually happening, which literally means it is, in fact, credible. But you can see why I'm reacting like this, right? Your dog sent us a secret coded message!" said Alexander.

"Yeah, yeah, we get it, Alexander, but that doesn't change my question. Now what?" Taisy repeated.

"Now we need a plan to get to Washington, DC!" I said, sitting up in my bed. "We have to save Elvis!"

5

Maybe it was the bump on my head, but no matter how hard I tried, I couldn't come up with a way to get us to Washington, DC, to save Elvis. I thought about it all night in the hospital, all the way home after Dr. Helen released me (I guess she really did have a map of my head, because she immediately declared it an old bump), and all the way to school the next day. I thought about it so much that my head hurt. Then, just when I was about to give up, I smelled watermelon. It was Taisy, of course. She came up behind me in the school hallway before lunch, grabbed my arm, and pulled me into the empty gym.

"I've got it," she said. "I have the perfect plan. We're going to DC."

"What is it?" I asked, totally eager to hear it, but also a little jealous of Taisy. How did she come up with a plan before me? Elvis was my dog, after all.

"The National Spelling Bee. The only problem is we have to get Alexander to agree. If he wins the school spelling bee, he'll go on to the citywide spelling bee, and if he wins that, he'll go on to the state spelling bee, and if he wins *that*, he goes on to the National Spelling Bee in Washington, DC. We go along with him to offer moral support. Bingo! We're all in DC."

"Taisy, in case you haven't noticed, Principal Kriesky is obsessed with the spelling bee, and he's posted signs all over the school. The school spelling bee is tomorrow. There's no way Alexander will be ready so soon."

"Alexander doesn't have to be ready. He's a human computer, remember? He remembers every single thing he's ever read, which means he probably knows how it's spelled too. He can make it all the way to the national championships without even preparing. Benji, it's our best shot at saving Elvis."

"Let's just say this plan of yours works. When would it get us there?"

"In six weeks."

"Six weeks? We can't wait six weeks! He could be dead by then!"

"What? Don't say that. Look, I wish we could get there sooner, but for now, this is all we've got."

I really didn't want to wait six weeks, but six weeks was way closer than waiting till summer vacation, which was what my mom said when I asked her the other night if she'd take me to DC to visit Elvis. "Have you run this by Alexander yet?" I asked.

"No." Taisy shook her head and gazed nervously at the basketball hoop above my head. "I wanted to talk to you first."

I have to admit it felt good when she said it. Like I was important. Like I was essential to the success of the whole plan. "Do you think he'll go for it?"

"No. Absolutely not. That's why you have ask him. You're the only one who can convince him to go. I'll be the one to coach him."

"Wait—why don't you think he'll do it?"

Taisy raised her eyebrows at me. Clearly she thought I should already know the answer to that. "Oh, let's see. Maybe because he hates being the center of attention, or because he doesn't like speaking in front of crowds, and also because he hates surprises. And this plan has all three of those things, so that's how I know."

"So what do we do?"

"I don't know, Benj. I was hoping you might take

the baton from me and run with it."

Ugh, I hate when Taisy uses sports analogies. I mean, sometimes I have no clue what she's talking about. Once she was talking about going full-court press, and all I could think of was grilled cheese sandwiches. But I did understand this particular reference. She was talking about those Olympic relay running races where some-one runs with a baton and then passes it to the next team member. But my problem was that now that I had the baton, I didn't have anyone else to pass it to. Or at least that's what I thought, until I heard a voice say, "Don't tell him ahead of time."

Taisy and I turned around, because we hadn't seen anyone in the gym when we came in. We still didn't see anyone. For a split second I thought, Oh brother, please don't tell me I have to deal with a talking ghost on top of dealing with a talking dog.

"Who's there?" Taisy asked.

Billy Thompson, the school bully, walked out from underneath the bleachers. I looked at Ripley, who was sitting by my feet, and whispered, "Thanks for the heads-up, Ripley." Ripley thumped his tail. He thought I was actually being sincere. He just didn't get sarcasm like Elvis.

Billy Thompson had bullied me for years at school.

I had been totally terrified of him, but when Elvis was here, Billy and I had a showdown. And Billy even helped save my life. Then I found out he has a secret fake foot. Since then, I wouldn't say we've been friends, but we do have an unspoken understanding. You don't bother me, and I won't bother you; you don't try to stuff me in the toilet in the boys' bathroom, I won't tell people you have a bunch of cool fake feet with different shoes on them. Anyway, I guess whatever unspoken understanding we had was now over, since he was talking to me out loud.

Taisy's a little friendlier with Billy than I am. She's not scared of anyone. "Billy, what are you doing under the bleachers? And how long have you been there?" She stood with her hand on her hip to show she meant business.

Billy shrugged. "Long enough to know you shouldn't tell someone something they don't want to hear until you have to. Trust me."

"Have you been listening to our entire conversation?" I asked against my better judgment. It's always best to avoid direct eye contact, conversations, and questions with Billy.

"I was here first. It's not my fault I heard everything."

What he said was true, but the way he said it was so

annoying. Talking to Billy made my stomach hurt and my heart pound. I really, really hoped I didn't faint.

"Yeah, that's true, Billy, but the polite thing would have been to let us know you were here," I said. Taisy gave me a funny look, which I knew meant that I should never think Billy will do the polite thing.

"Look, sometimes I hang out under the bleachers when I want to be alone, and today is one of those days. How did I know you were going to sit down and start yammering on and on about secret plans?"

I got nervous. What if I had said too much about Elvis? Then I remembered I hadn't said anything about his coded message. So basically all Billy knew was that we were trying to find a way to get to Washington, DC.

"So why do you think we shouldn't tell him?" Taisy asked.

I couldn't believe she asked him. Like I'd ever take any advice on anything in the world from Billy Thompson!

"Easy. If you have a kid . . ."

"His name is Alexander," I said, trying to be brave.

"Whatever. I don't care who it is. All I'm saying is if you have some kid who is scared of crowds and hates surprises, you should wait as long as possible before you tell him what you want him to do. That way he won't have any time to freak beforehand. If he finds out at the last minute, he'll be better at dealing with it, because he won't have spent the last twenty-four hours worrying."

I let Billy Thompson's words sink in. Weirdly, they made a lot of sense.

"That's a good point," Taisy said. "Benj, what do you think?"

"I don't know what I think. I mean, if Alexander hates surprises, he's not going to be happy if we just spring it on him at the last minute."

"Yeah, but it's tomorrow afternoon, so it's already going to be like springing it on him," said Billy. "Look, I don't even know the kid. But I'm telling you, I'm right."

I narrowed my eyes. "Why are you being helpful?"

Taisy shook her head at me and whispered, "Benj, that's not nice."

"I'm not being nice? Are you serious? I think you're forgetting who we're dealing with. If 'not nice' were a town, Billy would be the mayor of it. If 'not nice' were the name of a sandwich, Billy would be the one who invented it. If 'not nice' were a boat—"

"We get it, Benj, he'd be the boat's captain."

In case you haven't noticed, when I get nervous, I tend to start babbling.

"I don't need him to be nice to me. I don't care. I'm just telling you what I think, that's all. Take it or leave it. Anyway, I'm out of here." And just like that, Billy walked away.

Taisy elbowed me and mouthed that I should say thank you. I shook my head no. So Taisy did it for both of us.

"Thanks for your help, Billy! Have a nice afternoon. And your blue T-shirt really brings out the blue in your eyes," Taisy called after him. He didn't even turn around to acknowledge her. He just lifted his hand up over his head in a half wave and slammed the door behind him.

"The blue in your T-shirt really brings out the blue in your eyes? What does that even mean?" I asked.

"It means exactly what it sounds like. Don't you think he has pretty blue eyes? People would notice them way more if he didn't scowl all the time."

"No, I never really noticed Billy's pretty blue eyes. It must be because I was usually running for my life whenever I saw him. Or I was shutting my eyes when he was about to punch me. Or I was falling to the ground after he tripped me." Wow, it's amazing how fast all those bad memories came racing back to the surface.

Taisy sighed. "Benji, can we get back to talking

about Alexander? Pretty please with a cherry on top?" I nodded, happy to put the subject of Billy Thompson behind us. So Taisy and I talked it over for a few minutes, and we couldn't come up with any better ideas. Finally, I agreed. "I cannot believe what I'm saying, and I will deny ever saying this if you ever tell anyone, but I guess Billy is right. We probably shouldn't tell Alexander until right before the spelling bee. He'll either take the news well or he won't."

Well, let's just say he did not take the news well the next day. In fact, he took it pretty much the opposite of well. Taisy asked us both to volunteer after school and help Principal Kriesky run the spelling bee. But Alexander Chang-Cohen didn't know the kind of help we really needed. So there we were, standing backstage, with the spelling bee about to start, when Taisy nudged me in the side, pushing me closer to Alexander. I took a deep breath. Now, I've had a lot of experience with Band-Aids in my ten years on the planet, and that thing people say about how tearing it off quickly is better than trying to peel it off slowly is absolutely right . . . when it comes to Band-Aids! Not so much when it comes to delivering bad news.

"Hey, Alexander, thanks for helping out," I said, and then I just kept talking. "So what Taisy and I need you to do is to enter the spelling bee today. Then you can go to the citywide spelling bee, which we need you to win so you can go to the state spelling bee and win that, and then we'll all be able to go to DC, where you'll compete in the National Spelling Bee, and while we're there we'll be able to help Elvis with whatever trouble he's in. How does that sound? It's a plan, right?"

I realized that at some point while I was blurting the whole thing out, I had closed my eyes. When I finished, I opened one eye first to look at Alexander Chang-Cohen's face, and then I opened my second eye. It was hard to read his expression, and he didn't say anything right away. I guess it was a lot of information to digest, so it was fair to give him a little bit of time to take everything in.

He took about five seconds to take it all in, and then he bolted. It was so sudden, it was a moment before I realized what had happened. One second he was right in front of me and then he wasn't. I had no choice but to run after him. I passed Taisy as I ran out the side door that led back into the school hallway. "Did you see Alexander run by?"

She nodded and pointed to the right. "He went that-away. So I'm guessing it didn't go so well?"

I started to run down the hall in the direction she

pointed, and I called back, "You guessed correctly!"

She yelled back, "Hurry, Benji—you've got to get him back here quick! It starts in less than twenty minutes!"

I looked at my watch to check the time, which is when I heard Ripley bark, so I looked down at him, but I wasn't sure why he was barking. Then I looked up and realized he was barking because I was running straight into . . . Principal Kriesky, who was also not looking because he was reading through his index cards, which probably had his opening remarks written on them for the spelling bee.

I slammed right into him, and I would have bounced off and hit the floor, but he somehow managed to grab me in a weird awkward principal hug that I wanted to forget about even while it was still happening. So as my face was pressed into the belly of my principal, I felt something weird, warm, and sticky on my forehead. Oh no, surely I wasn't bleeding, which would mean another trip to the hospital for me. I reached my hand up and realized it wasn't blood. It was a warm frosted Cinnabon stuck on my forehead and in my hair.

I pulled away, and the smushed Cinnabon dropped to the floor along with his index cards. "Sorry, Principal Kriesky, I didn't see you."

Principal Kriesky and I have quite a history together, because he's had to deal with my mom a lot ever since I first started school. Which automatically means he's wary of all interactions with me, because my mom can be a little high maintenance.

I crouched on the floor and picked up the fallen cards as quickly as I could. I then handed them to Principal Kriesky, who was now examining the giant Cinnabon circle that was now on his navy sports jacket. "I would love to stay and chat, Principal K, but I was running in the hallway because I really, really have to go the bathroom, and if I don't get there soon, I might—"

"Just go, Benjamin, I'll be"—he paused and sighed—"fine."

"And I'm sorry about your Cinnabon too. That's probably the real tragedy here." I looked down at the ground so I could pick it up and throw it away. Then I noticed Ripley chewing something. Oops. "Well, at least someone got to eat it! C'mon, Ripley, we gotta go!" And we took off running again.

"Benjamin, don't run in the hall!"

I slowed to a fast walk. "Right! Sorry, Principal Kriesky!" I yelled back as I rounded the corner. I stopped when I was out of sight and leaned up against the wall to catch my breath for a second. I wiped my forehead and ended up with a handful of frosting, which I held out to Ripley to lick off. I guess even though my day was rapidly going downhill, his was getting better. Now I had no idea where Alexander Chang-Cohen had run off to, and I only had twelve minutes to find him.

Luckily, Ripley led me to the band room. I patted his head. "Good Ripley. Good boy." I opened the door quietly and peeked my head into the dark room. I turned on the light and scanned around, and I didn't see him. But then I remembered that in the back of the band room there's a large storage room where kids put their instruments during the school day.

I jiggled the door handle. "Hey, Alexander, it's me, Benji. Can I come in?"

"Yes." I heard Alexander Chang-Cohen's voice, even though I couldn't see him at first. After my eyes adjusted to the dark, I saw his hand wave me over to the back corner, where I found him sitting against the wall behind a few cellos. He had his face pressed into his legs. I slid down the wall until I was sitting right next to him. "I'm sorry to spring this on you like I did. I guess I should have done it differently."

Alexander Chang-Cohen didn't say anything.

"Alexander?"

Still no response. But then I heard a sniffle, which made me feel terrible, because that meant he was so upset he might even be crying.

"I'm really sorry, Alexander. Please don't be upset."

Alexander Chang-Cohen still didn't lift his face up, so his words were kind of muffled. "No, I'm the one who's sorry, Benji. I can't do it. I wish I could, but I can't. And if you don't want to be my friend anymore, I understand."

Just when I thought I couldn't feel worse, I did. As I mentioned before, I'm kind of new to the friend thing, so I wasn't sure what I was doing. "What are you talking about, Alexander? We're friends forever, and I'll always want you as a friend. I'm so, so sorry about all this. I should have known it was a bad idea, especially since Billy Thompson was involved."

"Billy Thompson? When did you talk to him?"

"It's a long story I'll tell you about later. You know what, forget I asked about the spelling bee at all. Let's just go home."

"I can't do it because it would be cheating," he said, finally looking at me. And he told me that because of his total recall, he could probably easily win the spelling bee, but it wouldn't be fair to all the other kids competing. I never even thought about it from his point of view before, but I understood what he meant immediately.

"I get it, Alexander. It's okay."

"But it's not. I have a chance to help you, but instead I'm hiding and freaking out."

When he put it that way, I didn't really know what to say. It was true, it would be helpful if he entered and won the school spelling bee. I should have just let the whole thing go, but then I thought about Elvis and what I'd do for him, which was pretty much anything.

"What if you got us to DC and then you threw the national championship so you didn't use your total recall to win the whole thing?"

Alexander sniffled and pulled his legs up even more. Uh-oh. "I take it back! I take it back!" I said. Okay, I definitely needed more practice in the friendship department, I guess. "What a stupid idea. Forget I said it."

Alexander Chang-Cohen stood up. "If it really means that much to you, I guess I could do it."

He sounded so sad, it made my chest hurt. I took a deep breath and stood in the dark, but I lost my balance and crashed into the cello case in front of me. Alexander Chang-Cohen helped me, and when I tried to help him pick up the cello, he stopped me.

"I'll do it. You just stay there until I turn on a light." Alexander Chang-Cohen went to flip on the light switch. He stared at me funny for a moment and then asked, "What's that white stuff in your hair?"

I patted my head. "It's Principal Kriesky's Cinnabon frosting." I looked at my watch and realized we only had five minutes to make it back to the auditorium. "It's going to start soon."

"Then let's go."

Alexander and I jogged toward the auditorium in total silence, but the closer we got to it, the more I knew what I had to do. I remembered something my mom once told me, which was that doing the right thing is rarely the easiest thing to do. So as we got there, I stopped and grabbed Alexander Chang-Cohen's arm. I guess being a good friend meant I needed to do the right thing for him, even though it wasn't what I wanted.

"I don't want you to do it, Alexander," I said. And this time I really meant it. "It's not worth it. I appreciate your being willing to do it out of friendship to me, but out of friendship to you, I can't let you. We'll find a different way to get to DC."

Alexander Chang-Cohen looked happy and relieved.

He smiled, and I knew for sure I had made the right choice. Then he frowned.

"So what do we do now?" he asked. "We still have to get to DC."

"We grab Taisy and figure it out over Cinnabons."

6

The following Saturday morning I popped out of bed, gobbled up my breakfast, and then told my mom Ripley and I were going to the park to meet Alexander Chang-Cohen to watch Taisy's archery practice. This was only half true. We were also planning to brainstorm about how to get to DC. I almost made it out the door too. Almost.

"Whoa, what's the rush?" my mom asked.

What I wanted to say was this: "Well, funny story, Mom, but Elvis, my former first dog who is now the country's First Dog, sent me a coded secret message over YouTube that says he needs my help. So it's really important I meet up with my friends *right now* so we can figure out a way to get to DC."

But what I actually said was: "Rush? There's no rush. Gotta go. Bye, Mom, see you later!"

"Stop! You look tired lately. Are you sleeping well enough?"

Moms just know, I guess, because she was right. I wasn't sleeping because I was worried about Elvis. When I did sleep, I had weird dreams about Elvis, and sometimes Ripley woke me up because I was talking in my sleep. "I haven't been sleeping well enough, Mom, you're right. But maybe it's because I need more sunshine. I hear that's a thing, lack of sunshine. So that's what I'm going to try. Bye, Mom!"

My mom laughed and shook her head. "Fine. Go." And I was already out the front door when I heard her yell after me, "Don't forget to put on sunscreen! And text me!"

Luckily, one of our town's biggest parks is in walking distance of our house. It had only been a month since I was even allowed to go to the park by myself (well, with Ripley). It took a lot of convincing, and the first ten times I had to stay on the phone with my mom while I was walking. Finally she said I didn't have to be on the phone with her, but I did have to take a picture of the park when I got there and text it to her.

As soon as I got to the park, I saw Taisy standing

in the distance. I took a picture for my mom. Taisy was standing so still, eyeing her target so intensely, it was almost like she was a statue. There was a small crowd of people sitting on the grass, quietly watching practice. I guess nobody wanted to distract one of these kids and somehow end up with an arrow in their forehead.

Everyone says kids are influenced by what they see in the movies, television, or books. And I will admit that Alexander Chang-Cohen and I have long conversations about what it would be like if we were roommates at Hogwarts Academy. It's just fun to think about all the many what-ifs of it all.

But the difference between Taisy McDonald and the rest of us is that she sees something like the movie *Brave* and she doesn't just say, "It'd be so cool to know how to use a bow and arrow," and then move on to something else a few days later. She says it once and then the next thing you know her dad has bought her all the equipment, set up a practice board in their backyard, and she's taking private lessons and learning archery.

"Benji, you can't find your passion unless you try lots of things," she once explained to me. "Besides, how will you know if you like something unless you try everything?"

So Taisy thought archery would be fun and might

help her miss gymnastics less. But of course, because Taisy is Taisy, she was already better at it than most people. This is where her dad came in. Taisy just wanted to have fun and compete with herself. He wanted her to go to tournaments.

Either way, I like watching Taisy practice. I just don't sit near Big Tate McDonald, because if he is too intense for Taisy, he's way too intense for me. So while he was busy videotaping Taisy, I found myself a nice spot in the grass away from him.

I settled in. I put down the towel I'd brought with me in my backpack, put down a different towel for Ripley, sprayed a perimeter of bug spray around my towel, applied SPF 75 sunscreen, and put on my baseball cap to block the sun from my eyes. Then I gave Ripley a rawhide to chew on and texted Alexander Chang-Cohen.

Where r u?

Alexander's mom thinks texting is ruining the English language and is making an entire world of short-attention-spanned lazy spellers. So she makes Alexander text in full sentences. It's weird, but not that weird if you know him.

I'm about forty yards southwest of you,

give or take a few feet.

I turned around, and sure enough, there was Alexander Chang-Cohen walking toward me with his rolling laptop case behind him. Some kids bring bats and balls to the park, some kids, or probably just this one kid, bring laptops. I waved at him and he waved back.

Alexander Chang-Cohen has his own ritual when he sets up in the park. He puts down a towel, and he has this folding chair thing that doesn't have legs, so he's sitting on the ground but he has back support. He also has a sun visor if he needs it. He doesn't use the sun visor to protect himself from the sun, but he uses it so he can see his laptop screen in the sunlight. But when he sits down, his first order of business is picking the grass out of the wheels of his laptop case. He has to do this right away, because he can't concentrate until he does it. I know it's quirky, but here's the thing I'm learning about friendship: It requires a tolerance pact. You tolerate all my weirdo quirky things and I'll tolerate yours.

When he was done, he looked over at me and said, "Hey, did you finish your social studies homework?"

"Alexander, who cares about homework! We have much bigger things to deal with right now."

"Oh, you mean our math test?"

"No, forget school. We've got to figure out a way to get to DC. Can't you invent a time machine and get us to summer vacation so we can go?"

"Even if I could build a time machine, if we used it to go to summer vacation, it's not like the next few months wouldn't exist. So I'm not sure how helpful it would—"

"Alexander, I was kidding. I'm just trying to let you know I'm getting a little desperate."

"What do you think it is Elvis needs help with?"

"I have no idea."

"You know, the more I think about Elvis's secret coded message, the more questions I have. If he was able to send us a message, that means he can spell, which I didn't think dogs could do, right?"

Uh-oh. I'd been waiting for these sorts of questions to come up, and I knew it would be Alexander Chang-Cohen who would ask them. I figured Taisy wouldn't ask about Elvis, because she definitely believes Princess Daisy understands her, so she probably doesn't think it's so odd that he contacted me, because I'm sure she'd expect if she were away, Princess Daisy would comfort her in a girlie way, like spell out her name in daisies.

"I haven't really thought about it that much. I just

figured with all the special training he got when he was a puppy that he was taught to read too. I mean, he is a trained service/therapy dog, so it makes sense they would teach him to read. You know, so he could read street signs and all." When trying to avoid more questions, I usually talk really fast and then try to change the subject as fast as possible. "Hey, you want to go to the snack bar?"

It worked, because he immediately forgot all about Elvis and instead told me he would love a slushie, but he didn't want to bring his laptop bag over there and then back and have to clean the wheels again. And of course he couldn't leave it behind, because it wasn't safe.

"You can see where I'm in a tough position, right? Plus I don't think my mom would want me to have a slushie this soon after breakfast."

"I guess you could say you're between a slushie and a grassy place, you know, as opposed to being between a rock and a hard place," I said.

"Very clever, Benji. That was really funny."

Sometimes Alexander Chang-Cohen does that. He says things are funny as opposed to laughing. It's another quirk about him I like. I told him to guard our stuff, and I'd go for both of us.

As Ripley and I were waiting in line at the snack bar,

someone put their hands over my eyes and said, "Guess who?" Even though Taisy was purposely making her voice much lower than it is, I smelled strawberry and knew it was her immediately.

"Hmmmm, let me see. Strawberry Shortcake?"

"No. Guess again."

"A talking giraffe? One with hands, I mean. Which would be kind of disturbing. So I take that guess back. Give me a hint."

"Who's one of your top three favorite people on the entire planet?"

"Oh, why didn't you say so? Taisy McDonald!"

She laughed and I turned around, looked up because she's much taller than me, and saw her smiling face. "How'd you know it was me? Was it my supercute archery outfit that you couldn't even see but you just sensed?"

"Yes, exactly that. So are you taking a break? I thought your dad didn't believe in breaks during practice."

"He doesn't, but remember, I'm controlling things when it comes to archery. It's making him crazy he can't tell me what to do. Who knew he'd be even crazier about competing when I wasn't even competing? Luckily, my mom's got my back on this one, so it's all good." The only person who isn't the least bit intimidated by

Taisy's dad is Taisy's mom.

"So are you having fun?"

"You mean watching my dad freak out? Yes, tons! Oh, you mean with archery. Yep. Sports are way more fun when it's not all about competing and winning. And it feels so good when I hit the bull's-eye. Plus, I love the sound it makes when it hits. *Thwwoooop!*"

I shrugged, mainly because I really didn't know very much at all about competitions and sports myself. She pointed at a flyer posted on the snack bar bulletin board. It was an announcement for a state archery competition that was taking place next weekend. The winners would go on to DC for a tristate competition. After that? The nationals. Then the Junior Olympics.

"My dad's been begging me to enter the tournament, but I keep telling him, no, no, no. I'm doing archery for me, not to win."

"Hey, pretty lady, can I buy you a slushie?" I asked when I got to the front of the line.

"Oh, Benj. You're so funny. I'd rather have an ice cream sandwich."

"An ice cream sandwich this early in the morning?"

"Yes. Doesn't it sound divine?"

It did, actually, so I ordered two ice cream sandwiches, a banana, and a slushie. The banana was for

Alexander Chang-Cohen to eat in case he ended up feeling too guilty to have a slushie at this time of day. While we were waiting, I told Taisy I was proud of her for standing up to her dad.

"I mean, why would you want to take up all your weekends with tournaments, and who wants to go to . . ."

I shoved my five-dollar bill into Taisy's hand. "Here. Pay, please."

And then I ran back over to the archery tournament flyer on the bulletin board and ripped it down.

"Benji, what are you doing?" Taisy said, coming up behind me with the food in her arms.

"Taisy, you know how I said you're doing absolutely the right thing by not competing in the archery tournament just because your dad wants you to?"

"Yes."

"Well, how would you feel about competing if one of your best friends begged you to?"

"What are you talking about?"

"If you win in your age division, you get to move on to the next round, which is in Washington, DC, in two weeks."

She caught on immediately. "And then I could go check on Elvis!"

"No, and then *we* could go check on Elvis together. No way I'm not going with you." Suddenly I realized what I was doing. Pressuring her to do something that she'd told me minutes before she absolutely didn't want to do. This was the exact same thing that just happened with Alexander Chang-Cohen a few days ago! I sighed, but I knew the right thing to do was tell her she didn't have to do it if she didn't want to.

"Never mind, Taisy, you absolutely shouldn't—"

"Benji, stop. I'll do it. I don't want to do it just because my dad wants me to be a super winner. But I'll absolutely do it it for you, and for Elvis. Besides, Princess Daisy would want me to do it too."

"Really? Are you sure? Because I don't want another Alexander freak-out in the band room over this. I learned my how-to-be-a-good-friend lesson on that one."

"Benji, I'm sure. Alexander and I are different. I like competitions—I just don't like competing when my dad is breathing down my neck. But to do it for Elvis makes it way more fun and cool. It's like I'm a female super-hero. With a purple cape!"

Suddenly I got nervous. This was our best chance of getting to DC. What if she didn't win the state tournament?

"What's wrong? Why does your face look like that?"

I shook my head. I didn't want to say it. Why did I always have to be such a worrier? Why couldn't I just be more positive? I didn't want to be like Taisy's dad and put even more pressure on her.

"It's nothing, Taisy. I'm fine."

"Whenever someone says they're fine, they're usually not. That's what my mom always says, and she's pretty much always right. Just tell me, Benji."

I shook my head. Sure, Taisy winning the tournament would certainly solve all our problems, but this whole Elvis thing was my responsibility, and if Taisy didn't win the tournament, then we'd just have to come up with another way to get there.

"Oh, I know what that face is. You're worried I might not win next week, but you don't want to say anything to me because I'm always complaining about how much pressure my dad puts on me, and so you don't want to be like that. Am I close?"

She looked right through me and read all my thoughts like they were written up on a chalkboard. I nodded. "Bull's-eye. You know I think you're the most amazing athlete in our whole town, and I'm even including the twins in that, but we both know you haven't been doing archery for very long, so maybe it's unrealistic to think you could win next weekend. It's only seven days away."

Taisy handed me my ice cream sandwich. She had graciously unwrapped the top half for me.

"Benj, don't you worry about me. I've been competing my whole life, and I know what it takes to win. Sure, seven days isn't much time, but it's enough. And honestly, it's kind of exciting for me, because I'm rarely the underdog when it comes to sports, but this time I will be."

I've never really heard anyone get excited to be the underdog, and I say this because I feel like I'm always the underdog and I'm never happy about it.

"Benj, it's going to be okay. I'm sure I can do it knowing I have your support and Alexander's. And I know I'll have my dad's support, so we're all good. If I said I wanted to practice around the clock, he'd have lights installed in our backyard by tonight. So don't worry. Though I know that's impossible for you, so try not to worry too, too much, okay?"

She sounded so confident, I actually believed her, and I started to feel hopeful again. "Breathe and believe, right?" I asked, which is a phrase Taisy taught me for whenever I start to lose hope.

"Breathe and believe. Absolutely!" she said, licking the edges of her ice cream sandwich. "C'mon, let's go make my dad's day by telling him I'm going to compete."

I'm pretty used to things in my life going all sorts of wrong. Here are just a few examples: There was the time it was my class's turn to sing in front of the assembly, and I'd spilled mustard all over my shirt and it landed in the shape of Alaska, so everyone whispered and pointed at me for three days, saying, "Juneau that kid Benji?" and I didn't even get the joke. There was the time the twins drew a twirly mustache on my face with a permanent Sharpie, knowing perfectly well it was school picture day. And there was the time in dodgeball when I miraculously made it to the very end. At first it seemed amazing, but then it was terrible, because I realized everyone was watching me and I didn't really have the upper body strength to throw the ball and hit my opponent, and my opponent had broken his glasses so his aim was off, and it took ten long, painful minutes for one of us to get the other person out. (Take a guess at who won and who lost.) Yes, that's the way my life usually goes. So dealing with things going badly? I'm an expert at that.

Things going well? Things going exactly as planned? That was all new to me.

Taisy practiced archery like a machine sent back from the future to show us humans what it means to be awesome. She got so good I would have felt pretty safe about letting her shoot an apple off the top of my head. (Okay, that's probably not true. Like I said, I have bad luck, so she'd probably sneeze or see a mouse when she was trying to shoot the apple off my head and I'd lose an eye or an ear.) But overall, Taisy was right. I didn't need to worry. She didn't just win that archery tournament, she dominated it. We all celebrated her victory when her dad treated us to burgers and banana splits.

Then things got even better. Alexander Chang-Cohen's mom decided they should take a trip to DC so Alexander could do a museum tour. And even better than that: Once Taisy and Alexander Chang-Cohen said they were going, my mom suddenly thought it was a great idea for us to go too. So she called up Agent Daniels to tell him we were coming to town, and he got us discounted rooms at a fancy hotel right across the street from the White House. The president would be out of town on our first night, so Agent Daniels arranged it so Elvis could spend the first night with me at the hotel. And the best part of all is we were invited to have dinner at the White House with some of Agent Daniels's Secret Service agent friends and the house staff on our second night!

On that Saturday morning when I was finally going to be reunited with Elvis, I woke up more excited than a kid on Christmas morning. As a kid myself, I don't mention Christmas lightly. When we arrived in DC a few hours later, we all dropped our bags with the porters at the Hay-Adams Hotel (this was by far the fanciest hotel I'd ever seen, and my mom had her mouth hanging open the whole time). Taisy and her dad immediately went to check out the tournament location. Alexander Chang-Cohen and his mom hopped a tourist trolley to start his educational tour.

So just like that, my mom and I were headed straight for the White House to get Elvis. Before we'd left home, my mom gave my father an entire instruction binder about the twins, and she also baked up a storm so she could thank Agent Daniels and the other Secret Service agents for being so great to us. She kept telling my dad she felt it was a privilege and an honor to bake for the White House.

She baked one of her cakes, of course, but she also brought a secret weapon. A big box showed up at our doorstep a few days earlier. My mom opened it to find a cake-pop-making machine my dad had seen late one night on an infomercial. He even sent a card: *A stick should be so lucky as to have a cake made by you on it! Love you more and more even though you're making me fat.* My dad is quiet, but he's always great with surprises like that, and my mom says he is very rare because most men are not so great with big romantic gestures. There are plenty of mornings when I wake up and find a cool new pair of wacky socks he's picked out or a book he knew I would like.

My mom went to work immediately, trying out and mastering all sorts of different cake pops to bring to DC instead of her usual cupcakes. So when we went through security at the White House and my mom was asked what was in the big box she was holding, she proudly said, "The most amazing cake pops you've ever had. Here, try one." And the security guy named Al, who was in charge of the X-ray machine, tried one, and his eyes got all big and he said, "Now that's a little morsel of heaven on a stick, right there." And my mom liked what he had to say so much, she gave him a second one for later.

This was the first time I had ever been at the White House, and I know I should say I was in awe of being there in person, and that I really stopped to take in the grandness of it all, and I was bowled over by how much history had happened there. Honestly, couldn't tell you a thing about it besides that it seemed big and fancy, because I had only one thing on my mind.

As soon as we made it through security, I just couldn't help myself. I racewalked with Ripley through the halls, calling out his name in a loud whisper. "Elvis! Oh, Elvis! C'mere, boy!" Meanwhile, as my mom was busy handing out cake pops to every Secret Service agent or White House employee she saw, she kept loud-whispering for me to wait up. "Benji, slow down. Hey, wait for me. Remember where we are! I'm sure the same rules apply here as at the swimming pool. No running, spitting, peeing, or splashing."

But I kept calling out to Elvis, because I knew how good his hearing was, so I knew he'd soon find me. "Elvis! Yo, Elvis! It's me Benji! Yoo-hoo!" And then I'd shout-whisper back to my mom, "Mom, you can give those out later. Please help me find Elvis."

What I didn't know, until Elvis told me about it later, was that he'd smelled me as soon as I walked up to the front gate. He was walking the perimeter of the lawn on the far side of the White House, not because he needed to do it for security—it was just something he liked to do for his own peace of mind. But when he smelled me, he immediately started running across the yard to find me. By the time someone let him in at the back door, my scent was all mixed up with the scent of cake pops wafting about the hallways.

So imagine the inside of the White House, which is pretty big and has lots of rooms. Then think about me speed-walking through the hallways, sticking my head into room after room to look for Elvis. Then picture this huge head of blond curly hair (that's my mom) chasing after me, all the while thrusting pink frosted cake pops into people's hands about twenty feet behind me. Now picture the biggest, blackest dog you've ever seen galloping through the White House two rooms behind us and zigzagging up to every person who just received a cake pop and scaring them half to death.

Finally, my mom, who got tired of chasing after me, did what any normal mom would do. No, I take that back. She did what only my mom would do. She took out a cake pop and threw it at me, hitting me square in the back. I know this brings up lots of questions, mainly what kind of mom throws a cake pop at her kid. But first off, she knew it wouldn't hurt me. And sure, it seems risky that she would even be able to hit a moving target, but you have to keep in mind that the twins got their athleticism from somewhere, and it wasn't my dad. But she knew the cake pop would drop to the floor and make a mess in the White House, and she also knew if Elvis was around, he'd zero in on the smell and he'd be more than happy to clean it right up.

I will admit the first thing I thought when I got hit was, Oh no, did I just get shot? I guess I thought that because I knew Secret Service guys had guns, and it occurred to me that running through the halls with a crazed look in my eyes was probably not the wisest thing I've ever done. But then I thought, If I got shot, I'm pretty sure it'd hurt way more than what I just felt. But what it did do, which is exactly what my mom wanted it to do, was stop me in my tracks. I turned around and looked on the floor and saw the now smushed cake pop lying on the floor nearby. Then I looked over at my mom, who was standing all the way down the hallway.

"Mom, did you just throw a cake pop at me?"

She shushed me and then started walking toward me. She whispered, "I needed to get your attention."

"Well, you have it."

"Benji, I don't think you should run in the White House. It's not polite."

"And you think it's okay to throw baked goods?" I didn't finish my thought because out of the corner of my eye I noticed something large, black, and furry behind her. It was him. It was Elvis! And he was running full speed toward me.

I will say I certainly remembered that Elvis is a big dog, because all Newfoundlands are big dogs. But you see, Elvis is big even for a Newfoundland, so it wasn't just a dog running toward me, it was a two-hundred-pound dog running toward me. I thought my face would break in half, I smiled so big.

"Elvis!" I yelled.

"Benji!" he barked.

I opened my arms wide to hug him, and then my last flicker of thought was, Man, he sure is running at me fast—I hope he stops in time or this may be the most painful reunion ever. Then I fainted.

I woke up seconds later to Elvis's wet tongue licking my face. His breath smelled like, well, it smelled like cake pop.

"Hey, did you stop and eat that cake pop on the floor before you came up to say hello?"

"No. Maybe. Yes."

I decided I didn't care and threw my arms around Elvis's furry neck, and as I did, I heard someone say, "Oh my, is that giant dog eating a small child?" I heard my mom's laugh and she replied, "No, they're just two old friends saying hello. Would you like a cake pop? I made them myself."

When I finally got off the floor, I just kept staring at him, because I couldn't believe he was actually right in front of me. All these months of missing him and we were finally together again. And then he opened his mouth, and I wondered what his first real words would be, whether he'd tell me he'd missed me the same way I had missed him.

But what he said was "Oh, I didn't know you'd be bringing him."

It took me a second to understand who Elvis was talking about, and then I saw he was staring at Ripley, who was sitting quietly a few feet away from me.

I rolled my eyes. "Of course I brought Ripley—he's my therapy dog. You know how you were my therapy dog before you left me."

"I didn't leave you by choice. It was just something I had to do. And I understand he's your new therapy dog, but you don't need him if I'm with you."

Okay, now it was all coming back to me. I remembered a lot of things about Elvis: his size, his smell, his giant head, his drool, how he's always hungry, his big vocabulary, but what I forgot was how difficult he was too.

"Elvis, c'mon, you haven't seen me in months and this is what you want to talk about? It's not nice to be jealous."

"Of course, I deeply apologize. I am being most rude." He then walked over to Ripley, who stood up to greet him. "Hello, Ripley. Welcome to Washington, DC."

"See, that wasn't so bad, was it?"

"No, it wasn't." Elvis turned back to face me. "You are looking quite well, Benjamin. I believe you've grown about a quarter inch since we last saw each other?"

"Whoa. I have. I mean I did. How did you know that?"

Before he could answer, my mom had finally managed to get past the woman who went from being worried I was being eaten by a dog to telling my mother that her cake pops were the best she'd ever had. My mom, never one for a quiet moment, literally fell to her knees and threw her arms around Elvis and pressed her face into his furry face. "Elvis, now you're a sight for sore eyes! You look and smell wonderful. What shampoo are they using on you here? Smell him, Benji. Doesn't he smell good? What, you don't want to tell me? Is it a state secret?" Of all my mom's many loud laughs, my favorite is the big, cackling, loud one she does when she cracks herself up. When she makes a joke, you can be sure she's the one who is laughing the loudest! Even though it was a corny joke, I couldn't help but smile.

I turned to Elvis and said, "As you can see, Elvis, Mom hasn't changed one bit." Elvis said nothing, but that was because he was still basking in all the attention he was getting, or my mom was squeezing him so tight he couldn't breathe, which was totally possible too. I'm sure that when it comes to absence making the heart grow fonder, it was definitely true in the case of Elvis and my mom.

"So where to now, Mom? Are we going to go see Taisy or meet up with Alexander Chang-Cohen?"

My mom looked surprised and asked, "Don't you want to spend some time with Elvis now that you're here?"

"Of course I do, but didn't you say that Agent Daniels said he gets to stay with us tonight?"

"I said Agent Daniels thinks it will be okay if he stays with us tonight. But we have to get official permission, because the last thing I need is for anyone to think we're stealing the First Dog."

"I think it'd be pretty hard to steal a dog as big as Elvis without anyone noticing, especially around here."

We heard him before we saw him, but Agent Daniels was now standing behind me. Even though I'd met him only once on one of the worst days of my life, I still felt happy to see him, since he's the one who's been reading my letters to Elvis for me.

"Hey, Agent Daniels! How'd you know we were here?"

"Well, it's kind of my job to know everything that is going on here, so the moment you went through security I was notified, and I did tell them to have you wait for me there, but I heard you took off in search of Elvis. I was finishing up a phone call, so I'm sorry I couldn't get here sooner. But it wasn't hard to find you. I just followed the trail of cake pops. Speaking of . . ."

My mom handed him one. He ate it in one bite. He closed his eyes because it tasted so good. "Mrs. Barnsworth, if I wasn't a married man, let me tell you."

"Agent Daniels, stop being silly, and trust me, you're not the first man to fall in love with my baking skills." My mom went from hugging Elvis to hugging Agent Daniels.

"I want you to know that there are a lot of people here who really want to meet you," he said to my mom.

"Me? Why me?" She looked genuinely surprised.

"Your cake has reached cult status here at the White House, and I'm pretty sure I'm the most popular Secret Service agent because of it. In fact, I received direct orders from the executive pastry chef, Pfeiffer Larue, that he'd have me fired if I didn't bring you by his kitchen to meet him."

"The executive pastry chef has the power to fire you?" I asked.

"No, Benji, I think he's teasing you," she said.

"Actually, I'm not. He couldn't fire me directly, but he's probably the most important guy here after the chief of staff to the president. The president has a major sweet tooth, and he'd probably do anything to keep Chef Larue happy."

I could tell my mom was very pleased by all the compliments. People tell her all the time what a great baker she is, but this was a whole different level. The executive pastry chef for the president of the United States wanted to meet her. She was actually blushing. Agent Daniels bent down to talk to me.

"I've discussed your request with the president, and he agreed that if you like, Benji, you can take Elvis for the night. Then when you bring him back tomorrow, I'll introduce you and your mom to Chef Larue and the rest of the staff, who love Elvis so much."

"I can have Elvis for the night! Mom, is that okay?" I was so excited I actually jumped up in the air.

"Of course it's okay," my mom said.

I looked down at Elvis. I couldn't help it—I gave him a big hug around his giant neck. I just couldn't believe that we were finally together again.

"Aren't you happy to spend the night with me?" I whispered into his fur.

"Yes," he said. "Now will you please ask your mom if I can have another cake pop?"

Normally, when I'm in the car with my mom, I sit right behind the front passenger seat so we can chat and she can look up at me in her rearview mirror. Ripley always takes his spot to my left, so he gets in first. So as usual, Ripley got in, I climbed in, and then I called for Elvis to get in, but Elvis just stood there looking at me. "Elvis, up!" I said. No reaction. "Elvis, what are you doing? Get in the car. We have to go." Still nothing.

"I want to sit next to you. Please."

My mom asked, "Why is he whining?"

I shrugged, even though I knew why.

"Do you think he needs to go potty?"

I shook my head and whispered, "I think he wants

to sit next to me."

My mom raised her eyebrows in amusement at me via the rearview mirror. But then she said, "Hey, Ripley, come on up and ride shotgun next to me. I'll roll down the window for you." My mom patted the passenger seat. Ripley barked and happily moved up to the front seat. I slid over to the next seat, and Elvis jumped up immediately and sat down.

"Sheesh, Elvis, all you had to do was ask," I said.

"I did ask, Benjamin, and I said please."

"Awwww, I think he missed you and just wants to be close, that's all," my mom said.

I smiled at her in the mirror. She always knows just the exact right thing to say. She threw me a wink and a smile. And then I saw another look cross over her face. It was the tiniest wave of worry, and I knew instantly what she was thinking. She was worried I'd get overly attached to Elvis again, and then it'd be a one-way ticket to heartbreak city when I had to go home without him. Well, she was right to be concerned, because it had already happened. But for once, I decided not to worry about the future. I would soak up every second I had with Elvis.

"Okay, guys. Let's go see Taisy compete in her archery finals," my mom said. Elvis's ears and tail perked up. "Wow, it's like he recognized Taisy's name. Do you think he remembers her, Benji?"

"Of course he remembers her," I said.

I knew without a doubt that Elvis remembered Taisy. More importantly, he remembered Taisy's dog, Princess Daisy. My mom got on the phone with Alexander Chang-Cohen's mom to talk about what they were going to wear to dinner at the White House.

With my mom busy in the front seat, I was finally able to talk to Elvis. I kept my voice low so my mom wouldn't hear me. I knew she'd be on the lookout to see if I talked to Elvis. I learned that lesson the hard way. The first and only time I told my mom Elvis talked to me, she freaked out, picked me up, and hauled me off to the emergency room to get a brain scan. I had never had a dog before Elvis, so how did I know that dogs weren't supposed to talk? If your dog talks to you, make sure you don't tell anyone, because they'll think you're crazy.

"Okay, Elvis," I whispered. "First things first. Brace yourself, but Princess Daisy didn't come with Taisy. I'm really sorry. She was going to bring her, but her dad thought it'd be a distraction for her at the tournament. Are you okay?"

Elvis let out the biggest, longest dog sigh you've

ever heard. And I thought *I* had a tendency to get melo-dramatic. "Yes, I suppose I'll have to be. Though I must say I am disappointed. Please tell me she's doing well?"

"She's great, as cute as ever. Now, moving on, I'm going to ask you a series of yes-or-no questions. Thump your tail once for yes. Thump twice for no."

"Really, Benjamin, must we be so covert?" Elvis stared at my face, which was probably blank. He realized I had no idea what covert meant. "Covert. Sur-reptitious? Clandestine? Furtive?"

It was so like Elvis to use one big word I didn't know and then use three more big words I didn't know to explain what the first word meant, all the while mak-ing me feel even dumber.

"Okay, Mr. Dictionary, I get your point." I rolled my eyes. It was funny how all of Elvis's obnoxious traits melted away so quickly when we were apart, but now that we were together, they came flooding right back. "Just tell me what covert means."

"Covert means secretive," he said with a sigh. "What I was asking before we were so rudely interrupted by your lack of knowledge was, must we be so secretive?"

"Why is Elvis making so much noise? Is something wrong?" my mom called from the front seat. "Does he need to go potty? Elvis, don't you potty in my car."

"No, Mom, I think he's fine. He was always loud. Don't you remember?"

I stuck my tongue out at Elvis and then shushed him with my finger to show him this was exactly why we needed to be covert, secretive, surreptiliousseshy or whatever stupid big word he said earlier that I didn't know. Finally, he saw my point. He thumped his tail once as if to say, *Fine. Go ahead, have it your way. I'll be quiet.*

Never a gracious winner, I whispered back, "Really, you think I'm going overboard by asking you to talk softly when you're the one who used Morse code? With your tail! Did you ever wonder what would happen if I hadn't seen your message?"

Elvis thumped his tail once. Yes. "But you figured I'd miss you so much I'd find it eventually?" He thumped his tail once again. Same old Elvis, just as full of himself as he'd always been.

"Do you still need my help?"

Thump.

"Are you in danger?"

Thump.

"Like big danger as in zombie apocalypse?"

Thump. Thump.

Okay, so it wasn't big danger like a zombie apocalypse.

"Is it small danger like the fire detectors aren't up to code in the White House and you're concerned for everyone's well-being?"

Thump. Thump.

Okay, so it wasn't big danger. It's wasn't small danger. Wow, this was taking longer than I thought. "Am I in danger?"

Thump. Thump.

"So I'm not in danger, but you're in danger, and it's a medium-sized danger. Let me think. Is there a time pressure to this danger?"

Thump.

"Okay, so we need to act fast?"

Thump.

"Do you already have a plan but you don't know how to implement it because you don't have thumbs and you're a dog?"

Thump. Thump. "Nice use of the word 'implement,' Benjamin," he couldn't resist adding.

Up front, the GPS announced that we were close to our destination.

"Okay, lightning round. Does it have to do with the White House?"

Thump.

"Does it have to do with the president?"

Thump.

"Really, this has to do with the president and you?"

Thump.

My mouth went dry. Just having a conversation about the president made my heart race. Suddenly, I didn't want to ask any more questions. I mean, we weren't playing a simple car game of Twenty Questions or I Spy with My Little Eye. This was big. Like, really big. Here I was in DC with my former dog, who was now the president of the United States's dog, the First Dog of the entire country, and he needed my help with a situation involving the president? Didn't he understand I'm just a sickly kid from Pennsylvania and not a superhero? I fumbled for the window switch to get some air. Oh great, the button wasn't working. I tried it both ways and nothing happened. Maybe it was jammed. Oh no, what if someone sabotaged my mom's car?

Ripley sensed I was about to have a full-blown panic attack, which could easily turn into an asthma attack, so he started barking. Elvis, not to be outdone by a Labrador retriever, joined in. I guess dogs really are territorial, which was fine by me as long as they didn't pee on me like a tree to mark their ownership. Two barking dogs in one large SUV with the windows rolled up was really, really loud.

"What on earth is going on back there?! Benji, are you okay? Benji?!" my mother called out.

"The window. I need air. It's not working."

"For Pete's sake, you know I keep the safety lock on so your older brothers don't get any funny ideas about dangling you out the window. Remember what happened when you were three?"

My window opened, and the warm, sticky DC air rushed over my face. I gulped it like a person who's been holding his breath. In fact, it's possible I had been holding my breath. Sometimes I do that when I get nervous. I forget to breathe.

"Benjamin, you're fine. Calm down." Elvis stuck his big face into my face and licked me with his giant tongue.

I nodded. I'd be okay. Obviously Elvis knew I wasn't a superhero. Clearly he needed the help only a ten-year-old kid and his two friends could supply. Maybe the president was planning on naming a new national holiday, like Banana Split Day, and he needed some kids to go in front of Congress to discuss why this would be a good thing even though every parent in the land was all about healthy eating these days. And of course, I'd be happy to help with that. I could definitely give one awesome speech about banana splits. Wow, if the president made Banana Split Day a national holiday, he'd get my vote. Well, if I was old enough to vote.

"Does this by any chance have to do with coming up with a new kid-friendly national holiday?" I asked.

No response.

"Did you hear me?"

Thump.

"But you're not going to answer?"

Thump.

"Why not?"

Silence. "Elvis, what's wrong?"

More silence. Elvis didn't even look at me.

"Oh, so now you're refusing to talk to me?" Now that's a sentence I never thought I'd hear myself say to a dog. My mom slowly pulled the car into a gas station and stopped the car.

"Benji, are you feeling okay?" she asked, turning her head to look at me.

"Sure, Mom, all good here. I just needed a little air, but I'm fine now," I said with a smile on my face. "I've just been catching up with Elvis. How are you?"

"Me? I'm fine. I'm going to get gas and maybe get myself a Diet Coke. Do you need anything? Maybe I should buy the dogs some water, since we're going to the park."

"Do what you gotta do. But I'm fine, Mom. Couldn't be better." And then I gave her a thumbs-up sign, which is weird because it's not something I really ever do. She gave me kind of a funny look, but luckily, she didn't push me.

"Okay, well, you guys hang tight then," she said, getting out of the car.

"Are you seriously giving me the silent treatment?" I asked Elvis as soon as my mom got out of the car.

"No, I am not. I don't partake in childish mind games, even when dealing with a child. But if you're not going to take my current predicament seriously, then I don't see any point in discussing it at all."

"Take it seriously? Are you kidding me? How am I not taking it seriously?"

"I have a very real situation I need to deal with, Benjamin, and I can say without a doubt that it's nowhere near a zombie apocalypse or the naming of a kid-friendly national holiday."

Okay, maybe Elvis had a point, but it's not like I was making fun of him. I was just trying to figure out what kind of situation we were dealing with. Could I help it if I happened to have the imagination of a ten-year-old? Who was he to criticize my line of questioning?

"I'll have you know I am taking this very seriously,

and you know how I can prove it? Because I'm here! In Washington, DC! You think it was easy for me to come help you? It's not like I'm old enough to drive or go anywhere on my own—and it's not like I could tell my mom my former dog sent me a coded message over YouTube! And it wasn't just me who had to work to get here, Elvis. Taisy and Alexander both helped. Taisy practiced her archery for a million, gazillion hours just to make sure she'd win so we had a cover story to get to DC. So don't you tell me that I'm not taking it seriously, because I've never taken anything so seriously in my entire life!"

Wow, I had no idea where that outburst came from. I guess all the stress I had been under the past two weeks finally got to me. I'm not exactly sure what I'd expected once I finally found Elvis, but it definitely wasn't a fight. I turned away from Elvis and watched the street traffic pass. I was afraid I'd cry, and I didn't want him to see, so I just started counting cars.

"Benjamin, I apologize. Of course I should have thanked you first for coming here to help me. As you know, I have spent the last few months apart from you in the company of adults who talk about very serious matters all the time, so when you brought up zombies and holidays, I overreacted. And I now understand it would behoove me to remember your age and accept the limitations of your knowledge and vocabulary."

"My limitations of knowledge and vocabulary? If you think that's an apology, then you are, like, the worst apologizer on the entire planet, Elvis."

"Benji, is everything okay?" My mom knocked on my window and put her face up to the glass to peer inside.

Without missing a beat, Elvis put his big furry feet across my lap and gave me a huge, disgustingly wet lick on my face. I laughed, which I guess was the whole point of why he did it. My mom smiled and waved at the two of us.

"Okay, you can get off me now," I said, but Elvis didn't move. Instead he whispered, "Benjamin, stop being, as you call it, a crankybutt."

"It's crankypants."

"Fine, stop being a crankypants. I feel uncomfortable discussing my personal business and feelings around a dog who I do not know," he said, nodding at Ripley. "But I see now is the time for me to step up and be honest. I have thought about you every single day I've been away. The days your letters arrive are my favorite days of the entire month."

Whoa, I couldn't believe what I'd just heard. Elvis

actually admitted he missed me the same way I missed him. It was a huge relief. Elvis and I hadn't changed at all, at least not with each other. That was the good news. The bad news was that now I loved him even more.

9

"Earth to Benji, come in. Come in. Earth to Benji. Do you copy?"

"Huh, what?"

I looked up as my mom parked the car at East Potomac Park. I saw a group of kids at the shooting line on a grassy field with bows in their hands and a crowd in the bleachers. We had arrived at the Youth Archery Championship. I put on the embarrassing safari hat my mom handed me, because it wasn't worth it to fight. Luckily, nobody knew me in Washington, DC. We piled out of the car: my mom, Ripley, Elvis, and me in my giant hat. As we made our way to our seats, people stared and pointed at us.

"Mom, what's going on? Why are people looking at

us?" I knew the hat was bad, but I didn't think it was that bad.

"I have a feeling they aren't looking at us. They're looking at Elvis."

Somehow I had forgotten. You can't really travel with a two-hundred-pound dog and go unnoticed. This time was a little different, though. They didn't just smile from a distance—they actually came up to us, asking questions, making comments, and taking pictures.

"Is that the president's dog?"

"Is that the First Dog, Elvis?"

"Is that a dog or a bear?"

"He looks even bigger in person than he does on TV."

"He's so handsome! I love his red, white, and blue collar!"

Before we knew it, a small crowd of a dozen people surrounded us. Elvis took it all in stride. Clearly he was used to this level of attention in public. When people took pictures, he even stood taller and shook his head to fluff up his ears. My mom volunteered to take pictures of families and their kids with Elvis.

And I, well, I was pretty much pushed aside. I mean, we were in a park with plenty of wide-open space. Why was everyone crowding in so close? For a minute,

I worried there wasn't enough oxygen. Then I remembered we were outside and that probably wouldn't be a problem. I slipped out of the center of the crowd to get a little space.

I walked over to a tree and sat down in the shade. Ripley, of course, followed me and quickly lay down by my side, putting his head in my lap. Good ol' Ripley. He always knew when I needed to pet his head to feel better.

I watched the crowd around Elvis, all those people smiling, petting, cooing over him. Ten minutes earlier I had felt super close to him. Now, from this distance, I felt like just another kid in the crowd. I mean, I knew he was famous, but I didn't realize how famous. There was no way he had as much time to miss me as I missed him. I was jealous. I only had one night with Elvis, and now I was supposed to share him with all his fans? What if he liked one of his fans more than me?

"Ripley, I want to say you've been an extremely good sport about all this Elvis stuff," I said, petting his head. "I hope you understand that none of this is about you. You've been an awesome and amazing dog, and I really appreciate everything you do for me. It's just, I have a history with Elvis, and the two of us have a very complicated relationship. I'd explain it to you, but I'm not sure I understand it myself."

"Are you talking to your dog?"

I looked up and saw a blond girl staring down at me and Ripley. She wore oversize pink plastic sunglasses with lavender lenses. They took up half her face. Her bright orange T-shirt said I'M A KID IN AMERICA.

"Yes, I was talking to my dog. This is Ripley, and I'm Benji."

"Does he talk back?"

"What? Why would you ask that?"

She smiled. She had lots of teeth, and suddenly her entire face was just sunglasses and a Cheshire cat grin. "I'm just kidding, silly. Are you always so serious? Me? I'm never serious. My name is Kimberly, but my close friends call me Kimmie. Also, can I say, I'm digging your hat."

I stood up because it was the polite thing to do and wiped my sweaty hand on my shorts. "Nice to meet you, Kimberly."

"Kimmie. I said, my friends call me Kimmie. Kim-mie, Kimmie, Kimmie. Well, just one Kimmie. I like the way my name sounds so much, I always throw in some extras."

"I know, but we just met, so I thought . . ." I trailed off. I don't understand why talking to girls is so difficult. Kimmie wasn't even paying attention to me anymore. She squatted down and petted Ripley.

"Why does your dog have a jacket on?" she asked.

"He's a therapy dog. And it's not really a jacket. It's more like a vest. The vest shows he's a working dog."

"What's he working on? A new song?" She laughed, and then quickly explained. "My mama's a country music songwriter, so she's always working on a new song. I want to write a Broadway musical when I grow up. I'm going to write it, direct it, and star in it. I'm what they call in the business 'a triple threat.' Do you want my autograph? It may not be worth much now, but one day it will be."

Whoa—I needed to introduce this girl to Taisy and fast, because maybe Taisy's mouth could keep up with her. Mine certainly couldn't. I nodded my head in agreement. You know what? I believed her when she said she was going to do all those things, even without her threatening me three times.

Kimmie pulled her sunglasses down her nose so I could finally see her bright-blue eyes. She nodded at the crowd gathered around Elvis. "That's the president's dog over there. He's bigger than me."

"He's bigger than me too," I said, and Kimmie laughed. "He's bigger than both of us put together!"

Her laughter was infectious, and I was happy to have a distraction. "He's bigger than me, you, and Ripley all put together."

"What do you think he's doing here?" she asked. "I know the president isn't here or there would be a ton of Secret Service around."

"You're right—the president isn't here. And there's no Secret Service needed either. He's actually here with me. We're watching my friend Taisy compete in the archery tournament."

Kimmie pulled off her sunglasses altogether so she could give me a proper stare down. Without her sunglasses on, she looked strangely familiar, but I couldn't quite figure out why.

"He's with you? Seriously? Don't kid a kidder." She was half impressed, half suspicious.

"Yeah, why would I lie about something like that?"

"I dunno." She shrugged. "I lie all the time. My mom's not really a songwriter."

Wow, I didn't see that coming. I know plenty of kids who lie, but normally we lie about lying, because we know it's wrong. But this girl seemed proud of the fact that she lied.

"Well, I'm not lying. He really is here with me."

"Okay, just say I choose to believe you, and I'm not

saying I do yet, why is he with you? Are you someone important too?" She took out her phone and snapped a picture of me.

"Nope, I'm not famous at all. I'm just here for the weekend to visit him from Pennsylvania. I knew him before he was the president's dog. It's kind of a long story."

"Do you know him from the farm in Tennessee where he was born and trained?"

I eyed Kimmie. She knew an awful lot about Elvis. "Nope. I met him after the farm, but before he came to DC."

"Well, you seem like you're telling the truth, or maybe you're just a very good liar." Kimmie put her sunglasses on so I couldn't see her eyes again.

I don't like anyone calling me a liar. I turned toward the crowd and called out, "Hey, Elvis!"

Elvis immediately broke through the crowd, trotting over to me. "Elvis, this is Kimmie. Kimmie, meet Elvis." Elvis sat and held out his giant paw.

"So Elvis, we meet again." Kimmie took it in her hand and shook it.

"Meet again? You mean you've already met him before?"

"Yep, plenty of times. I have friends at the White

House. Isn't that right, Elvis?"

Elvis thumped his tail once for yes, so I guess she was actually telling the truth this time. I couldn't help wondering what the story was with this girl. I wanted to ask Elvis, but there were too many people around to talk. My mom walked up to us and told us to hurry.

"It's almost Taisy's turn," she said. "We don't want to miss it."

Kimmie stuck her hand out and introduced herself to my mom. My mom shook her hand and told Kimmie she liked her sunglasses. The two of them walked off together ahead of me and Elvis.

"So do you really know Kimmie?" I whispered to Elvis.

"Her mother is a White House reporter, so I've seen her a few times. Whenever she's around, she takes pictures of me or videos. In fact, I wonder what she's doing here at the park. Do you think she's following me?"

"How should I know? I just met her five minutes ago. And she came up to me, not you." It was so like Elvis to make my meeting some wackadoo girl all about him. "She sure is some kind of different."

"Takes one to know one."

"What's that supposed to mean?" I asked.

"Nothing. I'm just saying Kimmie is quite an

eccentric character, and I personally believe it's the interesting people who add spice to life."

"Hey, don't act like I was saying she was different in a bad way, Elvis. I'm the last person on the planet who would ever say different was bad. Look at me—I'm as different as you can get. Especially since I'm standing in the middle of the park talking to a dog."

"Pardon me, of course you are right. I shouldn't have jumped to that conclusion. I know you are not a little kid who judges others."

"Don't call me a little kid. Technically I'm older than you."

"Maybe in human years, but in dog years I'm way older. In dog years I could see an R-rated movie, while you can't even see a PG-13 movie. But fine, I concede your point. Perhaps 'little kid' was patronizing. You are not a child who judges others. Is that more to your liking?"

"You make me crazy, Elvis."

"You're welcome. Now let's hurry along. I'm quite looking forward to seeing Taisy."

Finally, something Elvis and I could agree on.

As we walked toward the tournament, Ripley tried to take his normal place on my right side, but Elvis wasn't having it. He put his giant nose into the six-inch space between me and Ripley and pushed his way in. Do you know what happens when a dog whose head is wider than six inches tries to insert himself into a space that's way too small for him? I get knocked over and fall onto the grass. Honestly, the first time, I didn't even understand what happened. I'm used to mysteriously falling down for no reason. So I just got back up, brushed myself off, and started walking again. A moment later, the same thing happened. But this time I understood what really happened. I rolled onto my back on the grass, and Elvis's giant head blocked out the sky as he peered down at me.

"What are you doing, Benjamin?"

"What am I doing? What are *you* doing?"

"I'm not doing anything. But we're never going to see Taisy if you keep falling down."

"Oh, you think this is my fault? We're never going to see Taisy if you keep trying to walk on my right side when it's clear that Ripley walks on my right side. You know I do have two sides. You realize you could just walk on my left side!"

"I was doing nothing of the sort. But fine. I suppose I could walk on the left side. Though I prefer the right side. I have a splendid idea. Perhaps you could ask Ripley to walk on your left side. He seems affable, so I'm sure he wouldn't mind."

In a way, it was good to know Elvis could be just as petty and silly as the rest of us. To be honest, it kind of made me happy to see how jealous he was. And that warm, fuzzy, happy feeling would have continued except that a giant, slimy, sticky drool string hanging off the side of his mouth broke and fell right onto my face. Yuck!

10

I wasn't surprised Taisy made it to the semifinals. She'd only "gotten serious" about archery after we decided it was our best chance to get to DC, but Taisy's idea of "getting serious" is way different from regular people's. She's superhuman. She practices longer than you think is possible, and with absolute focus and determination. When she'd won the tournament to get us to DC, I asked her if she was happy she could finally relax now.

"Relax? Why would I do that?" she asked.

"Because you got us to DC. That was the whole point of this. Getting to DC for Elvis. It doesn't matter how you do in the tournament when we get there, right?"

"Of course it matters!" she said, and looked at me like I was crazy. "Why wouldn't I want to win the DC tournament too? Why do you think I can't win?"

At first I thought she was joking, but then I realized her completely serious face meant she was actually serious.

"Well, of course I believe you can win. But what if you don't win? You do realize that there are more nonwinners than there are winners. Not just in archery competitions, but like, in life."

"Benj, there you go with your stinkin' thinkin'," Taisy said, shaking her head.

Well, she had me there. I guess we could chalk it up to lack of experience. I've never really competed in much of anything. Well, unless you count a three-legged sack race (ended up in the hospital with a twisted ankle), an egg-and-spoon race (ended up getting egg all over David Tolentino's brand-new limited-edition Michael Jordan kicks), and the water-balloon toss (I'm assuming you know who ended up all wet, right?). In each of those cases I was forced to participate by my mom, who really wanted to go to the kids' birthday parties so she could check out the cake.

"Benj, in order to be a winner, you have to think like a winner. And it's not like I just expect to win a tournament without working for it. I practice. A lot," Taisy continued.

I nodded. Maybe Taisy was right. She should try her hardest and win the tournament in DC. I wondered what it felt like to be so good at something. I had never really experienced that feeling of being really great at something. I'm not brilliant like Alexander Chang-Cohen. I'm not an amazing baker like my mom. Obviously, the twins are male versions of Taisy, and I'm not great at sports like them. Even my dad has a talent. He has this weird green thumb. Everything he plants survives, even things that shouldn't grow in Pennsylvania.

"Benjamin, why does your face look like that?" Elvis asked, interrupting my thoughts. I immediately put my hands up to my face and felt around.

"What do you mean? What's wrong with my face? Do I have a rash? I don't feel itchy. Am I getting a unicorn horn? Because that's the last thing I need."

"No, you're fine. I meant, what are you thinking about? You seem a million miles away. And for your information, unicorns are creatures of fiction, so it's highly unlikely that a unicorn horn would grow out of your forehead."

"Shhhhhh!" My mom shushed us and pointed to the field.

Taisy walked up confidently, getting into position. It was her first set. She pulled the bow back slowly and eyed the target. Taisy would get three arrows. Whoever got the most points for hitting the arrow closest to the center would win that set. There are five sets of three arrows each, and the winner is the person who wins the most sets in a round.

Taisy shot her first arrow. It wasn't even close to the bull's-eye. The crowd murmured. My mouth went dry.

"That was not good. Normally she totally hits the center," I whispered to Elvis.

"Shhhhhh!" My mom and Kimmie shushed me.

Taisy's second arrow flew, landing dead center. Taisy's dad called out, "That's my girl!" You're not supposed to cheer until after all three arrows are shot, because you don't want to disturb the contestant's concentration. But Taisy probably didn't even notice. She has the concentration of a steel trap.

Taisy's third arrow hit so close to her second arrow, it was hard to tell them apart. The crowd cheered. Taisy had come from behind and won the set.

"So what's going on, Benjamin?" Elvis asked, leaning into me.

"Who cares about me? What's going on with you? Why are we here? What's going on with you?"

Elvis shook his head. A string of drool flew out of his mouth, slapping me in the forehead. I wiped it off as he whispered to me, "I don't want to discuss it here, out in the open. I'll tell you later."

"Out in the open? You're a dog, and as far as I can tell, no one understands you except for me."

"I'm not worried about people hearing. I'm worried about other dogs hearing," Elvis said, nodding toward Ripley.

"Ripley would never tell. He's such a good dog. So loyal and obedient and—"

"Yes, how lovely for Ripley. He's just the best dog ever. I wasn't talking about him. I was talking about Mr. Long Ears over there at three o'clock."

I turned my head toward three o'clock.

"Don't look right away!"

"Oh please, you're being paranoid, Elvis." I turned and saw a basset hound about twenty yards away, lying next to his owner's folding chair. First off, the basset hound looked asleep. Secondly, I could tell by all the white hair around his muzzle he was clearly a really old dog.

"You're worried about that dog hearing you? He's asleep."

"Benjamin, dogs can still hear better than you when they're asleep. Trust me. I belong to the school of It is better to be safe than sorry. I don't want my words being carried away on the breeze. My personal business is my personal business. You're here because I trust you implicitly. Now tell me what's bothering you."

Before I could speak, Taisy got up for her second set of three arrows. This time all three of her arrows hit the center ring. She barely paused between shots. Taisy easily won that set too.

"It's just that Taisy's only eleven and Alexander's even a few months younger than me, and they're both awesome at a lot of things. The only thing I'm really good at is getting injured and winding up in the hospital. And to be honest, I wish I wasn't so good at it."

"You're good at a lot of things, Benjamin, and remember your age. You have plenty of time to figure out what you want to do with your life. If I were you, I'd enjoy being a kid, because hanging out with adults all the time, I've learned that it's way more fun to be a kid."

Elvis and I stopped talking, and then I smelled

something, a sudden hint of a snowy mountain breeze. (Not that I know what that even smells like since I've never been on top of a snowy mountain. But I imagine that's what it would smell like.) I looked up and there was Kimmie, chewing minty gum.

"What are you and Elvis talking about? Hmmmm?" Kimmie asked. I was starting to wonder if Kimmie's passion was showing up at random times and asking random questions. She had changed her sunglasses. These were red, shaped like hearts, with blue lenses.

"Did you change your sunglasses?" I asked.

"I did. Thanks for noticing. I think it's important to have a second look ready at any time, just in case you have to blend in to a crowd and disappear. Don't I look totally different?" She sucked in her cheeks and made fish lips at me.

"Uh . . . yes?" No doubt about it. This girl was weird.

"Taisy just tied her third set," Kimmie said.

"Oh. Whoops. I guess I missed it." I had been so wrapped up in my conversation with Elvis, I'd missed Taisy's turn completely.

"So whatcha talking about with the president's dog? Spy stuff?"

"That's ridiculous. I'm not a spy. And neither is Elvis." I scowled.

"I didn't say you were a bad spy. I was thinking you were a good spy. Relax. This is Washington, DC, spy capital of the world. On any given day there are ten thousand spies in the city." She leaned in close. "For all you know, I could be a spy."

"Ten thousand spies? Where did you hear that?"

"It's just a known fact. We've got a lot of history here. You should stick around. You might learn something."

"Of course there's a lot of history here, but I'm from the Philly area, and we have a lot of history too. Big things happened, bells rung, I mean, rang, well, not many bells, but one bell in particular. Though I guess there were multiple bells ringing at times, because there are a lot of church bells too. Oh, you know what I mean."

I don't know why I only get all tongue-tied around girls. Okay, so when I'm flustered I tend to get tongue-tied around anyone, but it's always worse around girls.

"Do I? Know what you mean?" Kimmie pulled her sunglasses down to the end of her nose, staring at me intensely.

"You're a weirdo, Kimmie."

"Benjamin. That's not nice," Elvis barked softly. "And you should be careful around her. I'm not sure I trust her."

"What?!" I looked down at Elvis and threw my hands up in the air. Then I turned back to Kimmie. "I'm sorry, Kimmie. That wasn't nice of me. I didn't mean to name-call. I simply meant I find every single thing about you weird." I turned back to Elvis. "Is that better, Your Highness?"

"Oh, so I'm the weird one?" Kimmie said. "You're the one having a conversation with your dog. You do realize dogs and humans don't actually understand each other."

I guess my eyes got wide, because she squinted at me, peering close at my face. "Wait a second. Do you understand what he's saying? Are you saying your dog talks to you?"

"No. Of course not. Dogs don't talk. That would make me crazy."

"You're right, it would make you crazy. Crazy interesting. But your expression seemed to say otherwise. I'm good at reading facial expressions. I have a spy book at home, and I've learned you can tell a lot just from looking at a person's face. I also have a book that teaches you how to lie better."

"There's a book that teaches you how to lie better?"

"Well, technically, the book teaches you how to spot a liar. I figure if I make sure I don't do the things people can spot, I'll just naturally be a better liar."

"That weirdly makes sense."

"I know it does. And I don't mind you calling me weird. I take it as a compliment. I don't want to be like everyone else. I want to be an original."

"Well you're in luck, because you are a complete original."

Suddenly, it was like a solar eclipse. First it was super sunny, then it was super not sunny. I looked up and saw a shadow. I thought it was the moon covering the sun, but then I realized it was just my mom and her big hair.

"Benji, Kimmie. You two are not being very polite. It's Taisy's turn again. You two should stop talking and instead be supportive of your friend. This is the semifinals, so if she wins this, she's going to compete in the finals tomorrow."

"She's not my friend. I don't even know her."

OH NO, SHE DIDN'T!!!!! I wouldn't have believed it if I wasn't standing right there and witnessing it. Kimmie had just talked back to my mother. My mom has a high tolerance for a lot of things, especially because she raised the twins, which she compares to dealing with feral animals on a daily basis. But she is a stickler for kids' manners and how they speak to adults. And she is not a fan of sassy backtalk.

My mother leaned right into Kimmie's face. She had her hand on her hip. "Excuse me, young lady, I'm not sure exactly who you think you are, or who you think you are talking to, but you will not address me in that tone of voice. Where is your mother?"

Kimmie was speechless. Suddenly she looked like every other kid who has just gotten in trouble. My mom has a universal you-better-watch-out tone of voice that she can use at any time. She can be the most fun mom ever, but she can also be the scariest mom ever.

"I'm sorry, Benji's mom. Really. Please don't tell my mom. I'm sorry. She'll take away my laptop and then I'll die. Please don't tell! Please don't tell. Please don't tell. Please don't tell. Please don't tell. Please don't tell. . . ."

It was clear she was just going to keep going unless my mom stopped her. Another thing about my mom? She never, ever holds a grudge.

"Okay, okay, I won't tell your mother, but where is she? You're too young to be out here on your own."

Kimmie pointed over to a small tent on the other side of the field that said PRESS.

"She's a reporter. Normally she only covers the White House, but someone called in sick, so she had to cover this event for them. DC reporters are all about calling in favors. Now that person owes her one."

A cheer erupted, and we turned around to see Taisy jumping up and down for joy. Mr. McDonald raced across the field like he was scoring a touchdown and swept Taisy up in his big arms.

"I can't believe it. Now I missed it too! We're terrible. All of us. But you two especially," my mom said. "Do not tell Taisy we missed her big moment. We don't want to hurt her feelings."

"That won't be a problem for Kimmie," I said. "Apparently, she's a great liar."

"Benji, that is not nice. What is going on? Is it national Be Rude Day and no one told me? Apologize."

"But Mom, she's the one . . ." What was I doing? For Pete's sake, now Kimmie had me talking back to my mom. I looked at Kimmie and her giant red glasses. "I'm sorry for calling you a great liar."

"That's okay. And I'm not a great liar. I'm an awesome liar."

"See, Mom! Did you hear that?"

But my mom wasn't even listening. She walked toward Taisy, who was running over to us. Taisy had one of the biggest smiles I've ever seen on her face. It was kind of odd. She wins all the time, so I didn't think this win would make her this happy. Then she ran right toward me, her arms outstretched. What else could I do? I stepped forward and stretched my arms out too, ready to congratulate her. But then Taisy ran right past me, hurling herself at Elvis. She wrapped her arms around his neck and buried her face in his big, black, velvety cheek.

"Elvis, you big cutie patootie! I've missed you!"

Wow, if being embarrassed was a competition, I would have just won a gold medal. I quickly recovered, turning my hug-me arms into a fake yawn. I was hoping no one noticed. Then I looked over at Kimmie, and she gave me a smile that said she'd definitely noticed.

11

I once overheard my mom telling my dad that if a child asks for something forty times, parents eventually get so worn down they give in. She read it out loud from a magazine over breakfast one morning. I'm sure my dad forgot this little factoid by the end of breakfast, but I've always remembered it. I even put the theory to the test. Asking for something forty times is harder than you think. I tend to give up around twenty. It's not easy hearing "no" over and over again,

and it's even tougher to push forward once my mom says, "Do you want to know what'll happen if you ask for that glow-in-the-dark fish tank one more time?" I never wanted to know.

After Taisy's win at the archery tournament, we all went back to her room at the hotel to celebrate. While my mom and Mrs. Chang-Cohen had regular rooms, Taisy's dad got the presidential suite. It was a super-fancy two-bedroom suite on the top floor of the hotel. The room had French doors that opened to a small balcony and an amazing view of the White House. As soon as we walked in, I knew this was the perfect place to order room service. I also knew it was the perfect place to have room service without any parents around. While Mr. McDonald showed my mom and Alexander's mom the view of the White House, I whispered my plan to Alexander and Taisy. It was foolproof, and this is exactly what happened. I nodded at Taisy and Alexander Chang-Cohen, counted to three with my fingers behind my back, and then we all went for it. We even used our special high-pitched voices for effect. Taisy went first; then Alexander and I followed.

"Daddy, please let us order room service. Didn't you say I could get a treat for winning?"

"Mooooooom, please can we order room service? The

three of you can eat downstairs in the fancy dining room without having to worry about us being bored or being too loud or using the wrong fork."

"I will eat two vegetables, not just one, if we can order room service. Room service vegetables are extra good for you. I heard that somewhere like on the radio once."

"Please—we never get to stay in hotels."

"Room service is so cool and fun, and don't you want us to remember this trip forever?"

"I love that little wheeling cart thingie that turns into a table like I always see on TV."

"Can we?"

"Please, may we?"

"I could die happy, if only . . ."

"Just say yes! This is a vacation, or like a vacation."

"What's the harm in it? We're happy, you're all happy. It's pretty much a win-win situation."

"Please, Mom?"

"Please, Daddy. You know I love you."

"Please, Mom. I'll be your best friend."

"Just say yes."

"You know you want to say yes. I can tell by the way you're smiling."

"Remember how you told me that you love room service too, and it made you feel like a queen? Don't you want that for me? I mean, not the queen part because I'm a boy, but I could feel like a prince. Or a king. Please?"

"Did I tell you how much I love you and how you're the best mom in the whole world?"

"Please, let us?"

"I'll never ask for anything again . . . for the rest of the night."

"Can we get room service, please?"

"Say yes, please say yes."

"I'd be happy with a maybe, that I can work with. Did you know maybe is just a hop, skip, and a hug away from yes?"

"How lucky are we to be here in Washington, DC, with the best parents ever? We are truly blessed."

And then finally we joined in together and chanted, "Please, please, please, please, please, please, please, please, please . . ."

Taisy's dad caved first. "Enough! Everyone stop talking right now."

The three of us clammed up immediately and looked at one another. Mr. McDonald's voice is loud and deep in general, so sometimes it's difficult to tell whether he's mad. This was one of those times.

"Let's huddle up." And then he waved to my mom and Mrs. Chang-Cohen to follow him into the bedroom and closed the door.

I held my breath, wondering whether it had worked. Elvis bumped me, reminding me to breathe.

"Do you think it worked?" Alexander Chang-Cohen sounded hopeful. Taisy tiptoed to the door and tried to listen, but she shook her head and said the door was too thick.

"Was that forty? Did we make it?" We were all so busy asking that none of us had really kept track.

"I was keeping track of my own number of my own asks," said Alexander, "so if I multiplied mine by three . . ." He didn't finish his sentence, because the door opened so fast that Taisy had to jump away. She nonchalantly looked around, saying, "I just love the glass doorknobs in this hotel. They seem like they're original from whenever it is this place was built."

"You kids are too much," my mom said, laughing. "Okay, we have decided to grant your wish. The three of us are going downstairs to eat in the Lafayette Room. You three may stay here and . . . and . . ." She paused for dramatic effect. "Order room service."

We broke into cheers and did a happy dance. I'm sure if anyone saw us, they'd think we just received the best news in the world. And honestly, it's kind of what it felt like. That moment when they said yes, I looked around the room and realized I was in fact a really lucky kid. I had amazing friends, we had awesome parents, and Elvis and I were together again.

After our parents left, all three of us lay across the king-size bed with Taisy in the center, looking over the leather room-service binder. Taisy was the expert. She had traveled all over the country for gymnastics competitions, so she'd had room service plenty of times. Even Alexander had had room service once on a trip to Disneyland. But me? This was my very first time.

We read through every single item on the menu, twice. Taisy wanted French onion soup, a turkey club sandwich, and warm cookies with milk for dessert. Alexander Chang-Cohen tried to decide between the pepperoni pizza and a cheeseburger with sweet potato fries. He wanted the Oreo cheesecake for dessert. Me? Well, I'm more complicated because of my food allergies. No nuts, no cilantro, no pine nuts (which are technically seeds). I'm also allergic to some mushrooms, but not all of them. I do like tomato sauce but not sliced tomatoes. I also like salsa but not cherry tomatoes. I can eat American cheese but not cheddar cheese, because it makes my stomach hurt. I used to be allergic to fish, but then I think I grew out of it, because I accidentally ate half a tuna salad sandwich, thinking it was chicken salad, and nothing happened to me. Bay scallops give me itchy feet, while big scallops make my ears turn red. But I can eat crab. Go figure.

So, taking all that into account, I was leaning toward either the mac and cheese or spaghetti and meatballs (but only if the meatballs were made without oregano—oregano makes me sneeze). Taisy let out a sigh waiting for me to decide and then just picked up the phone to order.

"Hey, don't forget to order something extra," Elvis said, nudging me. "And maybe you and I can take a walk together. Just the two of us."

"Hey, Taisy. Order something extra for Elvis and Ripley," I said casually. "I'm going to take Elvis for a quick walk. Ripley will stay here and stand guard over you guys."

"Guard us? Why would we need a guard? What do you know? Is someone coming we don't know about? Are we in danger?" Alexander Chang-Cohen asked, in a panic.

"No! I was just kidding. But I am going to go out alone with Elvis."

"But what did you want for dessert?" Taisy asked.

"Surprise me. Just make sure I'm not allergic to it."

I looked Ripley right in the eyes and told it to him

straight. I felt it was a better way to go than beating around the bush.

"Ripley, don't take it personally, but I'm going out with just Elvis this time. So you stay here and be a good dog." If Ripley was upset, he didn't show it. He trotted over to Taisy and let her pet him. She cooed in his face. "Who's my Ripley Bipley Boo-bear?"

When we got out into the hall, I heard Elvis mutter, "I cannot believe *he* gets Taisy's baby-talk voice too."

"Did you say something, Elvis?" I asked with a smile on my face.

"No, I didn't."

I texted my mom, and she said it was fine for me to go but insisted I not cross any streets and I stay in sight of the hotel doorman so he could keep an eye on me. I texted her back and pointed out that I'd probably be safe with the two-hundred-pound dog at my side. As soon as we hit the sidewalk, I told Elvis he had ten minutes to tell me everything.

"What do you want to know?" he asked.

What did I want to know? Was he kidding? "I want to know everything. You're the one who was like, 'Benj, come quick and save my tail! Please hurry!'"

"I said nothing of the sort. Why must you always exaggerate so?"

"I don't know, because I'm a kid? Because I have an overdeveloped imagination? Elvis, I'm here to help you. Just tell me what's going on."

"It's an extremely complicated and delicate situation. I'm just not sure where to begin."

"Hmmmm, oooh, let me think. Oh, I have an idea. Why not start at the beginning?"

Elvis stopped walking and looked up at me. "You know, I missed a great many things about you, Benjamin, but your sarcasm wasn't one of them."

I rolled my eyes. Elvis sighed. We were quiet for a full minute while I waited for him to start. And then, finally, Elvis told me everything.

I know that everything you hear from a talking dog would probably be weird, but it's not actually true. I guess I'm just used to Elvis talking now, so I don't find it all that strange anymore. Well, until he told me his story. It was a very long story, and Elvis started at the very beginning.

"The earliest interactions between the United States and Japan date back to the seventeenth century, Benji, and that is known as the Nanban trade period, though to be clear, the United States wasn't the United States as we know it now. In the seventeenth century, it was the European colonies that would later become the United States."

"Uh, Elvis? I'm not really sure what you just said

and why it's important, but we have two blocks until we're back at the hotel."

"I was trying to give you an overview of the relations between the United States and Japan from the beginning, as you suggested. I believe this will give you the proper context to understand my current dilemma."

"Okay, but this is what I just heard: blah blah blah blah current dilemma. So why don't we fast-forward to the current dilemma part and save the history lesson for later when I'm having problems falling asleep tonight?"

"I believe our society is moving in the wrong direction with all this hurry, hurry, instant media access, birdy tweety nonsense. Patience is a virtue, and sometimes slowing down and looking at the whole picture of a situation is better when making an informed decision. The way I see it, we would all be better off . . ."

I stopped walking. Elvis continued ahead, still rambling. He stopped after a few feet and turned around. "Benjamin, don't dawdle."

"Come back here, Elvis."

"Why don't you come here?"

Before Elvis first arrived at my house, my dad gave me two dog books. I read them both, twice. Both books said it was very important to show your dog who's the owner and who's the dog. Somehow I felt like this was one of those moments. Even though technically Elvis wasn't my dog anymore, I still wanted to show him who was boss. Or at least show him he wasn't the boss of me.

It was a standoff. I stayed in my spot, and Elvis stayed in his. Finally, Elvis trotted back toward me and sat down. "I don't play games, Benjamin."

"I wasn't playing a game, Elvis. I don't think you get what's going on here. I'm here all day tomorrow and tomorrow night. Then we leave early Monday morning, because my mom still thinks we should all go to school even if it's only for a half day. I told her that was ridiculous because—"

"Benjamin." Elvis tilted his head to the side. We started walking again.

"Oh, like you don't ramble too? But point taken. I'm not here long, you have a problem that you need help with, so let's hear it."

"I'm afraid the president is going to give me away as a gift to the prime minister of Japan, and I don't want to go. I don't like sushi."

Out of all the things I had imagined over the last two weeks—and I had thought of a ton of different scenarios, from aliens to the zombie apocalypse—this had never been on the list.

"But why would he give you away? To Japan?" I asked.

And this is what Elvis told me. Of course, he gave me the long Elvis version, but I'm going to try to make it brief. About two months ago, there was a big fancy party at the White House, and the prime minister of Japan was there. When he saw Elvis, he had this crazy, over-the-top reaction. His reaction was so big there was a momentary panic, because he dropped to his knees in the Rose Garden, and everyone thought he was having a heart attack. Apparently, such showy behavior is very out of character for a Japanese dignitary, because they're known for being serious and unemotional.

Elvis, given the fact he is a dog, couldn't help himself. When he saw the prime minister with his arms outstretched for him, Elvis ran into them. A few of the prime minister's security guys moved in to stop him, which then caused some of the United States Secret Service guys to jump in there too, and it was just a big pile of Secret Service guys and a dog and a prime minister. Then the president called everyone off, because he realized the prime minister really did want to hug and say hello to Elvis.

"As you know, Benjamin, I am fluent in French, my

Italian is serviceable, but unfortunately, I do not know any Japanese at all," Elvis explained to me. We were back in front of the hotel again. I looked up to see if the doorman was watching me.

I called out to him, "Gotta do another lap. He hasn't done his business yet." Then I ducked down so he wouldn't wonder why I was talking to a dog.

"So even though he was saying things to me, I couldn't really understand what he was saying," Elvis continued. "But what I can tell you is that he had an extremely strong reaction to me, which I knew must have quite a story to it. I was right, of course."

Of course, Elvis was right. There was quite a story behind the prime minister's reaction to Elvis. Eventually the translators got involved and explained everything. The prime minister's love of Newfoundland dogs, and black Newfoundland dogs in particular, went back to when he was a little boy.

When the prime minister was about my age, he went on vacation with his parents somewhere in the part of Maine that is near Canada. Or maybe it was in Canada, but in the part of Canada that is near Maine? I can't remember what Elvis said exactly. Anyway, he was in the ocean playing, and he ended up too far out. The tide pulled him farther and farther away, and his parents weren't paying attention. He began freaking out, and in his panic he started drowning.

"He said that forty years after it happened, he could still close his eyes and taste the salt water. It was the most terrifying experience of his life, and even though he was probably too young to really understand death, he did remember feeling an intense sadness, because he felt like he was going to die and his parents would be heartbroken." Elvis paused for dramatic effect.

"Then what happened?" I asked. "And don't you dare say 'patience is a virtue' again."

"Well, suddenly a large black object appeared next to him, grabbing his arm. He thought it was a terrible sea dragon, which is probably the Japanese version of a sea monster. But it wasn't a sea dragon at all, Benjamin." Elvis took his second dramatic pause. "It was a giant black Newfoundland. The dog swam out to save this little boy's life. The Newfoundland swam in tight circles around him, keeping his head above water. Eventually the dog took the boy's arm in his mouth and swam toward the shore, dragging him behind him. The next thing the prime minister remembered was his dad pulling him out of the water. He felt the sun on his face, and heard the sound of his mother crying with relief."

"But where did this Newfie come from? How did he

know the kid was drowning? What happened next?" I asked breathlessly. Elvis then explained that the owners of the Newfie had no idea what was going on until the dog was already swimming back, pulling the boy with him. It was pretty chaotic after the rescue. The dog owners spoke in English, and the prime minister's parents spoke in Japanese. Somehow, though, they managed to trade information. The prime minister's parents wanted to repay the owners and their Newfie in some way.

"But for some reason, they were unable to contact the Newfie's family after they returned to Japan," said Elvis. "To this day, the prime minister regrets not getting the chance to properly repay and thank the dog who saved his young life. He literally said he would not be alive today if it wasn't for the unbelievable heroics of a Newfoundland. So now, whenever he sees one, which is very rare in Japan, he goes a little overboard."

"Wow," I said, thinking over Elvis's story. "What was that like for you? Getting all that attention?"

"I was very proud and pleased to hear about it, but I can't say I'm surprised. I believe any Newfie would have done the exact same thing if he had been there."

Leave it to Elvis to not be surprised by one of the craziest stories I had ever heard.

"Elvis, the guy is the prime minister of Japan, which I know is like the head honcho dude of the entire country. Think about what would have happened if that Newfie hadn't been right where he was right when he was."

"I'd prefer not to think about such things. Don't dwell on what could have happened, Benjamin. Concentrate on looking forward."

"Well, right now, I'm looking forward to room service. We should head back upstairs."

Elvis and I went inside. We said a quick hi to the doorman, who dropped down to pet Elvis for a minute. As we walked to the elevator, I paused and ran up the few stairs to the dining area, waving to my mom to let her know I was okay. She waved back and threw me one of her giant smiles. She looked really happy in that fancy dining room, surrounded by cloth napkins and real silver and giant bouquets of flowers.

After the excitement of Elvis's story, I almost forgot about his predicament, but as soon as we stepped into the elevator, I told him to tell it to me straight, no more storytelling. And that's when Elvis said that a week after that dinner he was in the Oval Office, sleeping behind the president's chair, when the chief of staff came in and mentioned they needed to send a gift to the

Japanese prime minister for his fiftieth birthday.

"Well, it needs to be good," Elvis heard the president say. "It needs to be personal. Japan is one of our closest allies."

"Right, and you'll be announcing the new trade agreement next month, so it'd be a nice gesture to make it special."

"Well then, what about a picture of Elvis and the prime minister in an antique frame? I mean, man, did he ever love Elvis."

"You know what would really knock his socks off?" the chief of staff said.

"What?" asked the president. Elvis completely woke up then. He wanted to hear this too.

"Just go with me for a moment," said the chief of staff. "Would you ever consider giving him Elvis? He and Elvis certainly bonded that night. And I think it would be the perfect way to show him how much we value our relationship with Japan."

The elevator door opened with a soft *bing*. We were back on the eighth floor. To be honest, in that moment I was worried that we had been gone so long, we'd missed the whole room service delivery part. I really didn't want to miss the part where the guy comes in with a cart and sets everything up for you. Anyway, I was so worried about that, it took a minute for Elvis's story to actually sink in.

"*Beep, beep, beep.* Back up. What did you say?"

"*Beep, beep, beep*? What does that mean?"

"That's the sound a truck makes when it backs up. It goes *beep, beep, beep.*"

"Oh, I suppose it does. That's very amusing, Benjamin. *Beep, beep, beep,* back up. I will have to remember that colloquial expression."

"Okay, this conversation has left the building. Go back to what you were saying about you being a gift?"

"If the president gives me as a gift, then I'd be the Japanese prime minister's dog. And I'd have to live in Japan. And I don't like sushi. Well, I don't mind a good fish stick, but you know me, I'm more of a cheeseburger sort of dog. Plus Japan is very far away."

And then I realized Elvis wasn't being completely honest. He didn't send me a secret message with his tail because he didn't like sushi. He sent me a secret message because he didn't want to lose me. If Elvis moved to Japan, I'd probably never see him again. One, because Japan is halfway across the world and I'm ten years old, so it's not like I can just buy a plane ticket and hop on over there. Two, I don't speak Japanese, so how would I be able to set up a visit even if I could get there?

When these things registered fully, it hit me like a ton of bricks. All I kept saying over and over was, "Japan? Japan? Really, Japan? Like *Japan* Japan? Japan? Whoa, Japan." I said it so many times, the words sounded all weird, and pretty soon it felt like I was just saying gibberish. Elvis licked my face to get me to stop.

Finally, I found my words. "But wait, you said this happened weeks ago. If they were going to do it, wouldn't they have done it already?"

"Well, his birthday is coming up soon, but I'm not sure when exactly. I need you to Google it." Wait, he wanted me to Google it? Maybe Elvis didn't care about leaving me after all.

"Oh. Is that why you needed my help? To Google someone's birthday?"

"Yes, Benjamin, I sent you a coded message for you to come to DC so you could Google one piece of information for me. I just wanted to know when I'd be leaving."

"Are you being sarcastic?"

"I'm trying, but if you're not sure if I am, then I'm certainly not doing a very good job of it, am I?"

I pulled out my phone and Googled "prime minister of Japan's birthday," which took me to Wikipedia, which said that it was . . . I swallowed hard—ten days from now.

"Now, are you absolutely sure this is happening? You know for a fact that the president is going to give you away? Because the prime minister's birthday is only ten days away."

"No, I don't know for certain, but I did hear his staff whispering about Japan and giving me odd looks. What I do know for certain is I don't want to go. I need you to figure out a way to stop this from happening."

"Well, why didn't you say so?"

"Benj, what are you doing out here in the hall talking to yourself?" I looked up and saw Taisy peeking through a crack in the door.

"What? Oh, I was just talking to Elvis, you know, catching up and all." I tried to laugh it off. Taisy talks to Princess Daisy all the time, so I was hoping she wouldn't think it was too weird. "Well, come in and be your normal weird self in here. Room service should be here soon."

I didn't have a choice. I had to go inside, even though I still had about a million questions. When we entered the room again, I ushered Elvis right into the bathroom, calling out, "Sorry! I think Elvis stepped in something gross outside. I should clean up his paws so he doesn't track it all over your room." My voice was all squeaky and high-pitched with anxiety. After I closed the bathroom door, I whispered to Elvis.

"What am I supposed to do to keep you here?"

"I don't know, Benjamin. I'm much smarter than you, but I still haven't been able to come up with an idea. Well, besides asking you for help. Look, at the very least I'm grateful that we got to see each other one last time."

"Whoa, whoa, whoa! Hold your horses. Don't say that. No one said you were going anywhere. This whole thing is crazy. You can't just up and move to Japan. There's no way I'm going to let this happen."

As big a problem as this was for Elvis, it was an equally big problem for me. There was no way I would let Elvis leave the United States of America and me behind. I had no idea what I was going to do, but I knew I would think of something.

As Elvis and I walked out of the bathroom, there was a knock on the door. Maybe room service would take my mind off my problems. I was either extremely hungry or my stomach was now all tied up in knots about Elvis. I reached up to take the chain off the door. Alexander bolted past me and threw his back up against the door.

"What are you doing?" I asked him.

Alexander Chang-Cohen whispered, "Stranger

danger. My mom makes me follow a strict protocol of answering the door when there are no adults around."

"But it's our dinner."

"How do you know that?"

"Because he knocked and said, 'Room service.'"

"The faster you let him do his thing, the faster we can eat dinner and get to dessert," Taisy called out.

"You do know a two-hundred-pound dog is in the room, and I'm pretty sure that's better protection than most adults," I whispered back to Alexander. He said he'd ask his mother to revise the protocol with regard to having a dog in the room, but for now he couldn't.

"Hi, sir," Alexander called through the door. "How do we know you're room service?"

"Because I am? I'm sorry, is there a problem? Is this room 818?"

"Yes, it is, but I just have to ask you a few questions before I am allowed to answer the door, if that's okay."

"Go ahead."

"What is your name?"

"My name is Petey Peterson."

"Is that short for Peter Peterson?"

"Yes, why?"

"I was just curious."

"Alexander!" Taisy and I both yelled at him together.

Alexander continued talking through the door. "Hi, Petey, my name is Alexander Chang-Cohen, and I'm here with my friends Benjamin Barnsworth and Taisy McDonald. That's our dinner you have out there."

"Well, it's very nice to meet all of you . . . through the door?"

"May I ask how long have you worked for the hotel?"

"Let's see, I guess it will be about two years this July."

"Great, now I'm just going to call downstairs and verify you work here, and then I can open the door. I hope you understand that we have to be extra careful because we're kids."

"I do understand, Mr. Chang-Cohen. I'm happy to wait."

"Lastly, what color is your hair?"

"Excuse me, sir?"

"Alexander," I whispered, "if he was a bad guy, I'm pretty sure he would have left by now, so I think we're all good."

"Your hair color? And eye color, if you don't mind," Alexander continued, ignoring me.

"Well, what hair I have left is brown, and my eye color is green with flecks of hazel."

"Alexander, come on," Taisy called out. Even she was losing patience. "I'm going to faint, I'm so hungry. Can't we just open the door? Please? I agree with Benj. I'm pretty sure he is who he says he is. I mean, who would lie and pretend they're room service?"

"Everyone! We're in a hotel. In every movie that takes place in a hotel, when some bad guy wants access to a room, they say, 'Room service,' or if it's a woman, they say, 'Housekeeping.'"

"Hey!" said Taisy. "Only women can be housekeeping? That's so chauvinist."

"I'm sorry, Taisy. You're correct. That was foolish of me. I take it—"

"Can we just get on with this?! Our food is getting cold!!"

Alexander nodded and called downstairs to ask if a Petey Peterson worked for the hotel and what color his hair and eyes were. He hung up the phone and gave me a thumbs-up.

I rolled my eyes, opened the door, and came face-to-face with the real, live Petey Peterson. He smiled and pushed a large rolling table into the room. The three of us sat on the bed and watched as he unlocked the sides of the cart, turning it into a round table covered in a white tablecloth. My favorite part? The domed silver covers over our plates. It was just so grand room service-y, especially since Petey Peterson had on such a nice uniform. The gold buttons were so shiny, I knew Taisy must like it too. He arranged the table and chairs so one of us could sit on the bed, and two others could sit on the chairs.

"Is there a fourth person?" he asked.

"Nope. The fourth dinner is for our dogs," Taisy said.

Petey Peterson looked around again and finally noticed Elvis sitting quietly by the window. Then he did a double take. "That's the biggest dog I've ever seen!"

"He gets that a lot. Petey Peterson, meet Elvis. Elvis, meet Petey Peterson," I said. Elvis wagged his tail a few times. Petey bowed slightly before Elvis, and in a surprising turn of events spoke in a really goofy, baby voice. "What a nice doggie you are, Elvis. Are you a nice doggie?"

I cringed a little. Elvis hates being talked to like that, well, unless it comes from Taisy. But when Taisy does it, she's not talking down to him as much as loving him up. Petey patted Elvis on the head a few times.

"Okay, kids, you have a nice dinner. Either you can call room service and we'll come remove the table, or you can just push it out into the hallway and someone will pick it up."

Taisy signed the check, and when Petey saw her signature he smiled. "That's probably the prettiest signature I've ever seen, and in my job, that's saying a lot, because I see tons of signatures."

"I'm so happy you like that one." Taisy beamed with joy. "It's new. I figure I have a few more years before I have to pick the signature I'm going to use for the rest of my life. Well, unless I happen to get famous sooner rather than later."

"One more thing: Before you guys check out, you should ask the front desk to call down to the kitchen," Petey said on his way out the door. "I'm sure they'll let you see our old-fashioned ice cream freezer. It's pretty cool."

"What's an old-fashioned ice cream freezer?" I had to ask, because I'm curious about anything having to do with ice cream.

"I know! I know!" Alexander Chang-Cohen raised his hand like he was in school. "It's a walk-in freezer that was originally designed to store those big tubs of ice cream."

Petey touched his finger to his nose with one hand and pointed at Alexander Chang-Cohen with the other.

"Right on the nose. And we've got thirty-plus flavors. It's pretty cool to see."

And as quickly as Petey walked into our lives, he walked out.

13

If you want to know whether room service maca-
roni and cheese is better than regular mac and cheese,
it is. We were so excited and hungry that for the first
five minutes of eating, we didn't even talk. We each
savored the experience in our own way. Taisy was very

proper, sitting up very straight
with her napkin in her lap.
Every few bites she picked
up the silver bud vase and
inhaled the scent of the
single red rose. Alexan-
der Chang-Cohen also
loved the domed covers.
After every bite he

covered and uncovered his food.

And me? I just kept repeating in my head, This is my very first room service meal of my entire life. This is my first bite of my very first room service meal of my entire life. This is my first twirl of spaghetti of my very first room service meal of my entire life. And then when I sucked up a lemon seed through my straw in my water and it started a huge coughing fit, I thought, This is my very first coughing fit of my very first room service meal of my entire life.

Ripley immediately stood at attention when I coughed, staring at my face to make sure I was okay. A second later Elvis, who was enjoying his kibble mixed with some hamburger in the bathroom (one thing I did not forget about Elvis was how messy an eater he was), came charging out of the room and showed up on my other side.

"If I didn't know any better, I'd think Elvis is jealous of Ripley," Alexander said.

"Duh, Alexander, are you just figuring that out? Benj has a very weird and very furry love triangle going on right now." Taisy giggled.

When she said this, I thought, This is my first very weird love triangle of my very first room service meal of my entire life.

After a minute, when I regained my breath, I told Ripley and Elvis to go back to their business. Ripley lay down next to me, and Elvis waited a moment longer and then turned tail and trotted back into the bathroom to finish his own meal. Alexander and Taisy leaned in to start their desserts.

"Before you eat, I have something really important to say." Taisy and Alexander held their forks in midair. I took a breath and blurted everything out. "Elvis is being given away to the prime minister of Japan. If we don't stop it, we'll never see him again."

"What are you talking about?" Taisy asked. Alexander waited for me to answer.

"Well, the president thinks it would be a great idea to give Elvis to the prime minister as a fiftieth birthday present. Apparently the guy was once saved by a Newfie, and he went crazy for Elvis."

All at once, Taisy and Alexander Chang-Cohen asked me a bunch of questions. Then their questions trailed off as we all got distracted trying one another's desserts. Room service meals on a scale of one to ten in awesomeness? Definite ten. Room service dessert on a scale of one to ten in awesomeness? Definite twelve.

"Wait, so how did you find out about this?" Taisy asked. There it was, the million-dollar question. I

164

started to panic. How could I lie to Taisy? But how could I tell the truth?

"Find out about what? What do you mean?" I said, pretending I didn't understand her question. Next I tried the vague approach, where I looked down at my hot fudge cake and said, "You know, I found out the *regular* way."

"What's the *regular* way?" Taisy asked, pressing me. So then I tried shrugging and changing the subject.

"Hey, I really want to see that ice cream freezer. Maybe we all sneak out and go check it out at midnight? Who's with me?" I asked, hoping to distract them.

It almost worked, because Alexander Chang-Cohen announced he had never snuck out anywhere in his whole life, and he wanted to know if I had snuck out before and if I had, why I hadn't told him about it.

"Alexander, I don't care whether Benj has ever snuck out before, though I'm assuming not, no offense, Benj. But can we just stick to one subject for a second? I want to know how he found out this information about Elvis."

Finally, I just had to tell Taisy the truth. "I can't tell you."

"Why not? And says who?" Taisy was using her offended voice, because she's a big believer that friends should share everything.

"I just can't. But it's true, I swear. So why don't we start brainstorming on how we're going to make sure this doesn't happen? If Elvis goes to Japan, I'll never see him again. None of us will ever see him again. And it's bad enough he doesn't even live near me, but at least if he stays in DC, it's close enough for me to visit him, or he can maybe even visit me. So guys, what are we going to do?"

Sometimes, when Taisy gets frustrated with me, she turns to Alexander Chang-Cohen for help. "Alexander, why won't Benji tell us who told him about this Elvis Japan thing?"

Alexander Chang-Cohen has a love/hate relationship with being put in the middle. On the one hand, he likes it because it makes him feel like part of our group. On the other hand, it never ends well for him or, really, for any of us.

"I'm not sure why Benji won't tell us, but knowing Benji like I do, it's probably for a very good reason."

"So you're taking his side on this?" Taisy asked, narrowing her eyes.

Alexander Chang-Cohen's eyes got big, and he rapidly shook his head no.

"Of course I'm not. I'm not on anybody's side. I'm

Switzerland. Which is a colloquial expression used to connote the fact that I'm not on anyone's side, because Switzerland is always—"

"Alexander! I don't need a history lesson about Switzerland right now. What I need is for you to tell Benji I want to know who told him about this Elvis thing."

"Benji, so Taisy wanted me to tell you—"

"Yes, I heard her, Alexander. I'm sitting right here at the table. But can you please tell Taisy I cannot reveal my source, and she just has to trust me that the intel is good. I'm invoking my Fifth Amendment right."

"Benji, you're not really using your Fifth Amendment right correctly, but I understood what you meant and it sounded cool. So I get it," Alexander said to me. Then he turned back to Taisy. "Taisy, Benji said that—"

"I know what he said, but I don't understand it or like it. Best friends aren't supposed to keep secrets from each other. Tell him that."

Alexander Chang-Cohen started to turn back to me but instead faced Taisy again.

"So when you say 'best friends,' am I included in that, or were you only talking about Benji? No pressure, either way."

"Alexander, of course I consider you to be one of my best friends, too."

Alexander beamed at this news and told Taisy that he considered her to be one of his best friends as well. While they smiled at each other, I thought about what to do. Taisy did have a good point. She and Alexander Chang-Cohen are my best friends, and honestly, let's not kid ourselves, they are pretty much my only friends, and I certainly wanted to keep them. Maybe it was finally time to tell the truth, the whole truth, and nothing but the truth. Plus, all this bickering was taking away from my enjoyment of my very first room service dessert of my very first room service meal of my entire life.

"Fine. I'll tell you both, but you have to triple pinkie swear you won't tell anyone what I'm about to say. Do we do the pinkie thing now or after I tell you?"

"Now," said Alexander.

"I think after is more official," said Taisy, and Alexander quickly deferred. I took a deep breath and finally said what I had wanted to tell both of them for a very long time.

"It was Elvis who told me about it. Elvis can talk."

I guess I was so nervous I closed my eyes, because I heard and saw nothing until I opened first my left eye and then my right eye. When I looked at Taisy and Alexander Chang-Cohen's faces, it was hard to tell what either of them was thinking. We all looked at one another across the table in silence. Then Taisy spoke first.

"Benjamin Barnsworth." Uh-oh. "If you don't want to tell us, then don't. But don't lie to our faces! This isn't funny, so stop trying to make it seem like a big joke."

I was just about to protest when Elvis came out of the bathroom and sat next to me. He thumped his tail twice for "No." I followed Elvis's lead and changed my story.

"Look, Agent Daniels overheard the president and his chief of staff talking about it, but he swore me to secrecy because he shouldn't have told me about it. He said I couldn't even tell my mom. And I couldn't tell you guys because I don't want to get him in trouble, so you both have to pretend I didn't tell you anything." Wow, so much for me not being a good liar, because I'm not sure where all that came from, but it sounded pretty believable to me.

"Thank you for telling us, Benji, and of course we'd never ever tell." Taisy finally smiled. "Right, Alexander?"

Alexander nodded, but he was still looking at me with a funny expression. Taisy then held up her pinkie, and we all pinkie promised this would stay between the three of us.

"Now that that's done, can we figure out a way to keep Elvis in the United States?"

"Well, what if we . . . No, that won't work. We could . . . Or maybe we should try . . . What if we . . . ?" Alexander said. He paused and scrunched up his forehead. I could almost see the wheels turning inside his brain. "Yeah, I've got nothing."

"Well, we better come up with something, because we don't have a lot of time. We only have one full day left in DC," I said.

Taisy added in, "Actually, we don't even have a full day tomorrow. We have my tournament in the morning. But then we do have the whole afternoon and evening. Okay, everyone, it's time to put our thinking caps on. I wish Princess Daisy were here. She has a cute doggy ski hat I put on her when I'm doing my homework sometimes. I call it her thinking ski cap."

Alexander Chang-Cohen mimed putting on his thinking cap, which he then proceeded to screw into his forehead. I don't know why I found this so funny, but I did, and I just started laughing. Taisy joined in, and even though I'm sure Alexander Chang-Cohen wasn't trying to make us laugh, he was still happy at the result, so he joined in as well. Laughter is a great stress reducer, and boy, did this situation require reducing stress.

Suddenly, the door opened, but then it was stopped by the chain. We screamed and Elvis barked. Elvis has a very loud and scary bark. It's really deep, even deeper than his talking voice.

"Taisy! It's me, Dad. Come open the door."

Taisy jumped up and ran over to the door. Mr. McDonald was by himself, and he told us that my mom and Mrs. Chang-Cohen were still in the lobby, talking to the concierge about the hotel spa services.

"How was your dinner, kids?" he asked.

"Really splendid, sir," said Alexander Chang-Cohen. Something about Taisy's dad makes kids super polite around him.

"I couldn't have asked for a better meal for my very first room service meal of my entire life. I had mac and cheese and spaghetti," I said, nodding in agreement with Alexander.

"And dessert, I see." Mr. McDonald looked down at all the empty plates. "You know, for a little kid, you sure can eat a lot. Where does it all go?"

"Big appetite, big personality." I don't really know why I said that, because it didn't really make sense, but that's what came to mind.

"Well, you two are supposed to go meet your moms downstairs in the lobby. I'm supposed to send you down."

"Can I go too?" Taisy asked.

"No, you need to get ready for bed. You've got a big day tomorrow."

"Bed? It's barely eight o'clock. It's too early. Can I watch a movie?" Taisy complained.

"Taisy, everyone got up extra early today to drive here. It's been a long day, and tomorrow is going to be even longer. So it's not too early, and you will be going to bed now." He was using his don't-ask-again voice, and Taisy knew it.

"Yes, Dad," Taisy said, turning to me. "Help me push the room service cart out into the hallway."

"Petey said you could—"

"Benj, Alexander, help me push, okay?" Taisy demanded, cutting me off.

And then it hit me. Taisy had something to tell us. Alexander Chang-Cohen got down on his hands and knees and crawled under the tablecloth to figure out how to fold the sides of the table down. A second later, he popped back out.

"Okay, you two push all the plates toward the center and then tell me and I'll let the side drop."

"Don't you think it would be better to not let any food go to waste?" Elvis whispered to me. "I could certainly use a little snack."

"Snack? You just ate dinner!" When I finished my sentence, I looked up and noticed Taisy and Alexander Chang-Cohen staring at me. I chuckled and said, "C'mon, guys, you recognize Elvis's 'please feed me' whining? And he's right, we might as well give him the leftovers." I scraped the leftovers onto a single plate.

"I never give Princess Daisy table scraps. She has a delicate stomach." At the mere mention of Princess Daisy's name, Elvis couldn't help but whine a little. It was a shame Taisy couldn't have brought her to DC, though there was a tiny part of me that was happy because I kind of wanted all of Elvis's attention.

I grabbed the plate off the table and headed into the bathroom. Elvis followed with his tail about as high as a dog can have it. When we were alone, I whispered, "Hey, don't come up and talk to me like that when other people are around. I forget that talking to you is a big secret."

I scraped the food into his bowl, which he had already licked so clean I could see my reflection in the shiny silver surface. I picked up one of the rolls.

"What are you doing with that roll?" Elvis asked.

"What's it to you? You have a ton of food in there. Eat it and let's go."

"Are you giving it to him?" Elvis nodded toward

Ripley, who was dutifully waiting for me on the outside of the doorway.

"As a matter of fact, I am. Don't compare, Elvis. It's not nice."

I've probably heard this exact phrase a million times in my house. My mom says it to me and the twins all the time when one of us complains or says something like, "Why did you give Brett the frosting spoon to lick?" Her standard answer is always the same: "Don't compare. It's not nice." And if we push harder, insisting it really isn't fair, she always says this: "Well, you should learn right now that life is definitely not fair."

Elvis didn't answer me. He wolfed down the leftovers, and I tossed the last roll to Ripley, who lifted his head and caught it easily in his mouth. As he chewed, he looked to the side, and something he saw made him quickly step into the bathroom. A second later, Taisy pushed the room service cart past the bathroom doorway. She smiled and said, "Hop on." I looked down and saw the tablecloth move.

"Is Alexander under there?"

"Wouldn't it be so funny if someone rolled him down to the kitchen? Talk about one funny surprise."

I know I should be too mature to ride underneath a table, but I'm not. I lifted the tablecloth, peering at

Alexander. He waved to me and moved over to give me some space.

"Taisy, are you sure you can push both of us?"

"Benj, I'm almost a champion archer. I'm sure I can manage. And if not, Elvis will help me. Right, big boy?"

"Anything for you," Elvis said.

"Did you hear him bark? It's like he understood what I was saying!" Taisy said.

"See? That's exactly why I talk to him so much. I feel like he understands me."

Taisy moved to the other side of the cart so she could open the door. She tried to pull the table into the hallway, but it was too hard. Elvis walked out of the bathroom to the other side of the cart. He put his head down, pushing the cart. Alexander and I sat quietly under the tablecloth as the cart rolled.

"Thanks, Elvis, for helping out! I can't believe how smart you are. Who knows, maybe Benj wasn't joking and you can talk," Taisy joked.

"Scoot over," Alexander whispered to me.

"Scoot over? I'm as scooted over as I can be. Fine, I'll get out on my end."

All of a sudden, I smelled Taisy. Peaches. "Taisy, I don't know if we can all fit under here."

"We're not driving cross-country. And it's only for

a second. It's the only place we can talk. Look, we need to figure out this Elvis thing. I say we sneak out and meet up later tonight."

"I was joking when I brought up sneaking out!" I informed Taisy.

"Yes, Benji was joking," Alexander Chang-Cohen whispered.

"But I'm not. C'mon, we'll be fine, we're in a hotel. We're not going to leave the building or anything. It will be a super-fun adventure. A night we'll remember forever."

"Yeah, one that could get us grounded until we're old enough to drive," I said.

"Stop worrying, Benj. We'll be fine."

"But shouldn't you get a good night's sleep before your tournament tomorrow?" Alexander asked, always the practical one.

"I'll be fine. Okay, I gotta go back in before my dad comes out here."

Taisy crawled out from underneath the table. Alexander Chang-Cohen followed her. And then I followed him. Right then the elevator dinged at the end of the hallway, and a couple exited the elevator. They took one look at us, turned, and walked in the opposite direction. You'd think it'd be weird to see three kids crawling out from under a room service cart, but the couple were in their eighties. Maybe they'd seen this kind of thing before.

"Taisy, get in here now." Mr. McDonald stuck his head out the door. "And you two better head down to the lobby. Your moms just called, and they're waiting for you. Oh, and one more thing: you forgot one."

Poor Ripley walked out the door. It was odd that he wasn't out in the hall with us already. I looked at Elvis and wondered whether he'd purposely blocked Ripley from getting out. Sounds just like something a jealous dog would do, especially a jealous dog named Elvis.

14

We probably should have worn all black. But when we packed for our trip, none of us thought we'd be sneaking out of our rooms in the middle of the night. Our pajamas had to do. The plan was to get up at the designated time, put on our shoes, and slip out of our hotel room (Alexander and I were sharing a room on the fourth floor that adjoined with our moms', so they wouldn't hear us). Then we would run to the stairwell, walk up the four flights, make sure the coast was clear, and walk past Taisy's while coughing twice. The cough would be just loud enough so she could hear, but not loud enough to wake Mr. McDonald.

This was Taisy's signal that we would be waiting at the rendezvous point. Apparently "rendezvous"

is this fancy-pants French word that spies in movies use instead of the words "meeting place." If Taisy didn't hear us cough by fifteen minutes after the designated time, she would just go back to sleep and assume our mission was compromised (i.e., we got caught, we chickened out, we slept through the alarm). The same went for her. If she didn't show up at the designated rendezvous place within fifteen minutes after the double cough, we would assume she was unable to get out. Alexander and I would hightail our pajamaed bottoms back to our room. ASAP.

Now here's something I bet you didn't know. Alexander Chang-Cohen came up with this entire plan. Who knew he would be such a natural about sneaking out? Here's how it happened.

After we found our moms in the lobby and went up to our rooms, we heard every single detail of their dinner: how pretty the dining room was, how gorgeous the chandeliers were, how beautifully the table was set, how polite the waiters were, how fresh the flowers were on the tables, and how scrumptious the chocolate lava cake was. I guess these two don't get out much, because clearly they had forgotten how much fun it is to eat with people their own age.

When they finally stopped talking,

they told us to go get ready for bed. They wanted us well rested for our big, exciting dinner at the White House. Mrs. Chang-Cohen informed us we'd even get up extra early so we could all go to the Lincoln Memorial before Taisy's archery finals. Under normal circumstances, I would beg my mom to let us watch a little TV, but I was still distracted with helping Elvis, and I was actually tired too.

I was in my bed long before Alexander Chang-Cohen. He has a very long and complicated oral hygiene ritual. He brushes, flosses with flavored floss, brushes again, and then does two rounds of gargling with fluoride mouthwash. I saw this firsthand the first time Alexander Chang-Cohen and I had a sleepover. He said he knew the gargling was overkill, but he found the sound of gargling amusing. Plus he believed it helped clear his nostrils, giving him a better night's sleep.

While he worked on his nightly routine, I lay in the bed closest to the window. Elvis was on the floor between the two beds, which put Ripley on the other side. Ripley was already asleep and snoring. I wondered if he liked having Elvis around. It did give him a little vacation from constantly watching over me. I mean, when you think about it, therapy dogs never really get a day off.

"Benjamin, are you asleep?" Elvis asked.

"Nope." I turned over to look at him.

"I'm not sure I can condone this sneaking-out idea."

"First off, it's called 'The Great Hotel Late-Night Secret Sneak-Out.' And what does *condone* mean anyway?"

"It means to approve or sanction. And in terms of your overly long title for this sneak-out, it's a little redundant. Obviously, it's late night because if it was in the middle of the day, it'd hardly be a sneak-out, so the late night is implied. And furthermore, the 'secret' part is also redundant, because the word 'sneak' already implies that it's a secret."

Jeez, it's a wonder I missed this dog at all.

"Oh yeah? Well, your butt is redundant."

I know that's the most immature comeback ever, but it was all I could think of. And it's the one the twins use all the time. Like if I say, "Hey, Mom says you have to come help me empty the dishwasher," they say, "Oh yeah? Well, tell your butt to help you empty the dishwasher." Or if I say, "Pass the salt, please," they say, "Oh yeah? Tell your butt to pass the salt, please."

"What I'm saying is I'm not going to let you sneak out."

"Let me? You're not my mom. You can't stop me."

"I weigh four times as much as you, Benjamin. I could easily stop you by sitting on you. I could hold you down with one paw."

"Don't be such a spoilsport. We're staying in the hotel. It's totally safe."

"It's not a matter of safety, and of course you'll be safe because I'll be with you. But the reason I am against it is because your mother would not be pleased. And it's a pretty risky move for all of you. I don't want Taisy to get in trouble."

"We're not doing it just for kicks, we're doing it because we need to meet up and talk about how we're going to save your hairy butt from getting shipped off to Japan."

"Well, perhaps we don't need to come up with a plan. Upon further reflection, perhaps it's best if I go."

"What? Why would you say that? I thought you didn't want to go!"

"I don't want to go, but if the president wants me to, and if it will strengthen our relationship with Japan, then I owe it to him as my master, not to mention the leader of the free world, to do as he wishes. It's my duty, Benjamin. Perhaps I should accept my fate if that is what he feels is best."

"He's not your only master, and I don't want you to

go. What about me? Don't you care about my feelings?"

"Don't be silly. Of course I do. But some things are bigger than us. We have to think of others. We have to think of the country."

"Elvis, get a grip. You're going to be a birthday present with a big red bow. It's not like you're going to end a war or stop a famine. Why can't they give the prime minister a different Newfie, or even better, a Newfie puppy?"

"Pffffft. Like a Newfie puppy would be better than me. I'd be a wonderful gift."

"You don't speak Japanese, you don't read Japanese, you'd be totally bored there. You wouldn't understand anything the Japanese dogs were saying."

"No, they would not speak Japanese. They would speak dog, which I know. But you do have a point. It would be frustrating not to know what anyone is talking about. I suppose I'll just have to learn Japanese."

"Or you just don't go."

"Benji?"

Whoops, I guess Alexander Chang-Cohen was finally done with the world's most elaborate teeth-cleaning ritual.

"Yeah?"

"Who are you talking to?"

"I'm talking to you."

"No, I mean when I came out of the bathroom, it sounded like you were talking to someone. Were you talking to Elvis?"

"I was. Uh, you see, it's kind of like talking to myself, but yet better. Whenever my mind gets all cluttered, I feel it's good to get some of the thoughts out in the open so as not to clog the"—okay, now I was just blabbering—"thought pipes?" I winced, waiting for Alexander Chang-Cohen to call me out.

"That makes sense. I wish I had a pet to talk to as well. I suppose I could create an imaginary pet to talk to, but I'm past that developmental stage when having an imaginary friend is appropriate. Oh, and by the way, I'm totally, completely, absolutely against sneaking out of our room tonight."

"Oh. Why?"

"I've assessed the risk factor, and it seems pretty high. There are just so many things to consider. Whether we can make it out, whether Taisy can make it out, where we're meeting, what we're doing, how we don't get caught. Even if we make it out safely, you must remember we have to make it back in too."

"I never thought about it like that. I was just sorta going with the flow. Taisy said 'Let's sneak out and meet up later,' and I thought, sure, why not?"

Alexander checked all the pillows on his bed to see which was best for sleeping. He likes softness, but firmness too. Don't ask. I made that mistake before, and he told me the entire history of pillows, which sounds like it should be interesting but really isn't. He found the best pillow, turned off the lamp, and faced me in the dark.

"Frankly, your boldness surprises me, Benji. Don't you know we're not the kind of kids who sneak out? We're nervous kids, way too scared to sneak out. We don't want our moms to be disappointed in us. I'd like to be able to drive when I turn sixteen. If I get caught doing this, I'd probably never even make it to sixteen."

"So you're saying this is mission: impossible?"

"No, I didn't say that. I'm sure it's totally mission: possible, though maybe it's more like mission: unlikely."

"But what if you're the one who figures out the plan? Won't that increase our odds?"

Suddenly, a tiny light appeared, and I could see Alexander Chang-Cohen's face. It took me a second, but I realized the light was coming from his supercool spy watch. He got it as his one souvenir from the Spy Museum on a stop on his trolley tour with his mom.

"You think I'd be good at coming up with a secret plan?"

"Sure. Much better than me and Taisy. We were kinda thinking we'd text each other later and then meet up."

"Really? You call that a plan?"

"No, I guess not. But I did come up with a cool title. What do you think about 'The Great Hotel Late-Night Secret Sneak-Out'?"

"Whoa, that sounds way cool. Though I don't know if you need the word 'secret' because—"

Elvis lifted his head up and looked at me with a total I-told-you-so face.

"I know, I know, it's redundant. But it sounds better that way, and sometimes sounding better is cooler than being grammatically correct."

"Oh yes, I absolutely agree with that."

He flipped off his light, and the room went dark again.

"I suppose I could come up with a plan that would work."

"Sure, but only if you want to. I don't want to make you do anything you don't want to do. I can just go out and meet Taisy on my own."

"You mean you'd go without me?"

"I wouldn't want to go without you, but the bottom line is I don't want Elvis to go to Japan, and if I can do something to stop it, I'm going to. And I'm willing to risk getting in trouble for it."

"Can you give me five minutes to think this through?"

"Of course. Take all the time you need."

I heard a series of tiny beeps. Alexander Chang-Cohen was setting the five-minute timer on his watch. The room went silent again, and then five minutes later I heard his watch alarm go off.

"Benji?"

"Yes, Alexander?"

"I'm in. And I have the plan."

"You sure?"

"Yeah. I feel better knowing we have a good plan to follow. So now, maybe we have a better chance of it all working out. I'll text Taisy with the details."

"What's the plan?"

And then he told me. And then we did it.

15

I now know why movies like *Mission: Impossible* have those awesome theme songs. You need all that loud music to drown out the sound of your own heartbeat when you're attempting to sneak out of your hotel room with your mom sleeping on the other side of the wall. I had fallen asleep, but when my phone began to vibrate at 12:12, I woke in an instant. I did ask Alexander Chang-Cohen what the significance of 12:12 was, and he said, "No significance, it just sounds cool, don't you think?"

Alexander Chang-Cohen and I put on our shoes, grabbed our room key (thank goodness his mom trusted him enough to give him a key, because my mom said no), and crept to the door. Elvis whispered it would be best if Ripley stayed behind. I held out my hand and told Ripley to stay and that I would be back. I felt a little bad, so I waved him up. He quickly jumped up and lay down at the foot of the bed. I'm sure if he could have, he would have stuck his tongue out at Elvis.

Alexander Chang-Cohen left a note on his pillow. He switched on his watch light battery so I could read it.

Dear Mom and/or Mrs. Barnsworth,
    I know it may seem alarming that Benji and I are not where we are supposed to be, but please do not worry. We (along with Elvis for protection) have snuck out of our rooms to wander around the hotel because we think it will be cool, and kids will be kids. Of course, if you are reading this, we have gotten busted, and you should know that we will accept any and all

punishment graciously and respectfully. But don't worry. We have not been kidnapped, nor are we in any peril.

P.S. This was not my idea, and I did point out we shouldn't do it, but I was outvoted. Also, I am leaving you the chocolate that was on my pillow as a small token of my sorriness. Also, I forgot to eat it before I brushed my teeth.

Warmest regards,

Alexander Chang-Cohen and Benji

Alexander Chang-Cohen clearly thinks of every detail. And he has extremely nice penmanship for a boy. I gave him the A-OK signal, and we continued to the door. We rock-paper-scissored to see who had to open the door as quietly as possible, and I lost, of course, no surprise there. My palms were sweating, and I turned that doorknob as slowly as I could, and then I pulled the door open as slowly as I possibly could. There was the tiniest creaking sound, and Alexander Chang-Cohen shook his head at me, miming pulling open the door fast. I did what he said, pulling back so fast I accidentally smacked Elvis in the snout with my elbow.

Alexander Chang-Cohen peered out into the hallway

and looked both ways. He motioned for us to follow. I waved Elvis to go ahead of me. For some reason, closing the door was even louder than opening it, and when I finally heard the door click, I was so relieved that it was over I . . . fainted.

A minute later, I woke up with Elvis's face pressed so close to my face, I breathed in his doggy breath.

"Ewwww, gross. Elvis, move! I just inhaled your exhale."

"I told you this wasn't a good idea."

"I'm fine."

I looked around and saw that Alexander Chang-Cohen was already down the hall. I stood up and ran to meet him. He held his finger to his lips to let me know that even though we had made it safely into the stairwell, we still had to be quiet. There was a draft in the stairwell, and you could tell it was echoey even though none of us made a noise that could produce an echo. We tiptoed up the stairs. Alexander typed something into his phone. I wondered who he was texting in the middle of the night. Then my phone vibrated in my pajama pocket. I pulled it out.

Are you okay? Do you need to sit down
and rest for a moment?

I shook my head and pointed up the stairs. When you go round and round in a stairwell, I can see where you lose track of where exactly you are. We overshot the eighth floor. The floor above was the empty banquet room on the roof of the hotel. So when Alexander tried to push open the door, it was locked. He stopped so suddenly in the doorway, I walked right into his back.

"Sorry, A."

"This is the wrong floor. I don't know how I did that. We've got to go back down."

I turned around to tell Elvis, but he wasn't behind me, which made me panic until I looked down the stairs and saw him standing one landing below, looking up at me. I could read his eyes perfectly. They said, "You should have let me lead, because I know where I'm going." I gave him my best smirk and shrug. So we all trudged back down, and Alexander Chang-Cohen opened the door to see if the hallway was clear.

He was just about to open it wide when Elvis said, "Someone's coming. Don't open the door." So then I whispered to Alexander Chang-Cohen, "Don't open the door, someone's coming."

"How do you know? Did you hear something? Because I didn't hear or see anything," Alexander said, closing the door.

We all stood in the stairwell, and a few seconds later we heard the elevator open and the sound of two people talking in low tones as they walked out. Of course Elvis was right, and I knew he was bursting to tell me he told me so, but I didn't turn around to give him the satisfaction.

"Now do you think the coast is clear?" Alexander Chang-Cohen asked me.

I looked down at Elvis. He thumped his tail once for yes. I nodded to Alexander Chang-Cohen. He opened the door a bit, popped his head out, and then opened the door fully. We all followed, and I forgot to hold the door, so it made a loud noise when it closed. Oh well.

"Are you going to cough? Or should I cough when we pass Taisy's door?" I asked.

Alexander Chang-Cohen shrugged and then pointed to me. I guarantee I knew what he was thinking. He was thinking that since I've been a sickly kid my whole life, I'd be a better fake cougher than him. I smiled. It was pretty funny to be so close to a friend you know exactly what they're thinking.

We passed Taisy's door, and I put my mouth into my fist to do my best, deepest, double fake cough. Right after I finished, Alexander Chang-Cohen ran down the hall to the stairwell, and I quickly followed.

"Why did you run?" I asked when we were back in the stairwell.

"I don't know, I just felt like the sooner we were out of sight, the better."

Alexander Chang-Cohen walked up half a flight of stairs. He wiped the step with his hand and sat down. I sat down next to him. Elvis was too big to sit on a step. He stayed one landing below. Alexander set his watch for fifteen minutes, and now it was just time to wait.

Barely thirty seconds passed. "Guys?" Taisy called out softly, walking into the stairwell.

"We're up here," I called out. Elvis thumped his tail wildly on the concrete floor, and the sound echoed.

"Shhhhh!" we all whispered, and Elvis's tail stopped immediately. Taisy giggled, stroking Elvis's head. Alexander Chang-Cohen and I sat up a little taller. Taisy looked amazing. She had on purple silky pajamas with little daisies on them, with a matching robe and cute purple fuzzy slippers, and pushed up on her forehead was one of those eye mask things, which had two embroidered closed eyes with long eyelashes on it.

"Wow, Taisy. That's some outfit you've got on. Too bad the whole point of sneaking out is to not be seen by anyone, because you look totes adorbs," I said, which is what she sometimes says about Princess Daisy's outfits.

Taisy gave me a huge smile at my compliment. I couldn't believe that anyone would ever waste such an outfit on sleeping.

"Well, look at us sneaking out in the middle of the night in Washington, DC," Taisy said. As she was about to sit down, Alexander Chang-Cohen leaped up. He went down to Taisy and scooted his flannel-pajamaed butt across the step she was going to sit on. Taisy and I stared at him in shock.

"What? It's the polite thing to do. I didn't want her to get her purple pajama outfit dirty."

"Alexander Chang-Cohen, that may be one of the nicest things anyone has ever done for one of my outfits. Thank you so much."

Now it was Alexander's turn to beam with happiness. I wasn't sure exactly what I felt in that moment, but I wondered if it was how Elvis felt about Ripley. I know Taisy isn't more my friend than Alexander Chang-Cohen's, but I do feel like the bridge that linked them together in the first place. Though, to be honest, I doubt we'd all be sitting here together in a hotel stairwell in the middle of the night without Elvis. I guess he was the original bridge.

"Okay, guys, let's get started," I said. "How are we going to make sure Elvis doesn't go to Japan? Did anyone come up with any brilliant ideas yet?" Alexander Chang-Cohen and Taisy shook their heads no. I nodded and said, "I wish I could just bring him home with me and then the whole Japan thing wouldn't even matter."

"You're saying you want to kidnap the president's dog? I don't know, Benji. I think you would get in serious trouble for that," said Alexander.

I explained I didn't mean we'd kidnap Elvis. I was simply thinking I could ask for Elvis back. I looked at Elvis, who was lying at Taisy's feet. If he heard me, which I know he did, he showed no reaction.

"Maybe we tell the president you're sick and your dying wish is to have Elvis back."

Whoa! I couldn't believe Taisy said that. I was really thankful my mom wasn't around. She absolutely forbade me to ever talk about dying. She said I'd understand when I was older and had kids of my own.

I guess I must have made a funny face, because Taisy continued on. "Hey, I'm not saying it's the right idea." She shrugged. "And I know it's bad to lie, but I thought we were just brainstorming here. We should all be able to say anything we want, right?"

"Well, she has a point, because no one would refuse a dying child's wish," Alexander said.

"Easy for both of you to say. You're not the kid who is supposedly dying! Let's just say we tell the biggest lie of our lives and then what? I bring Elvis home and everyone just waits for me to die, but I don't because I'm not dying, and then we say a miracle happened and I was cured? Or what if they find out about the lie and they not only take Elvis back but I go to prison?"

"I don't think you would go to prison for lying," Alexander said.

"I know that, I was just saying it to make a point. That's a stupid plan, sorry, but it is."

"Hey, don't call my plan stupid. Maybe it is, but you don't have to be mean about it." Taisy shot me an angry glare.

"I'm sorry, Taisy. Just because I called your plan stupid doesn't mean I think you're stupid."

"You know, if you look back in history, a lot of stupid plans have worked. But I'm not saying I think we should do it, because I don't. But it would probably work. But yet, I feel ashamed to even be considering it," Alexander said. He looked confused, but I knew it was just his thinking face. He was running ideas through his head, hoping to hit on a better one.

"Okay, sorry I brought it up. Benj, no hard feelings, okay? You know I don't want you to kick the bucket,"

Taisy agreed, putting her hand on my shoulder.

"I know, Taisy. I don't want me to kick the bucket either."

We all sat in silence for a moment, thinking. Alexander Chang-Cohen yawned, which made me yawn, which then made Taisy yawn. It was kind of crazy that we were sitting on these hard steps in the middle of the night when none of us had any real ideas to discuss. I was about to suggest we wrap up The Great Hotel Late-Night Secret Sneak-Out when Elvis lifted his head. There was something about the way he did it that made the little hairs on the back of my neck stick straight up. He stood up and turned, looking right at me. Then I heard the door open one flight above us. The door that had been locked only ten minutes ago. We all jumped up, but it was too late. We heard footsteps coming down the stairs. I completely froze.

I'll admit it. I held on to the railing and squeezed my eyes tightly shut. I was too scared to know who it was, and I didn't want to know what would happen next. In my heart of hearts, I knew there was no way Elvis would let anything really bad happen to me. But there was absolutely nothing he could do to keep us from getting . . . busted!

16

As surprised as we were to get caught on our Great Hotel Late-Night Secret Sneak-Out, I'm pretty sure the person who caught us was just as surprised, if not more. I didn't actually see the look of surprise on his face. I still had my eyes shut when he found us. But he told me about it later, over a banana split. In fact, he said, "I'm pretty sure I was just as surprised, if not more, when I saw you three, or rather, four in the

stairwell. What a weird night."

But I'm skipping over the exciting part. Sorry. Sometimes I do that when ice cream is involved.

If you hit the rewind button, this is where we were. My eyes were squeezed shut and I was frozen in fear that a bloodthirsty half vampire, one-quarter werewolf, one-quarter zombie monster had found us in the stairwell and was about to eat us. I was gathering my courage so I could be the one to jump in front of Taisy and let myself be eaten first. I figure this was a no-brainer, since Alexander Chang-Cohen had already sacrificed his pajama bottoms for her earlier. Instead of getting attacked, this is what I heard:

"Mr. Petey Peterson, is that you? Hello, sir, do you remember me? I'm Alexander Chang-Cohen, the overly cautious stranger-danger kid from earlier today." Then Alexander Chang-Cohen continued, "I'm the one who ordered the cheeseburger, well done, and the sweet potato fries with a side of broccoli and spinach? Those dark green vegetables sure are important."

I opened my eyes, turned my head to look up, and sure enough, it was indeed Petey Peterson.

"Hey, guys, uh, what's going on here? And is your dog friendly? Because he sure is giving me the evil eye."

Elvis was looking pretty fierce. He was even

showing more teeth than I've seen before.

"Elvis, it's okay, boy. He's the room service guy we met earlier. Alexander Chang-Cohen called down and verified him as a hotel employee, so he's cool. Unless your doggy sense says he's not?" I took a step down and away from Petey Peterson and thought about it and asked, "Hey, what are you doing in the stairwell in the middle of the night?"

"What am I doing? What are you three doing? Aren't you guys a little young to be out so late? Where are your parents?" Petey stared at us, and then he caught sight of Taisy's pajamas. "Can I just say your outfit is really darling? I have a niece who is about your age, and I know she'd love it."

"Why are you changing the subject? You're acting suspicious," I said.

"I'm not acting suspicious. I work at the hotel. I went up to the roof to make a phone call."

"I agree with Benji. Your voice sounds funny. You seem nervous." Alexander Chang-Cohen took a step down and stood next to Elvis.

"Okay, you've busted me. I'm acting like this because I'm embarrassed by what I was doing up there."

"Were you throwing water balloons off the roof?" I asked. I don't know why I said it, but it was the first thing that popped into my head. Also, it seems like it'd be a lot of fun.

Petey smiled. "I wish, but no. I was calling my girlfriend, who works at the White House. She was on the lawn and we like to wave at each other while we're talking. I know it sounds juvenile and silly, but . . ."

"I don't think it sounds juvenile or silly at all!" Taisy interrupted. "I think it's totally romantic and supercute! It's kinda like a reversed Romeo and Juliet. So could you actually see her?"

"Well, I stood by a light so she could see me better. She sat by the fountain, and I thought maybe I saw her, but honestly I wasn't sure."

"What does your girlfriend do at the White House?" Taisy asked.

"She's a Secret Service agent."

"She is???!! That's so cool!" Taisy and Alexander said at the same time. "Maybe that's what I should be when I grow up, a Secret Service agent," Taisy said. "Though, does that mean I have to wear a plain suit to work every day?"

While no one was paying attention to me, I leaned in and whispered to Elvis, "Is he telling the truth?" Elvis thumped his tail once for yes, and I immediately relaxed a little more.

"Okay, I told you my secret. Now it's your turn. What are you three doing here in the middle of the night?"

And so we told Petey Peterson about Alexander's secret plan and my great name for the plan. We also asked him not to turn us in and said this was our first-ever sneak-out and how we were normally very responsible kids who all had good report cards.

"Well, I snuck out once from my hospital room to go to the morgue, but that's not exactly the same thing. My mom was at home, so I wasn't really sneaking away from anything. Also, I was with my friend, a hospital nurse who also happens to be Taisy's uncle Dino," I said.

Petey Peterson took my news in stride, nodded his head, and then admitted that when he was our age, he snuck out all the time. Of course, he just snuck out of his bedroom and went into his backyard tree house with a sleeping bag. The first time he did it, his mom woke up, discovered he was missing, and called the police. Then Petey woke up to a policeman shining a flashlight in his face.

"Don't worry, Mr. Peterson. We left a note for our moms in case they found us gone," Alexander Chang-Cohen said.

203

"Hey, Mr. Peterson?" asked Taisy. "Now that we're all here anyway, do you think we could go up to the roof where you made your phone call? I bet it's an amazing view. We'd really love to see it."

It was obvious Petey wasn't sure what he should do. I'd bet big money he had never dealt with two ten-year-olds, one eleven-year-old, and a two-hundred-pound black Newfie in a stairwell at one a.m. This kind of thing probably wasn't in the Hay-Adams employee manual.

"Pleeeeeeeeeaaaaase? I bet it's so pretty at night from the roof," Taisy pleaded again.

"Sure, why not?"

Two minutes later we were gazing out at the White House. It was lit up, glowing white and beautiful. It was so quiet and still it felt pretty magical.

"I feel like we're in a snow globe that hasn't been shaken yet, so there's no snow." After I said this, I felt like everyone was looking at me. When I checked, everyone was looking at me.

"That's exactly what it feels like, Benji," Alexander Chang-Cohen agreed.

"Totally!" Taisy agreed too. Even Petey smiled broadly. Maybe he was thinking about his Secret Service girlfriend who was in the very White House we were all staring at right now.

You know that feeling when you're already in such a weird mood because you feel like you're living in a dream, or in our case, in a snow globe that hasn't been shaken up yet? Well, there is something about being in an odd situation that makes you braver than you would normally be, and after a few minutes, I decided to be bold and just ask for what I wanted even if it seemed crazy.

"Hey, Mr. Peterson?"

"You can call me Petey, Benji."

"Thanks. So, Petey?"

"Yes, Benji?"

"Would it be too much of an over-ask for you to show us that old-fashioned ice cream freezer you told us about earlier?"

"I don't know. I'd like to, but it is the middle of the night. You kids need your rest." Petey put his hands in his pockets. He spoke softly, with just a hint of hesitation in his voice.

"Come on, Petey. It would be really fun, and even though it's the middle of the night, we're already up and we are on vacation after all." I pushed him.

"Well, that's a good point. Let me think about it." Petey leaned back and closed his eyes for a minute. Then he opened them. "Okay, let's do it. Why not?"

Alexander Chang-Cohen raised his hand. Petey just looked at him until Taisy explained this is what Alexander does around adults he doesn't know very well.

"Yes, Alexander?"

"Can we take the elevator? Or do we have to take the stairs?"

"Sure, we can take the elevator. But you have a much better chance of not getting caught if you take the stairs."

"You know, according to my watch we've already been gone forty-seven minutes and twenty-two seconds, twenty-three seconds, twenty-four sec—" said Alexander as we headed back down the stairs.

"We get it, Alexander, thanks," I said. "I'm up for ice cream, but Taisy, I'm a little worried you need your sleep before your big tournament."

"Tournament? What tournament?" I guess Petey felt like he was one of the pack now.

Taisy told him all about the archery tournament and how she would be in the finals the next morning. I filled him in on the part where Taisy is an amazing athlete, and how she wasn't even all that serious about archery up until recently, because we had to get to DC.

"Why did you have to get to DC?" Petey asked.

"Maybe we should tell him," Alexander Chang-Cohen

suggested. "It may be good to have an adult's help. We don't have much time left."

"Well, now I'd really like to know!" said Petey, looking at me and Alexander. "Why did you all have to get to DC?"

"You know, Petey, I'd love to tell you, but it's a really long story and we don't have time. That ice cream isn't going to eat itself, now, is it?"

I walked down the stairs, and Elvis followed me. Taisy, not one to miss out on an adventure, fell in line behind me, then Alexander Chang-Cohen. Petey was at the rear.

One hundred and eighty-two steps later (Alexander Chang-Cohen counted), we were downstairs in the hotel kitchen making banana splits. The kitchen was smaller than you would expect, but I guess that was because it's a pretty old hotel. Even though it looked old-fashioned, I noticed that the appliances, the rows of ovens, and the stove tops all looked pretty modern. What I will say about the kitchen is it smelled great, probably from all the cookies that are constantly being baked.

Petey introduced us to Graham, the nighttime cook, who was sitting on a stool reading a graphic novel. Then we met Kylie, the night manager of room service.

Graham just grumbled at us. He wasn't the least bit curious about us suddenly showing up in the kitchen. Kylie was clearly nervous about getting in trouble. Petey swore it was fine and said we were just going to have some ice cream and then we'd be gone.

Once you see an old-fashioned ice cream freezer with more tubs of ice cream than you can imagine, well, one thing leads to another and the next thing you know, you're having a banana-split ice cream party that's so fun, even Grumpy Graham has to put down his book and join in.

It turns out everyone has their own idea of a perfect banana split, though.

Grumpy Graham was totally on my side. "Benji is right. A banana split has to have strawberry, chocolate, and vanilla ice cream."

"No, it doesn't. I make mine with sorbet some-times," Kylie said.

"Whoever heard of a sorbet banana split?!" Petey said, laughing.

"As long as there's a split banana, it should count. Besides, I like mine with frozen yogurt," Taisy said, and high-fived Kylie. "Us girls have to stick together."

"Alexander, do you have any facts about banana splits?" I asked.

"Just that David Evans Strickler, a twenty-three-year-old apprentice pharmacist at Tassel Pharmacy, located at 805 Ligonier Street in Latrobe, Pennsylvania, who enjoyed inventing sundaes at the store's soda fountain, invented the banana-based triple ice cream sundae in 1904," said Alexander Chang-Cohen totally casually.

The whole kitchen went quiet as Petey, Kylie, and Grumpy Graham stared at Alexander in amazement. Taisy and I were so used to him and his amazing brain we sometimes forget that to strangers it's pretty amazing.

"And that's why we call him the human computer!" Taisy said proudly. I picked up my glass banana boat and held it up. "Let's do a banana-boat toast to David Evans Strickler!" And everyone started laughing and picked up their banana boats, and we clinked them with one another's boats and said, "To David Evans Strickler!"

Here's a thing I've learned about being a kid. We're always dying to grow up and get older because we have so many limitations. Kids get bossed around all the time. We have to go to school, we have to clean our rooms, we have to do our homework. We get told when to go to bed, when to wash our hands, when we can watch TV, and when we can't. We can't do whatever we want because, well, we're just kids. So every now and again we like to feel free, to know what it's like to forget about all the rules and do something like eat a banana split in the middle of the night.

And that's exactly what this night was, what it felt like, what it tasted like. The Great Hotel Late-Night Secret Sneak-Out was the kind of freedom every kid dreams about, and let me tell you, it was even better than I ever imagined. Think about it. Me with my two best friends, my first and favorite dog (sorry, Ripley), and three strangers whooping it up in the kitchen of one of the most famous hotels in Washington, DC. Elvis was totally right: being a kid is really fun.

I'm pretty sure our late-night ice cream extravaganza (which is a fancy word for party, by the way) was great fun for Petey, Grumpy Graham, and Nervous Kylie too. Because the thing about being an adult that they don't tell us kids is, sometimes it's not so fun, and sometimes they wish they could go back to being kids, even if it's just for an hour in the middle of the night.

It was Grumpy Graham who recognized Elvis first. Don't worry, Elvis was partying it up with the rest of us. He had a big ol' bowl of vanilla ice cream with bacon bits sprinkled on top. Graham just kept staring at Elvis while he ate his sundae.

"Hey, he looks just like the president's dog," he finally said. "I knew I recognized him from somewhere."

"He is." I nodded. "He's Elvis, the president's dog."

Petey and Kylie were flabbergasted. I gave them the short version of how Elvis showed up on my doorstep a few months ago and explained that this was our first reunion. Petey asked if he could get some pictures with Elvis. His mom was obsessed with dogs. He said she had four of her own, and she loved them as much as she loved him, so she'd be really thrilled to have a picture of her son with the First Dog.

"My mom knows everything about all the White House dogs," Petey said. "Did you know that Fala, President Franklin Delano Roosevelt's dog, was the only president's dog that has a memorial in DC? In fact, he was later buried next to the president in Hyde Park."

Petey stood proudly next to Elvis and put one arm around Elvis's big furry neck. Taisy used his phone to take a few pictures. He had a giant grin on his face, and he put his chin right up to Elvis's snout.

"Yes sirree, Fala was a national treasure," said Petey. "He was there during some of President Roosevelt's most important meetings during World War II. I bet he was a very calming influence for the president. That man had a lot on his shoulders. Dogs have that effect on people. Don't they, Elvis?"

"A national treasure? What do you mean, a national treasure?" I asked Petey. "Can you tell me what that means?"

Taisy took a picture of Elvis and Grumpy Graham, who finally, after a big banana split and a lively debate about graphic novels with Alexander Chang-Cohen, smiled.

"Well, Fala was considered a national treasure because he boosted the country's morale in a time of need," said Petey. "He was a bright spot for our country during a dark time of war, Benji. That's what a national treasure does. It gives us all a sense of pride. And Fala made the people of America feel proud. He was the loyal companion of a great president. You know, my mom has even said Elvis reminds her of Fala. Wow, I can't believe I didn't put it all together sooner. I mean, how many two-hundred-pound black Newfoundlands could possibly be running around in Washington, DC?"

"Don't feel bad, Mr. Peterson. You probably didn't put it together because why on earth would the president's dog ever be with a kid like me?" I just spoke the truth. I was pretty sure that was what he meant.

"Why, Benji, that's not true at all." Petey stopped scraping the bottom of his bowl and looked right at me. "I think you're a pretty extraordinary kid, and I couldn't be happier that I had the opportunity to make your acquaintance and meet your wonderful friends. I would say Elvis is just as lucky to have found you as you are to have found him."

Alexander's watch alarm went off right then. I was kind of relieved when I heard it, because Petey had pretty much left me speechless.

"Okay, troops. It's two in the morning, and we're pushing our luck," said Alexander. "And Petey, I have an idea how we could use the elevator this time."

"Oh yeah, what's that?"

And five minutes later, the three of us were all smushed together underneath a hotel service cart in the elevator trying not to giggle, not that it mattered, as we weren't in the elevator with anyone.

"Benji, you have the pointiest elbows ever," Taisy whispered.

"Sorry." But I couldn't help it. I was texting her and Alexander Chang-Cohen:

Petey solved our problem! We have to
get Elvis declared a national treasure.
There's no way a national treasure can
move to Japan!!!!!!!!!!!

Picture this: three sleepy kids sitting on the steps of the Lincoln Memorial while their parents are taking hundreds of photos of them and everything around them. When Mrs. Chang-Cohen said we were getting up early, she wasn't kidding. It wasn't even seven o'clock and we were already out. That's early under normal circumstances, but considering we all went to sleep after two a.m., we could barely keep our eyes open.

Taisy pointed to the engraving on the step below us, where Martin Luther King, Jr., stood for his famous "I Have a Dream" speech.

"What am I thinking?" she asked.

Alexander Chang-Cohen raised his hand.

"Alexander, you don't have to . . . you know what, I'm too tired for this. Yes?"

"You were going to say you have a dream too, and it was that you were still asleep and dreaming, right?"

I laughed, and Taisy did too. We were so tired, we were a little punchy, which isn't a good thing considering it was the beginning of a day and not the end of one.

"Benji, what's so funny? And why are you three so tired? I slept great last night. I'm so excited to walk over and see the Korean War and the Vietnam War memorials. Who's with me?" my mom asked.

"Mom, can we just hang out here for a while?" I yawned.

"You don't want to see them?"

"I do, but just not right this second. Can't we just sit here and eat our bagels with Elvis and Ripley, and then we'll come and join you guys?"

My mom gave me a long, hard stare. I knew if Taisy and Alexander Chang-Cohen weren't sitting right next to me, she'd absolutely grill me to find out exactly why I was so exhausted. Her mom senses told her something was up; she just couldn't figure out what.

"Mom, nothing is wrong. I'm just tired. I went to sleep late. Elvis snored a lot and it kept me up." At the mention of his name, Elvis shifted to look at me. I'm sure he was staring daggers at me, but I didn't turn to meet his gaze. Meanwhile, my mom relaxed a little. Staying up late with Elvis snoring made perfect sense to her.

"Loud snoring. Gee, I wonder what that's like, Daddy," said Taisy.

Mr. McDonald was taking a picture of his feet standing in the spot where Martin Luther King once stood. He was so engrossed he wasn't even listening.

"Taisy, I love you too, sweetie," he said absently, and she giggled.

"Mom?" Mrs. Alexander Chang-Cohen turned at the sound of her son's voice. "Is it okay if I eat with Benji and Taisy and then I'll come join you? Maybe you should start at the Vietnam War Memorial and we'll be done by the time you get to the Korean memorial?"

"But what am I going to do without my own personal tour guide?" Mrs. Chang-Cohen smiled.

My mom looked at her quizzically, and Mrs. Chang-Cohen explained that because of her son's remarkable memory, he usually read up about the places they would be visiting. Then he recited all the interesting facts about a place and their historical significance as they walked around.

"Mom, just give us ten minutes, and then I'll be happy to be your personal tour guide."

"I didn't think they'd stop wanting to hang out with us for at least another couple of years," my mom joked, but I heard a tiny hint of hurt in her voice.

I had the urge right then and there to stand up and tell her everything. To tell her about Elvis's secret code, how I didn't want Elvis to go to Japan, how we snuck out last night and I was still so full from ice cream I didn't know how I was going to eat my bagel. But instead I forced myself to keep my mouth shut. I opened the bag of bagels.

"Why do I have four bagels in my bag?" I asked her.

"One's for you, one's for Ripley, and two are for Elvis. I had a feeling one bagel wouldn't be enough for him."

I stood up and walked down seven steps, straight to my mom. I threw my arms around her waist and pressed my face against her stomach. "Thanks for taking care of me and my dogs, Mom. I really do appreciate it."

My mom hugged me back, kissing the top of my head a few times. "What on earth is this? My, my, someone definitely didn't get enough sleep. Maybe you've had too much excitement. I see a nap in your future."

Even though I wasn't thrilled that she was babying me in front of my friends, I didn't really care because she already sounded much happier. I let her go, but she didn't let me go, which meant I couldn't move.

"Mom, hug's over. You can let me go now."

"It's over when I say it's over." She chuckled, gave me one more squeeze, and then released me. "Okay, now it's over."

Then I ran up the stairs and almost tripped on the last step, but I caught myself somehow, which almost never happens. As soon as our parents hit the bottom step, we waved good-bye to them, and then we huddled together and got down to business.

"So, what do you guys think of getting Elvis declared a national treasure?" I asked. "Once we do that, there's no way he can leave the country. We'd never give away our national treasure. Can you imagine, 'Hey, Mr. President of random foreign country, happy birthday, and here's the Declaration of Independence. Enjoy!' Right?! That would never happen."

"Like the president would ever give away the Declaration of Independence! That's the most ridiculous thing I ever— Oh my goodness, you were doing that exaggeration thing you do to make a point. I get it now! It's a brilliant idea, Benji!" said Alexander Chang-Cohen.

"Taisy, what do you think?" I asked.

"I think while we're at it we should also have this blueberry muffin declared a national treasure, because it's sooooooo yummy delicious," she said, looking up from her breakfast. I handed Alexander Chang-Cohen some of my bagel.

Over our picnic breakfast, we discussed ideas, and I was pleased, but not entirely surprised, that Alexander Chang-Cohen had already done some research on his iPad about national treasures. It turned out there was no specific way to be declared a national treasure. Someone important in our country just had to declare that something or someone was a national treasure, then it got printed in the newspaper and *voilà!* Suddenly everyone believed it.

Here are a just a few of the great, and not so great, ideas we came up with for Elvis:

- Shave his butt and get a tattoo that says NATIONAL TREASURE.
- Have him save a small child's life.
- Have him save the president's life.
- Have him rescue a kitten stuck in a tree.
- Have him rescue a fireman stuck in a tree who was trying to save a kitten.

- Fly a plane when the pilot gets sick and land it safely.
- Catch a bad spy and turn him in to the FBI.
- Help a good spy save the world.
- Swim across the Atlantic Ocean while carrying an American flag in his mouth.
- Bark "The Star-Spangled Banner" at a baseball game on live television.

Obviously, most of our ideas were unrealistic, if not impossible, to pull off. But I did notice that the ideas had one thing in common. A national treasure performs a heroic act. How to get Elvis to perform that act was the key. It was Sunday morning, we were sightseeing for another hour, then we were all heading to Taisy's tournament, and finally were going to spend the rest of the afternoon and early evening at the White House. Then we'd leave first thing the next morning so we could make it to school for the second half of the day.

Alexander Chang-Cohen's phone buzzed. He read the message. "My mom says we need to come meet them now. And that we should make sure we collect every last bit of our trash, because littering is very bad." We stood up and cleaned, and the five of us headed down the steps to go meet our parents. We all walked as slowly as we could so we could continue talking.

"We have to come up with a plan right now, figure out how to do it by tonight, and somehow get it on the news by morning? I guess that's doable. Maybe," Taisy said.

"Do you think it's impossible, T? Should we come up with a different idea?" I was worried. I couldn't remember ever hearing doubt in Taisy's voice before.

"No," said Alexander. "This is the best idea we've had so far, and we'd still have to execute any other idea in the same amount of time. Maybe Taisy's right, though. This is truly mission: impossible. I wonder what Tom Cruise would do."

"Hey, I never said the word 'impossible.' Did you hear me say that ever? No, I didn't. I don't even believe in the word!" Taisy exclaimed. "I'm just saying it's not going to be easy. We have to go in with our eyes open and know what we're up against. But know that when you work hard, and you succeed, it's even more rewarding. It's like we're already at the finals. We have only one shot to get this right."

"One chance. It's like sudden death?" Alexander's voice squeaked.

"I guess so. But what if we can't pull it off?" I asked.

"Stop it, Benj. We can't think like that. Vince Lombardi said, 'The difference between a successful person and others is not a lack of strength, not a lack of knowledge, but rather a lack of will.' And we have the will."

"We do!" Alexander squeaked, nodding his head enthusiastically, and then tried to make his voice sound lower.

"We do? I mean, we do! Who's Vince Lombardi again? Is he the guy who makes those square frozen pizzas?" I said.

"No, he was a famous football coach. My dad quotes him all the time."

"So, what's the plan?" I asked, trying to be as confident as Taisy.

"I don't know. Alexander, you were the mastermind behind last night's plan. What do you think our best chance of success is off the list?" Taisy looked at Alexander. He rubbed his chin thoughtfully.

"Well, a lot of these may be difficult to engineer because they require the saving of someone, and unfortunately, we have no way of knowing who will need saving tonight since we don't own a crystal ball, we are not equipped with superpowers, nor do we have a time machine." He paused and looked at us. We stopped for a second and then continued walking. "I'm just talking out loud, okay? We could look into finding a police scanner, but that feels a little dangerous. I suppose we could stage one of these things, and then let Elvis rescue the person, but that's probably illegal and also morally wrong. I mean, it's not like we're going to set fire to a burning building just so Elvis can save someone."

We were almost at the Korean War memorial. I saw my mom's big blond hair coming toward us. We were running out of time. I had to think of something.

"What about if I let him save me?" I blurted the words without thinking.

"That's crazy, Benj! What if something happened to you? Like by accident? I'm all for a big plan, but not a stupid one," said Taisy.

"But Elvis wouldn't let anything happen to me, right, boy?"

Elvis sniffed a bush, deciding whether he wanted to make it his. He trotted over to me, barking softly. "Benjamin, I'd never let anything happen to you. But I won't let you put yourself in harm's way to save me. So don't even think about it."

"I don't think he likes your idea, Benjamin, and neither do I. You know, out of all of these, the easiest one to pull off is Elvis rescuing a kitten from a tree. All we need is a kitten and a tall tree," Alexander said.

"Ooh," Taisy cooed. "Can it be a little white kitten with a light-blue ribbon collar and a little gold bell? Those are my favorite kinds of kittens."

"Sure thing, now do you want the kind that has two blue eyes or the kind that has one blue eye and one green eye?" I asked.

In case you can't tell, I was being sarcastic. This was yet another example of how boys and girls are different. How in the world did Taisy have a favorite kind of kitten? I mean, I don't have a favorite kind of kitten. I didn't even know that was a thing to have. I have a favorite color (blue, sometimes orange if I'm feeling like shaking things up). I have a favorite dessert (banana split, duh). I have a favorite kind of pizza (double pepperoni, double cheese, double sauce, double awesome). But I do not have a favorite kind of kitten.

"Well, if you must know, I prefer two blue eyes on white kittens, but I do enjoy the different-colored eyes if it is an orange-striped kitten, or a fat gray smushed-face Persian kitten. Those would be my two alternates."

"I was being sarcastic!"

Taisy laughed and rolled her eyes. "Benji, that *is* my favorite kind of kitten, but I'm not crazy enough to care about exact eye color. I was just being sarcastic because you were being sarcastic. You know, sarcasm rarely helps a high-stress situation."

"Did Vince Lombardi say that too?"

"No, Taisy McDonald said it! Benj, why are you being a big meanie today? I feel like you're trying to pick a fight with me." Taisy's eyes went wet. Her forehead crinkled.

"I'm not, I swear," I said. Alexander Chang-Cohen looked down at the floor when I spoke. He always looks down when he doesn't like what someone says.

"Alexander, do you think I'm picking a fight?" I asked.

"I don't like it when you two fight." Alexander shrugged, still looking down.

"WE'RE NOT FIGHTING!" Taisy and I said at the exact same time.

Then we looked at each other, startled, and burst out laughing. Here's what I was learning from this situation: When the going gets tough, Taisy gets tougher. When the going gets tough, I feel like throwing up and freaking out. And poor Alexander Chang-Cohen, he just ends up stuck in the middle.

"So—now we all know the plan," said Taisy.

"We do?" Alexander and I said together this time. At least I wasn't the only one having trouble keeping up.

Taisy nodded and motioned for us to huddle up. We

leaned our heads together, putting our arms around one another. It was a good thing, not just because we had stopped fighting, but also because all the tension and excitement was making me weak in the knees.

"I'll win the archery tournament. Alexander Chang-Cohen will go look at paintings of famous dead people at the National Portrait Gallery with his mom, and Benj will find a kitten that Elvis can rescue from a tree tonight. Also, Benj, you have to figure out how we can capture the rescue on national news. It would be helpful if you could find a hysterical owner as well. Ready? And break!" She clapped her hands, and Alexander Chang-Cohen joined in a second later. I didn't clap because I was still absorbing what Taisy had just said.

"So I'm supposed to go find a kitten and figure out how to get this whole thing on national news?" I asked.

"Well, Alexander and I would help, but we're kind of busy."

"Hey, maybe you should call your new friend Kimmie. Isn't her mom a reporter?" Alexander Chang-Cohen asked.

"That's true," I said. "And very convenient, now that I think about it. But there's one problem. I don't have her number."

"Oh, I do." Taisy pulled her phone out of her purse and texted me her contact. Taisy had her listed as "Kimmie Sunglasses."

"So I'm just supposed to call this girl I met for the first time yesterday and ask her if she can help us tonight with our plan to make Elvis a national treasure? She's going to think I'm crazy. And that's saying a lot, because she's a little crazy herself."

"Trust me, she'll be thrilled to hear from you," Taisy scoffed.

"What is that supposed to mean?"

"It means she clearly liked you, so I'm sure she'll be happy to help. And if I didn't have to go win a trophy, we wouldn't need her help, FYI. But beggars can't be choosers. We need all hands on deck to get this done!"

I looked over at Elvis, who was discreetly watering some shrubbery to my left, and wondered how on earth this was suddenly my life.

18

My mom and I had two hours of downtime before we needed to get to the park to see Taisy's tournament. Alexander Chang-Cohen and his mom went to the National Portrait Gallery. Taisy went ahead to the park with her dad to warm up, check out the competition, and get into the "zone." My mom said she forgot my safari sun hat and insisted

we go back to the hotel to get it.

"You need it for Taisy's tournament," she argued. "It's very sunny out, and you don't want to be sunburned at the White House later, do you?"

I should have known right then she was up to something. My mom rarely forgets anything. She's got one of those steel-trap minds and remembers everything. By the way, yes, it is true that elephants are famous for their amazing memories too, but never, ever compare your mother to an elephant. They don't like that. Trust me, I found out the hard way.

"Mom, first off, it's doubtful even half a UV ray could get though the SPF ten thousand I'm already wearing, so it's unlikely I'm going to get sunburned. And secondly, it's not like we're meeting the president at the White House. We're hanging with Agent Daniels and some of his Secret Service buddies at the White House. Big difference."

It was too bad I forgot to ask Petey for the name of his Secret Service girlfriend. It would have been fun to meet her. I wanted to tell her how much I liked Petey, and to use one of my mother's expressions, what a good egg he is. I'd also tell her he makes a mean banana split, which is not a compliment I just throw around.

When we got back to our hotel room, my mom's true

intentions came out. She not so subtly suggested I take a nap by saying, "Benji, baby, you should take a nap."

"Mom, who ever heard of taking a nap at ten in the morning?" I said.

"You don't want to be a crankypants for your last big day in DC, do you?"

"I'm not a crankypants."

"I know you're not a crankypants right now, but you will be. Or worse."

Ohhhh, now I understood why my mom was acting so like a mom. She was afraid. She thought I hadn't gotten enough sleep last night, which was true, although she didn't know the real reason why. She knows when I'm tired, I get emotional and, admittedly, kind of crankypants. And when I'm any and all of these things, the probability of me ending up in a hospital emergency room goes way up.

On top of that particular worry, I knew my mom was already bracing for the end of the night, when we'd be leaving Elvis at the White House and I'd be sad. Wow, if she only knew what was really going on.

"Mom, I'm not sleepy," I said, not very convincingly, because I was actually extremely sleepy.

"Okay, but I know you, and you're tired. You look tired."

I couldn't believe she'd just said that! She always hates when people say it to her. She believes that what people are really saying when they say "you look tired" is "you look terrible."

"So by saying I look tired what you're really saying is I look awful?" Maybe my mom was right. I was tired.

Suddenly my face burned hot, and I started crying. It's like it came out of nowhere, a flash flood of emotion just built up in me like a volcano. I mean, how the heck was I supposed to find a kitten in Washington, DC, on such short notice?

"Mom?"

"Yes, dear, what is it?" She was no fool. She knew something big was going on with me, but she was trying not to overreact to my tears so I wouldn't get embarrassed.

"Can I ask you for something that would mean an awful lot to me?"

"Of course, you can ask me anything."

"Really, anything at all? And you'll say yes?"

"I won't say for sure I'll say yes, but we can probably work something out." She handed me a Kleenex, "Benji, just tell me, what can I do to make you feel better?"

"Can we go to a local animal shelter and rescue a kitten?"

"Of course we can, anything you want. . . . Wait. What did you say? What's this about a kitten? What are you talking about?"

Oh boy, I needed to come up with something fast. So I opened my mouth, and it was like I had no control over my tongue. It just started wagging, and this is what came out:

"Funny story, Mom. Over breakfast me, Alexander Chang-Cohen, and Taisy were talking about the nature of competition and trophies, and it turns out that Taisy has won over fifty ribbons and trophies in her lifetime, and while she likes them and her father really really likes them, they leave her feeling a little unsatisfied these days. Sure she wants to win today, but she's also wondering what one more trophy is going to add to her collection. So then we were thinking why it is that some hard, shiny object symbolizes your hard work and dedication and the thrill of victory. We were thinking, why couldn't it be something else? Something more meaningful, more special, something that would really make you remember the day you beat everyone else with your awesomeness. We took turns saying what would be more meaningful than a trophy, and when it was Taisy's turn she said she had a favorite kind of kitten. Even though she's technically a dog person, she thinks it's okay to have a favorite kitten too. Hers is a white one with a blue ribbon around its neck. I was thinking since she's obviously going to win the archery tournament, the same way she wins every tournament, perhaps we could get one of her favorite kinds of kittens for her. I mean, she doesn't have to keep it or anything, but even if we found one we could borrow just for the night, and we could return it tomorrow morning on our way back home, I think she'd be super excited and happy. What do you think?"

"Benji, that's a really charmingly kooky story, but there's no way we're getting a kitten for Taisy. First off, there are no kitten-rental places, and secondly, you're allergic to cats. But maybe we can find a toy store and buy her a stuffed-animal kitten. I do think it's sweet you want to get her a present."

"Okay, maybe we can't rent one. But maybe we can borrow one? And I know I'm allergic, but I'm taking allergy shots for Elvis, I mean for Ripley, so won't they work for cats too?"

"I don't know—I never thought about it before. We can certainly ask Dr. Helen on your next checkup, but it doesn't matter for now because we're not getting one."

I spent a brief moment deciding whether to push my luck. Then I decided I'd given it my best shot and it was a no go. I needed to come up with something else. My mom's phone rang. It was my dad, of course. He was driving the twins all around town, trying to figure out which sporting event they needed to get to. They play so many, it's hard to keep track. My mom walked out of my room into her own, leaving me, Elvis, and Ripley.

"Elvis, do you know how I can get a kitten by the end of the day?" I asked.

"Not really. Kittens aren't something I normally concern myself with. But if you want to know who has the best Peking duck in the city, now that I can tell you. And I have been meaning to speak with you about this kitten idea. Do we really think this is the smartest way to go?"

"Of course it's not the smartest idea, but we don't have time to figure out anything smarter. It just has to work, and in order for it to work, I need a kitten. Besides, Alexander Chang-Cohen is working on the logistics of the specific plan, and he's plenty smart."

Elvis didn't say anything back, which is odd because he usually seems to have something to say about everything. "Why are you so quiet? What are you thinking about?"

"Nothing."

"I don't believe you."

"Fine. If you must know, I'm feeling a bit guilty about getting you and your friends involved in something that may be out of all your hands and my paws at this point. Though at least you did learn a few things at the Lincoln Memorial this morning, so there's that."

"Are you giving up?"

"I can't give up, because we're not exactly doing anything yet."

"Please don't give up, Elvis. We've got to try. Maybe you're right. Maybe this is a stupid plan and it will never work. But I wouldn't be able to live with myself if we didn't at least try something."

"My, my, my, aren't you a feisty little David," said Elvis.

"David? Who's David?"

"David and Goliath?"

"David and who?"

"It's a famous story that's often quoted from the Bible, where David, the little guy, has to go up against Goliath, a giant, and in an unlikely turn of events, David is able to defeat Goliath. Now it's an expression used to describe the little guy going up against big odds."

"You know, Elvis"—I smiled—"I've been an

underdog my entire life, and I'm pretty sure it's not going to stop anytime soon. All I do is go up against the bigger guys, figuratively and literally, because I'm small for my age. Of course I rarely win, so that's not very David of me, but well, that's beside the point."

"Yes, Benjamin. In fact, I do know what you mean. And may I thank you in advance for all your efforts on my behalf. What you and your friends have done for me has not gone unnoticed. If I could give you a medal, I would. But know that no matter what happens, it meant everything to me to have you come and try."

I threw my arms around his furry big neck and hugged him. "I love you too, Elvis." And I almost started crying again.

"Easy now, Benjamin. I must say I concur with your mother. A nap might do you some good. And I love you too."

"Okay, maybe a little nap would do me some good." I yawned. "Want to get up on the bed? I guess it's okay, because we're not at home, so we're not breaking the no-dogs-on-the-furniture policy."

"Hip hip hooray! I thought you'd never ask." Elvis hopped up and stretched out, taking up most of the bed.

"You know what would be the nice thing to do, don't you, Elvis?"

"Fine, if we must."

"C'mon, Ripley, you too! Up. Jump up." Ripley barked happily and jumped and curled in the space below my feet, leaving plenty of distance between him and Elvis.

The next thing I remember is waking up three and half hours later to the sound of my mom yelling.

"Oh no, oh no, oh no, oh no, oh no, no, no, no, no!!!"

I sat up and rubbed my eyes. Elvis was already on the floor, standing at the door between our adjoining rooms.

"Mom?! Mom?! What's going on?" I called. She burst through the door.

"I can't believe it. After I finished talking to your dad, I came in here and you were all asleep, and I took a few pictures because it was so cute. Then I decided I'd read a little while you napped, and I fell asleep and I just woke up!"

"Well, I guess someone else needed a nap besides me!"

"Benji, we slept for over three hours!"

"What? Wait, did we miss Taisy's . . . ?" I ran over to my phone. When I looked at the screen, I saw five missed calls. I had over twenty text messages from Alexander Chang-Cohen.

11:45. Where are you? Mom and I just
arrived at the park.

11:52. I am surprised you are not here
yet, but I'm sure you are on your
way.

11:54. I am standing in line at the snack
bar. My mother said I could get
a Gatorade. I'm debating between
lemon-lime flavor and blue.

12:05. I chose lemon-lime. I don't want a
blue tongue for pictures.

12:07. In case you were wondering, the
National Portrait Gallery was
amazing. My mom bought a souvenir
book. I can show you in the car
on the drive home tomorrow.

12:14. Taisy is probably going to start
in fifteen minutes. She asked
where you were, and I didn't want
her to worry, so I said you said
you were stuck in traffic and you
would be here shortly.

12:20. My mom said she called your mom's
cell phone but she didn't get an
answer. Should I be worried?

12:21. I hope you are okay. Taisy is starting in ten minutes.

12:23. You are still not here.

12:24. I'm not sure why I texted you that last text, because obviously you know you are not here. I must be nervous.

12:33. Taisy did an excellent job in her first round. Her opponent is eleven years old and is even taller than Taisy. It is pretty impressive to see.

12:36. Callie, Taisy's opponent, won this tournament last year when she was only ten years old. She is from New Jersey.

12:44. They are tied at the end of the third round. Should I start calling local hospitals? My mom tells me not to worry, but I can't help it. She is pretending she is not worried, but I know she is.

12:52. Oh. My. Goodness. They are tied after the fifth and final round!!!!!!!

12:57. I hate tiebreakers.

12:58. They are each shooting three arrows for the tiebreaker, and whoever's are closer to the center will win. I'm sure Taisy will win.

1:01. I think I understand why people who bite their nails, bite their nails.

1:03. Taisy lost.

1:04. I have never seen the expression on Taisy's face that I'm seeing right now. She's acting like she's okay with losing.

1:15. Taisy received a really small trophy. She showed much grace as she shook Callie's hand.

1:16. Callie received a really large trophy.

1:18. What am I going to say to Taisy? I wish you were here. I wish I wasn't here. I wish Taisy had won.

1:20. Poor Taisy. (I know that wasn't a complete sentence, but sometimes you just have to be a rebel.)

After I finished reading the last text out loud, I looked up and realized my mom was no longer in the room, so it was just me talking to Elvis and Ripley. My mom was on the phone with Mrs. Chang-Cohen. I heard her say she was sorry over and over again. I could tell by the sound of her voice she felt awful for missing the tournament.

Now that I knew Taisy had lost, part of me was relieved I'd slept through the entire tournament. It would have been really tough to sit there and watch Taisy lose. And it would have been even tougher talking to her when it was over. I mean, what do you say to a winner who doesn't win?

19

Taisy, her dad, Alexander Chang-Cohen, and his mom all headed back to the hotel for a quick lunch before we all walked over to the White House to meet Agent Daniels and the executive pastry chef. Time was clearly running out, and I still hadn't managed to find a kitten. I didn't have a choice. I pulled out my phone and texted Kimmie Sunglasses.

```
Hey, Kimmie, it's Benji from the park.
```

```
Hey, Benji from the park! ☺ U texted!!!!!
I knew you would!!!!
```

(She knew I would? What was that supposed to mean?)

Weird request, but do you know where I
can find a kitten? I need one today. I
also need a reporter and a cameraman.

What color kitten?

White with a blue ribbon?

That's my favorite kind!!!!!

Wow, I guess it was a girl thing to have a favorite
kind of kitten.

Taisy's too!

I knew I liked her. Where is the
rendezvous?

I hadn't used the word rendezvous in my entire life,
and now two days in a row I found myself discussing
secret meeting places. My life was definitely not boring.

Not sure yet. White House? Probably. U
think u can find one?

U can count on me! (She added a picture of an aba-
cus. Wow, they really do have an emoji for everything.)

Thanks for your help. More later. Over
and out. Is that spy talk?

Close enuf!!! ☺ ☺

I know I had just met Kimmie a day ago, and I didn't
really know anything about her, but I have to say I did
believe she was exactly the type of girl who could find
a kitten on short notice. It was pretty impressive that
she was totally on board with my weird request. She
acted like it was totally normal for her to get texts from
strangers asking for baby animals. Then again, for all
I know, maybe she did get texts like that all the time.

Now that item one was off my worry list, I had to
deal with item two. I went to look for my mom. I found
her on the floor in her room, packing her suitcase.

"Hey, Mom. Whatcha doing?"

"What does it look like I'm doing?" She stopped
folding her shirt and turned toward me. "I'm sorry for
snapping, honey. I'm just feeling so bad about missing
Taisy's tournament. It's so embarrassing."

"It wasn't your fault, though. I'm sure Taisy and her
dad will understand. It could have happened to anyone."

"Yes, I suppose that's true. But those things don't
usually happen to me."

"Welcome to my life, Mom. I mess up all the time, and you're always telling me it's okay. So now it's my turn to tell you it's going to be okay." I sat down on the bed.

"Thanks, sweetie."

"Okay, now your turn's over. I need help."

"How did I get lucky enough to have such a funny kid?" she said with a laugh.

I shrugged. I was pretty sure that was one of those questions that sounded like a question but didn't actually need an answer. Which was good, because I really didn't know what to say.

"What am I going to say to Taisy? You know, about her losing the tournament? It's weird because I'm the one who usually needs cheering up, so I don't really know how to be the cheerer-upper person."

It's true. I can't tell you how many times I've seen that look on people's faces when they know things aren't great with me, but they have to face me and come up with the perfect thing to say. Even the twins look a little pained when they visit me in the hospital sometimes. They never know what to say. Of course, given the fact that they are guys of few words, and they rarely know what to say ever, this isn't that big of a reach.

Once, I woke up in the middle of the night with a crazy high fever from a kidney infection, and my mom was so freaked out, she drove me to the hospital in her nightgown and a pair of furry bear-paw slippers we gave her for Mother's Day. Anyway, I was pretty sick and ended up in the hospital for a week, so my Sunday school class came to visit me. I could tell most of those kids had never even been to a hospital ever, except for when they were born, and they were scared. They had each written me a get-well poem or drawn me a picture, but most of them just sat there silently while my Sunday school teacher, Mrs. Jinky, talked to my mom out in the hallway. It wasn't the most pleasant experience, and I remember feeling worse after they left.

"Wasn't it nice of everyone to come and see you?" my mom had said.

"It would have been nicer if they actually wanted to come and see me," I said. I remember the look on my mom's face when I said it. It was one of the few times in my life that she didn't have a quick response.

So now it was my turn to deal with an uncomfortable situation. My mom stood up and then sat down next to me on the bed.

"First you apologize for missing her tournament, which you can totally blame on me. And then you tell her she's awesome and it's a big accomplishment to have made it to the finals at all," my mom said.

"You mean I should lie to her?"

"What? No. I'm not telling you to lie."

"You don't believe that, though. You're supercompetitive, and you're always telling the twins, 'There is no room for second place.'"

"Oh please, that's just a famous sports expression. I don't mean it."

"Let me guess, Vince Lombardi?"

"Why yes. Benji, how do you know who Vince Lombardi was?"

"I've got a few surprises up my sleeve, Mom. Can we get back to my problem now?"

"Just know Taisy may not want to talk about it at all. So follow her social cues."

"What's a social cue?"

"It's when you can tell how a person is feeling by how they're acting. So if she seems like she wants to talk about it, you let her talk, but if she doesn't want to, then respect her feelings and don't. You're really sensitive, Benji. I know you'll do the right thing. Now go get changed. You have a weird stain on your T-shirt."

I looked down at my shirt. "That's not a weird stain, it's the world's largest drool spot from the world's largest dog."

I walked back into my room with Elvis. I noticed

Ripley was still lying on the bed. I guess he finally realized this hotel room was too small for me to have a dog on two sides. I went over to my backpack to find another shirt.

"I know my mom thinks I'll know what to say to Taisy when I see her, but do you think it's true? I just don't want to act weird and make her feel worse."

"Benjamin, there will be a lot of these situations in your life as you grow up, new situations that aren't just about you and your own feelings. You'll have to learn to navigate them. These are character-building moments. I believe you have good character. In fact, because of all you have been through in your young life, which is much more than most children your age, you're probably more empathetic, which means you're more likely to have an innate understanding of the pain of others. Put yourself in Taisy's shoes and think about how you would want to be treated. All that said, please don't make her cry, because I don't think I can handle that."

"Thanks a lot, Elvis. That was a really inspiring speech . . . until it wasn't."

We didn't have any more time to discuss it, because just then Alexander Chang-Cohen texted me to say they were back at the hotel, getting a table for lunch downstairs.

On the elevator ride down, my palms started to sweat. My mom didn't even notice. I could tell she was nervous about what she was going to say too. We walked to a large table in the back of the room by the window. Taisy was studying her menu, and she certainly looked fine. As soon as I saw her, my heart pounded in my chest. I really didn't want to say the wrong thing. It was really hard to come in here, and suddenly I empathized with all those Sunday school kids. They must have felt scared too.

But this wasn't about some sick kid they barely knew; this was about Taisy McDonald, one of the most popular kids in my school, the tallest girl in my fourth-grade class, my favorite nurse Dino's favorite niece, and one of my favorite people in the whole world. I realized I knew what I had to do. I knew what she needed from me. And I knew this because I knew what she didn't need. She didn't need me to be sad for her, pity her, or be disappointed in her, mainly because she was probably already feeling all those things and more for herself. She needed me to be normal and treat her the same as I always do.

"Hey, Tais, guess whose mom forgot to set an alarm? I'll give you a hint. She's got the biggest, blondest, curliest hair in the room!" I walked right over and sat in the empty chair next to her. "I'm super sorry for missing your tournament. You know me and my morning naps."

Taisy smiled, and I knew I had picked right and I felt really happy and hopeful. Ever since I'd heard about Elvis's problem, I had felt so tense, but just then it all fell away and I was more relaxed than I'd been in days.

"It's okay, Benj. Out of all my tournaments to miss, this wasn't a bad one."

Wow, Taisy is so cool she was already joking about her loss.

"Are you kidding me? It'd be just as fun for me to see you lose as to see you win." And just like that, my moment was gone. "Sorry, that came out wrong. I didn't mean that. I meant that I like watching you even if you don't win, not that I've ever seen that before, but if I did I know I'd like it just as much, well, maybe not as much, but you know."

"Actually, I do know, Benji. It's okay. And I'm totally fine with losing. Really." Before I could study Taisy's face to see if she was telling me the truth, a phone started ringing. Everyone in the restaurant started frowning, and I said what everyone was thinking. "Uh-oh, someone forgot to turn their ringer off. Shame on them. Tsk. Tsk. Tsk."

"Uh, Benji. That's your phone ringing," Alexander Chang-Cohen said. I turned bright red and reached into my pocket and took out my phone. "Kimmie Sunglasses" popped up on my screen.

My mom gave me a funny look. I almost never use my phone as a phone, mainly because the only person who ever calls me on it is her.

I told everyone I had to take the call, and I politely excused myself from the table, walking down the stairs into the main hotel lobby.

"Hey, Kimmie, what's up?" I said.

"Not much. I just called to say hi."

"Oh, you did? Hi."

"No silly, I called to give you an update on the itten-kay," Kimmie said.

"The what?"

"Don't you know pig latin?"

"Of course I know pig latin. Itten-kay. Right, the kitten. Did you find one?" I asked.

"Not exactly, but it's close enough. It's a smallish, youngish-looking black cat that may or may not be my neighbor's."

"You can't take your neighbor's cat!"

"Relax, B, it might not be. It wasn't wearing a collar. And I like to think of it as borrowing. I mean, you're

251

not going to kill it, are you?" she asked.

"Of course not! Why would you even say that?"

"I don't know, just to get a reaction. Anyway, if the black cat doesn't work out, I have a few other ideas. Like I said, I got this. So what's the dealio with when we're meeting?"

"Well, we're heading to the White House in a couple of hours to hang out and then having dinner there around sixish. Can you make it there?"

"Sure, I'll just go to work with my mom. Apparently, the president is making some announcement, so she has to be on standby. Later, Tater Tot. Signing off, this is Green Bean McCoy."

"Green Bean McCoy?" I asked.

"I'm trying out different code names. What? Is that one too much?"

"Maybe a little. I thought when you spy, it's better to blend in."

"You're right, but that's hard for me when I'm oozing with charisma."

And just like that Kimmie Sunglasses hung up.

"Yeah, you're definitely oozing something," I mumbled.

"What was that, Benj?"

Taisy was standing next to me. I told her Kimmie

had found a kitten, or a young cat, and she would meet us at the White House later.

"And we're in luck. There will be lots of news crews at the White House because the president might be making some kind of announcement," I said.

"Great. Or rather, should I say that's purrrrr-fect!"

I shook my head. "That was terrible, Taisy. It wasn't punny at all."

"I couldn't not say it! Now let's go eat lunch so we can go the White House! I'm really excited to see it." Taisy started back up the stairs toward the restaurant.

"Hey, Taisy?"

"Yeah, Benj?" She stopped and turned around to face me.

"You're always a winner with me. You know that, right?"

"I know. Thanks." Taisy bounded back up the stairs, and I turned toward Elvis.

"So, how'd I do?"

"Very smooth, Benjamin. There may be hope for you yet."

I was already dressed for the White House, so after lunch I went with Taisy to her room. As soon as we opened the door, we saw a giant bouquet of helium balloons waiting for her. Taisy ran and opened the card. They were from Petey and the Hay-Adams Hotel to say congratulations on the tournament.

She looked up at the balloons with a worried expression on her face. "Oh no, do you think they think I won? Did they send these because they think I won? Should I give them back? These seem too big to be sorry-you-lost balloons."

"Taisy, I'm sure they don't care if you won or not. It was just Petey being nice and supportive. I'm sure he's saying congrats on even making it to the finals. It's a big accomplishment."

I guess my mom's words came into play after all. Taisy bought what I was selling. She picked up the phone to call downstairs to thank Petey and the hotel staff. It was an amazing bouquet. The balloons were all different colors and sizes. This hotel probably knew the best balloon place in DC. It only made me love hotels even more than I already loved them. Maybe when I grew up I'd live in one. I also love balloons. I especially love it when balloons drop from the ceiling at the end of a big event. I've never experienced that in person, but I hope to one day. It's on my bucket list.

"I hate balloons," Elvis said while Taisy was on the phone.

"Who hates balloons? You can't hate balloons. People love balloons."

"People love balloons. Me, I'm not people. I'm a dog. Dogs don't like balloons. They're suspicious of them."

"Suspicious? Why? What has a balloon ever done to you, or any other dog?"

"Benjamin, dogs do not like things that pop. Balloons, firecrackers, the backfire of cars and motorcycles. I can't explain it, it's a dog thing. We have sensitive ears, and loud noises are not something we enjoy in general. So keep them away from me. Now if you don't mind, I might try to take a little nap before we leave."

"Again? We took a nap before lunch."

"What can I say? I'm a dog. I nap a lot."

"Apparently, and you hate balloons. I'm learning so much.

"Taisy, I'm heading downstairs to my room. I think we're leaving for the White House in an hour."

She was still on the phone, so she gave me the thumbs-up sign, and I left. I was getting nervous. It was almost time for Operation Save Elvis. On the elevator ride downstairs, I imagined the morning newspaper headline: FOUR-LEGGED NATIONAL TREASURE SAVES KITTEN IN TREE AT WHITE HOUSE.

When I got back to my room, I found Alexander Chang-Cohen brushing his teeth. No surprise there. I told him about Taisy's balloons and the fact that dogs apparently don't like balloons. And then I told him about the newspaper headline I'd imagined in the elevator. "What do you think?"

"I think that headline is a little long, but I like it." I barely could understand him, since his mouth was full of toothpaste foam.

"Not about that. What do you think of our plan working?"

He nodded to indicate that he thought yes, it would work.

"What are the odds?"

Now Alexander Chang-Cohen shook his head violently back and forth, meaning *don't do this*. (Can I just say that he looked like one of those cartoon rabid dogs with all that toothpaste foam coming out of his mouth?) He spit, rinsed, and finally turned to me as he was wiping his mouth with a towel.

"Benji, c'mon, don't ask that. Don't go there. You know what it means to ask me like that."

I did know, but I asked it anyway. Here's the thing about Alexander Chang-Cohen: You couldn't find a more loyal, positive, upbeat, hardworking, and honest friend. He always sees the best in everyone, and he also believes pretty much every single thing can be done if you work hard enough. It's how he was raised. So not only is he a super brainiac, but he's also the hardest-working brainiac I've ever met.

So when I asked him whether he thought the plan would work, he gave me the best-friend, upbeat, positive answer. The answer he knew I needed to hear, which was, "Sure, why not?" But when I asked him the odds, that totally changed the whole question. That made it about numbers and math and reality, which is how his big brain really works.

"Benji, let's just hope everything works out tonight and leave it at that, okay? Now can you please hand me my dental floss?"

"Which flavor?" Alexander Chang-Cohen has a wide array of flavored dental floss. Did you know they make cotton-candy-flavored floss? Which I think would make a dentist scratch his head, because it seems like the opposite flavor floss should be, don'tcha agree? Shouldn't floss be healthy flavored, like spinach or broccoli? And then shouldn't it be green too?

"Surprise me."

I handed Alexander grape bubblegum floss. As I watched him getting ready to set a good example for kids hoping to be their dentist's favorite patient, I thought about what he'd said. I knew I should let it go, that he was giving me an out and I should take it. But when I got nervous about things, it made me feel better to talk about them.

"Just tell me the odds of success. Please?" I pushed.

"Success of what part?"

"I don't know, whichever part has the best and most positive odds."

"I believe, which isn't to say it's true, that if we manage to get Elvis declared a national treasure, he will not be given away as a gift to the Japanese prime minister."

"What percent?"

"High nineties. Easy."

"Go on."

"You know, let's go call Taisy and see if she's ready. Maybe Petey will let us go back up to the roof so we can make balloon wishes. That is, if Taisy will let us."

When Alexander was little, someone told him that if you write down a wish on a piece of paper and tie it to the bottom of a balloon and set it free, one of two things will happen. One, someone finds that balloon and they get the wish, which means you shouldn't ask for something specific like a new pair of walkie-talkies, but instead wish for something that's good for any number of people. Like having more love in your life, or less cauliflower in your life, or that you'd find a candy bar in your backpack you had forgotten about that wasn't melty. But if no one found the balloon (and how you're supposed to know this, I have no idea), and it sailed up and up and up and an angel found it, then they would grant your wish for you. Apparently, balloons are hard to come by where angels live, so they get super happy when they get one. I wondered if angel dogs hated balloons the way Elvis proclaimed earthly dogs did.

"Taisy's on the top floor. It's basically the same. We

can do our balloon wishes later off her terrace," I said.

"She's on the top floor of the guest rooms, but I feel it'd be better to make the wishes off the roof. And besides, it'd be nice to see what the view looks like during the day as opposed to the middle of the night," Alexander Chang-Cohen said.

"You never really answered me before, Alexander. Do you think our plan to save Elvis will work?"

"Please, Benji."

"You don't. Oh no, you don't think we're going to be able to pull it off! That's why you don't want to answer."

"That's not true. I don't know, there are just too many unknowns to calculate the odds properly. You do realize we're only ten years old, right?"

"What's that supposed to mean?"

"It means this is big stuff we're dealing with. And we're just kids who aren't superheroes, who don't know any superheroes, and can't even reference a single comic-book superhero who has ever dealt with this particular situation. Trust me, nothing like this has ever come up in the Marvel or DC Comics universe! Maybe we're going about this all wrong. Are you sure we shouldn't talk to our moms? Or some responsible adult? We could call Dino, or maybe even talk to Petey and his Secret

Service girlfriend. Petey was the one who gave us the national treasure idea, after all."

"Are you crazy? How can we do that? What would we say? The whole story sounds ridiculous."

"It does and it is, which is why I can't give you the odds. But what I can offer you is this. There is a famous saying in Hollywood, or rather in the movies, when it comes to big endings in the final act. And they wouldn't say it so much if it weren't actually true."

"And what's that?"

"'This plan is so crazy, it just might work.'"

The way Alexander Chang-Cohen said it, so seriously, but with the slightest touch of a gangster accent, made me giggle, so I said it this time while waggling a pretend cigar. "'This plan is so crazy, it just might work.'" This made me giggle harder, which turned into laughing, and soon I was laughing so hard I was crying, and then I started coughing, which led to Alexander Chang-Cohen slapping me on the back and caused Ripley to whine, and Elvis to charge into the bathroom to rescue me. He clearly didn't realize I was sitting behind the door, on the edge of the bathtub. When he came in, the door hit my foot and I toppled into the bathtub, banging my head. My first thought when this happened was that I was pleased, because as yet nothing all that bad had happened to me in DC, and I didn't want the bad thing to be our plan failing and Elvis getting shipped off to Japan. Besides, I've bumped my head so many times in my life, it's a wonder I even made it to ten. I guess I have a really hard head.

I could already feel a bump rising, but I can tell when it's a serious bump versus a not-so-serious bump. I needed a bag of ice. I told Alexander Chang-Cohen.

"Aha! I'm going to call room service and see if Petey can bring up an ice pack for you. And maybe two Shirley Temples." Alexander pulled out his phone and started texting.

"You have the room service guy on your phone?"

"No, silly, I'm texting my mom. We can't just order room service without permission. I'm no fool. I'd like to see the age of eleven."

She said yes, and Alexander Chang-Cohen specifically asked if Petey Peterson could deliver it to us if he happened to be working and not on break.

"Hey, Alexander, can I ask you one more thing?"

"Sure, Benji. You can ask me anything."

"Do you think the president would really give Elvis away to the prime minister of Japan?"

"I honestly don't know, Benji, but what I do know is that a big part of the Japanese culture has to do with gift giving, and Elvis would be a pretty spectacular gift. I guess the president would only do it if he thought it would help our country."

"What are the odds?"

"Fifty-fifty, maybe?" I nodded; that seemed about right to me.

I'm a pacer, and so is Alexander Chang-Cohen. We paced back and forth across the room. At first we tried to pace right next to each other, but our paces were a little off, which is odd because he's barely taller than me, so you would think our pace would be about the same. But Alexander must take faster steps than I do, and it just didn't work out. So then we decided to start from opposite ends of the room and pace back and forth, crossing in the middle.

"Can we high-five or something when we meet up in the middle?" Alexander asked.

"I guess so. *Or* I could teach you the *Top Gun* high five, which is a high five up top but then you swing your hand all the way around and then do a low five as you're walking past. Want to try that?"

This maneuver proved to be a little harder than we thought, mainly, I would say, because neither one of us is particularly well coordinated. We got the top high five, but we couldn't get the bottom one.

Ten minutes later we heard a knock on the door. I went to open it, and got it about an inch wide when Alexander Chang-Cohen ran over and slammed it shut again.

"What are you doing? That's not the stranger-danger protocol. You can't just open the door like that."

"But he said it's room service, and we know Petey!"

"I know that, but how do we know it's Petey from behind the door?"

"Mr. Barnsworth, Mr. Chang-Cohen, it's me, Petey Peterson. I have your two Shirley Temples, one with extra cherries, one with extra ice. And the ice pack you requested."

"See? Now can we let him in?"

Alexander Chang-Cohen shook his head. "Petey, I'm going to stick my phone out and take a picture of you, and once I verify that it's really you, I'll take the chain off and open the door."

And that's what Alexander Chang-Cohen did, but he only got a picture of Petey's belly, shoulders, and neck and didn't get his face. He tried again, but this time he managed to get part of his chin. Finally Petey grabbed Alexander Chang-Cohen's phone from him, took a selfie, and then handed it back.

"Oh, it's definitely him," said Alexander, showing

me the photo of Petey.

"Of course it is! You're being a wackadoo."

"Well, this here wackadoo won't be getting kidnapped anytime soon, I'll tell you that much! What are you just standing there for? Open the door, Benji!"

I shook my head and opened the door. Petey had obviously seen his share of weirdo hotel guests, because he didn't let on that we were any weirder than anyone else he'd met at work. He entered the room carrying a silver tray.

"Who needs the ice pack?" he asked.

"That would be me." I raised my hand. "I managed to bump my head in the bathtub. But not while I was taking a bath. I was just sitting there. But it wasn't totally my fault, because I was laughing so hard it turned into a choking fit, which was when Elvis tried to rescue me and the door hit me . . . and anyway, now that I'm telling you all this I realize you didn't ask how it happened, just who needed the ice pack. So sorry. I get a little talky when I'm nervous."

"Oh, don't worry about it. That happens to me too."

"Hey, Petey, while you're here, do you think we could run a scenario by you?" Alexander asked.

"A scenario? What kind of scenario?"

"We have this 'friend' who has this 'plan,' and we

were hoping to get an outside opinion on whether it would work," Alexander said, using air quotes around "plan" and "friend."

"So we need an outside grown-up adult opinion," I chimed in.

"Well, I'll try to find you someone to talk to, then," Petey said, so seriously both Alexander Chang-Cohen and I didn't realize he was joking. Well, not until he said, "I'm joking. I was implying that I'm not a grown-up adult. But I actually am one, even though my girlfriend would tell you otherwise. That's a joke too, but a true one." He looked at both of us, realizing we weren't following. "Put your ice pack on your head and tell me what's going on."

After we finished telling Petey everything, it was pretty hard to read his facial expression. A few times during the story, he said, "Are you being for real?" And we would nod and continue.

"So what do you think, Petey? Will our 'friend's' plan work?"

He looked at both of us carefully and then opened his mouth to speak. "Well, first off, that's a heckuva story you two told about your 'friend' with the 'giant dog.'" As he said this, Petey looked over at Elvis, who was snoring loudly in the far corner of the room. Then he continued. "But I happen to think your 'friend's' plan is so crazy, it just might work. My favorite part, of course, is the national treasure idea, because whoever gave you that idea must certainly be a genius."

Alexander Chang-Cohen and I were so excited, we leaped off the bed and starting jumping up and down! "Yes! Yes! Whoo-hoo! Awesome!!!" Then I realized we were acting a little too excited for something that had to do with our "friend." So I elbowed Alexander Chang-Cohen, who was pumping his fist in the air, calling out, "I said it! I knew it! Right again! I'm right again!"

"Okay, thanks so much, Petey, for your thoughts about our 'friend's' predicament, and we'll be sure to let him know what you said."

"Okay, you do that. And . . ." He grabbed some paper and a pen, jotted something down, and handed it to me. "Give this to your 'friend' too. My girlfriend isn't working tonight, but her younger brother is. This is his name and phone number, and you're in luck because this is his first week on White House detail. So if your 'friend' gets into trouble, don't hesitate to call him, okay? He's gotten me out of many similar predicaments. Well, not similar, but equally crazy. I'll text him and give him a heads-up, okay?"

"Thanks, Petey, we really appreciate your help

with this. I mean, this hotel really offers the best room service I've ever had. Of course, this is my first room service experience so far, but I'm pretty confident this one will hold up over time. Oh, and was it your idea to send Taisy the balloons?" I asked.

Petey nodded and said that the hotel management always looks for ways to show appreciation to guests whenever they can. Alexander Chang-Cohen asked Petey if he'd like to join us in making balloon wishes. He explained the whole thing, and surprisingly enough, Petey said he could take his break and wanted to join us.

"Okay, let's go to Taisy's room now and get balloons. Besides, we probably need all the help we can get for today," said Alexander.

I nodded, because I already knew what I was going to wish for. It wasn't a general wish, it was a specific wish, a very, very specific wish. I figured the odds of a wish-granting angel finding it over a regular human had to be at least fifty-fifty too.

21

We were all quiet on the walk over to the White House, each of us lost in our own thoughts. We had done so much during our two days in DC, and even though it seemed like the days and nights were long, suddenly time was moving really fast. I can't quite explain it, but I felt a little older. Like I learned a bunch of life-lesson stuff, and my brain was still trying to figure out what to do with it all.

I was also so used to having Elvis around again. It was amazing how easily we fell back into our bickering ways, but also how much fun it was to burrow my face into his black velvety cheek when he was trying to nap in the hotel room. He looked so huge all stretched out on the floor, like a giant dog-shaped rug. When I lay next to him, I felt even smaller than normal. But now I also had the memory of him sitting next to the Lincoln Memorial, labeled under the only time Elvis ever seemed small to me.

I just couldn't bear the thought of driving away and leaving him behind. I asked my mom whether he could spend tonight with us and we'd drop him off in the morning on our way home, but my mom said she thought it would be better to say our good-byes tonight. She tried to soften the blow by telling me she'd talked to Agent Daniels and he'd agreed to let me FaceTime with Elvis every now and then. That way, I'd be able to still see him from time to time.

I didn't want to think about it. I just wanted to enjoy every moment I had with him while I could. When we arrived at the White House, there were lots of news trucks already parked there. Mrs. Chang-Cohen said she heard on the news that the president was going to "announce a new trade treaty with Asia."

Alexander Chang-Cohen's eyes got big and he looked at Taisy, who looked at me. "With Asia, or with Japan?" I asked.

"Japan is in Asia, Benji," Mr. McDonald said, smiling.

"I know. I just was wondering if it was one country

in particular, that's all."

"Actually, I think it is about Japan. Didn't the prime minister visit the White House recently?" Mrs. Chang-Cohen asked.

"I think you're right," my mom said.

"Well, if they're going to make a treaty with Japan, it should be an antisushi treaty. I prefer my food cooked." Taisy's dad laughed.

Elvis barked in agreement, and all the adults laughed, while I suddenly felt nauseous. If the president was announcing some new trade treaty thingie with Japan, it'd make even more sense he'd want to send an extra-special two-hundred-pound birthday present to the prime minister to seal the deal.

This time the guards at the gate told us our passes were for the main doors versus the side doors, where my mom and I entered the last time. The first time we came to the White House, all I could think about was seeing Elvis again. I didn't really take in the fact that I was standing in *the* White House. But this time, when we walked into the grand entryway, the enormity of it really hit me. I mean, here we were, me, my two best friends, and our parents, all in the White House together because of a crazy mix-up that had brought Elvis into our lives a few months ago.

The White House felt different from the last time I was there. The president was on the premises, and he was delivering a speech. There was a buzz in the air. People walked faster, with more of a spring in their step. The White House is such an amazing place because it's so many things to so many people. It's actually a house where the president and his family live day to day. They even have their own movie theater. It's also the place where he works and runs the country and makes some of the most important decisions in the world. Just being inside those famous walls made me stand a little taller.

We were first given our own private tour. We were so overwhelmed, we could barely talk. It was one thing to see this place lit up in the middle of the night from a distance. Actually being inside was, well, kind of mind-blowing. Of course, Elvis just walked around like it was no big deal. Taisy's favorite part was the flower shop, where they made all the White House bouquets. Alexander Chang-Cohen told us lots of facts about the Diplomatic Room. It's where President Roosevelt gave his fireside chats during World War II. I pictured Fala at his feet while he gave his addresses. I agreed with Taisy's dad that the Map Room was supercool. Mrs. Chang-Cohen almost fainted when we got to see the

Lincoln bedroom. She just thought it had been decorated so perfectly, and she said it was the most famous bedroom in the entire house.

"Even more famous than the bedroom where the actual president himself sleeps?" I asked.

"You know, Benji, I never thought about it. I guess this is the most famous guest bedroom in the entire White House."

"Hey, Mom, you haven't said which is your favorite room yet."

"Oh, I already know that my favorite room is the pastry kitchen. It's where all the White House desserts are made. I don't even have to see it to know it'll be my favorite. I can't believe I'm about to meet our country's executive pastry chef."

"He's had your cupcakes," said Mrs. Chang-Cohen. "So I'm sure he's pretty excited to meet you too."

We passed through the main kitchen, which was enormous, but it had to be big because of all the huge parties and dinners they had at the White House. I pulled my mom back from opening all the cabinets to inspect the pots and pans. And then our tour guide said she had specific instructions to end the tour in the pastry kitchen.

"Saving the best for last," my mom said.

I don't know if I had ever seen my mom so excited. For once, I almost felt like the grown-up, while she got to be the excited kid. When we entered the kitchen, we saw a short, round man wearing all white and a chef hat on his head. He was using a cookie cutter–like object to cut out disks of extremely frozen ice cream to put on top of circular pieces of yellow butter cake. He turned around and looked at us. He had plump cheeks, a tiny mustache, and bright-blue eyes.

"Hello, hello. Welcome to my kitchen. I am Chef Pfeiffer Larue, and these are the beginnings of my famous baked Alaska dessert. I am making them for the president's dinner. But don't worry, I'll make extras for my special guests."

"Oh, who else is coming here tonight?" Alexander asked.

"You!" Chef Larue laughed. His mouth opened so wide when he laughed, I saw all his teeth. His cheeks were bright red, his eyes wet and shiny. "It is for all of you. You're my special guests! Now who wants to try my marshmallow meringue?"

We all raised our hands, so he took out six spoons, dipped them into the bowl, and handed one to each of us. It looked like whipped cream, but it was actually denser, stickier, marshmallowier, and probably one of the best things I've ever tasted in my entire life.

"This is the president's favorite decision-making dessert. He always requests it whenever he's working on something that needs all his concentration. He says it helps him think."

Taisy spotted a beautiful golden birdcage in the corner of the room. She leaned up to the bars and whistled at the yellow canary inside. The canary whistled back. "You are the most beautiful bird I've ever seen. Yes, you are," Taisy said in a soft voice. Chef Larue came right over and proudly told Taisy his prized canary had the most beautiful voice and that was exactly why he'd picked her.

"When I went to pick out the canary, all the birds seemed the same, but when I pressed my face very close to the giant cage like this"—Chef Larue demonstrated just how close he pressed his face to the cage by picking up a giant whisk off the counter and looking at us through it—"it was Genvieve who flew to the front and sang for me right away. I knew in that moment that she was the bird for me."

Chef Larue went on to tell us all a really long story about his bird. She was extra special because she sang, and normally it's the male canaries who sing. As he told us, he kept working on the baked Alaskas on the tray.

It was kind of distracting. The more we watched him, the more we couldn't wait to try them. My mom was nodding and smiling too, but instead of standing still like the rest of us, she kept walking around and marveling at everything in the kitchen. She couldn't help herself, and I couldn't hold her back. She opened drawers and cabinets. She even opened a refrigerator. She was like a kid in a candy store.

So this is the story Chef Larue told, or at least the bit I remember when I wasn't thinking about that baked Alaska. When Pfeiffer Larue was a young boy living in France, his parents owned a small restaurant in the countryside called Le Canari Qui Chante, which means "The Singing Canary." They named the restaurant for the canary his mother always kept in the kitchen. She said since she spent so many long hours in the kitchen, she needed a little company. And when his mother first started teaching him how to bake when he was even younger than us, well, those were some of the best memories of his entire life. His mother passed away ten years ago, and he inherited her canary François Chevalier, but sadly the canary died only a few months after his mother, from what he believes was a broken heart.

"I tried to take over the restaurant when my mother died," Chef Larue said, sighing. "But after François

Chevalier went to canary heaven, I ended up with the worst case of baker's block I've ever had."

"Baker's block? Is that like writer's block?" my mom asked.

"Yes. Like a writer can no longer write, I could no longer bake. Weeks turned into months, months turned into one year, and finally, I sold my restaurant and moved to Paris."

If the chef's story had ended right there, you'd already be amazed, but his story was far from over. This was just the beginning. You see, four years ago he received the strangest phone call of his life, which was that the White House was looking for a new executive pastry chef and his name had been submitted by the French prime minister, who had eaten at Le Canari Qui Chante only once but had never forgotten the desserts. Even though Pfeiffer Larue lived in France, he actually had dual citizenship, because his mother was French but his father was American. They asked if he would be interested in interviewing for the job. He, of course, thought it was some sort of silly joke that his friends were playing on him, but after a while he realized they were serious.

"I tried many times to explain that I was retired from baking because of my baker's block." Chef Larue tapped the side of his head. Then he threw his hands up in the air. "But they wouldn't take no for an answer, so finally I agreed to fly to America for an interview."

When he got to DC, Pfeiffer Larue was so nervous, he called around to all the pet stores and bought himself his very own canary. He brought the canary to his interview, which he knew would probably be seen as odd, but the head butler, who was in charge of the entire household staff of the White House, wasn't surprised at all. They had an extensive file on him. Every potential White House employee is thoroughly checked out by the Secret Service, so they knew all about how Pfeiffer Larue learned how to bake from his mother at their family restaurant.

"When I cracked my first egg in the White House, I noticed my hand was shaking, and I really wondered whether I would be able to do it, but then I looked around this kitchen and thought of all those who have baked for presidents before me, and suddenly I was filled with a sense of purpose I had not felt in a very long time. And then, like magic, Genvieve Larue began to sing, and everyone who knows anything about canaries knows they only sing when they are happy, and I took that as a sign that she felt like she could make a home for herself here in this kitchen. And the rest, well, the rest is history. I have now been at the White House for two presidents."

We all looked at the tray of baked Alaskas before us, and boy, did they look scrump-dilly-icious. I completely understood how the president could get inspired by a dessert like that, which means baked Alaska was the president's SuperDuperScooper banana split. Chef Larue picked up a baked Alaska and put it on a plate, setting it on fire with a tiny blowtorch. The whole thing lit up for just a second and then it went out, leaving behind a light browning on the meringue. He let us all sample it. Inside the meringue was a circular disk of buttery yellow cake that melted in your mouth, and on top of that was strawberry ice cream. It's the only thing I have ever tasted in my life, besides my mom's cake, that was almost on a par with a banana split. And believe me, I would never say that lightly. I don't joke when it comes to my love of banana splits. Some things in life are sacred and should be treated as such.

"Whoa—if I were the president, I'd want to make a tough decision every day just so I could eat that! It's amazing," I said.

"It is . . . ," my mother said, holding out her verdict, "excellent!"

"Well, after dinner, everyone will get their very own one to enjoy."

Chef Larue bowed slightly to my mother, and I could see he was smiling. I guess he could tell my mom does not praise a baked good unless it's worth it. She's super picky about such things, and by super picky I mean she's very critical. In general, my mom is totally easygoing and is extremely understanding and forgiving about pretty much anything. But not when it comes to desserts. She has a very high bar, mainly because she always thinks her baked goods are better than everyone else's.

"Now, Mrs. Barnsworth, what must I do to persuade you to share with me your cupcake recipe?"

"Normally, I'd tell you there's nothing you could do to get the recipe out of me, but now that I've tasted some of your dessert, I don't know if I can say that with confidence. Maybe if you share your recipe, I'll share mine." My mom smiled.

"You, Mrs. Barnsworth, you, I like very much," Chef Larue said, and laughed. "Come, let us bake something together."

My mom's face lit up at the chance to spend a little time baking in the White House pastry kitchen. I was so proud of her and happy for her at the same time.

"I'd be honored to bake with you. But I'm going to need an apron. I'm a messy baker. I really like to get my hands dirty."

Chef Larue handed my mom one of his own aprons with his name embroidered across the front of it. I took out my phone and took a bunch of pictures of the two of them wearing matching aprons.

"Look, you two are twinsies!" Taisy said. "Can I help bake too?"

"Of course, my dear. Now, what should we make?" Chef Larue asked.

And right on cue Genvieve Larue started to sing. It's like she knew what they were about to do. I wondered if maybe the canary understood what Chef Larue said in the same way Elvis understands me. Somehow I think she did.

22

Now, if you think Chef Larue's story was the best one of the day, you'd be sadly mistaken. Because after two hours of Mom and Chef Larue's bake-off, Agent Daniels showed up in the kitchen, and right behind him, rolling a bright-pink Barbie suitcase behind her, was the one and only Kimmie.

"Look who I found wandering around by the press tent. She says she knows you guys?" said Agent Daniels. Kimmie stepped forward. She was wearing a bright-pink trench coat and knee-high lace-up yellow

Converse high-tops.

"I do know them. For once I wasn't lying. I make a point of telling the truth a few times every day, just to keep things interesting."

And of course, she was wearing sunglasses even though it was evening. These sunglasses were yellow and shaped like lightbulbs. They were actually pretty cool, and probably my favorite out of all the ones I had been lucky enough to see.

"Hey, Kimmie, glad you could make it," I said.

"Well, it's obvious the party can't get started without me. And speaking of getting the party started, everyone meet Sally Claws. Sally Claws, meet . . . everyone."

Kimmie unzipped her Barbie rolling suitcase, and I kid you not, an orange ball of fur shot straight up five feet into the air, letting out a sound that could only be described as a cross between a screech and a hiss. Everyone screamed and jumped back. Ripley moved closer, barking up a storm.

It seems the only thing Sally Claws liked less than being zipped up in a pink Barbie suitcase was having a yellow Labrador barking at her. She landed and then sprang back up in the air, lunging for Ripley with her claws out like she was Wolverine going after his archnemesis. Taisy screamed. My mom grabbed me and picked me up to protect me. Elvis charged forward to help his fellow dog.

I guess Sally Claws's name was no joke, because she had hers stuck in Ripley's ear. He bucked like a bronco to get her off. He slammed into the cart where Pfeiffer had placed his tray of baked Alaskas, and pretty soon there were twelve baked Alaskas flying through the air. They landed on the floor, splat, splat, splat, splat, splat, splat, splat, well, you get the gist.

If you want to know what happens when you have twelve baked Alaskas landing on the floor, well, basically it was marshmallow meringue everywhere, and soon both dogs and Sally Claws were sliding and wrestling around in it. When the baked Alaskas went down, Pfeiffer started yelling in French, and Big Tate McDonald started laughing. (If I hadn't been so scared about Elvis or Ripley getting their faces clawed off by that crazy cat, I would probably have been laughing too.)

Then, suddenly, Taisy flew into action. She grabbed the lid off a pot on the counter, held it up like a shield, and grabbed a long wooden spoon. She moved forward, into the whirling mess of animals. She poked Sally Claws with the spoon, trying to get her off Ripley. But she kept missing and jabbing Elvis and Ripley instead.

Taisy's dad stopped laughing. He lumbered into the center, grabbed Elvis's back legs, and dragged all two hundred pounds of him backward like he was a fifty-pound bag of flour, which is exactly what you're supposed to do in a dog fight. He then dragged him by the collar over to my mom and told her to hold on. She grabbed him and let me down on the floor. Next, Mr. McDonald went in to help poor Ripley. Sally Claws still wouldn't let go. Ripley squealed like a pig. It was a terrible sound.

"Benji, grab a pot of water and throw it on them! That's supposed to work," Mr. McDonald shouted.

I looked around the giant kitchen and saw a large pot on the stove. I quickly tested the outside to make sure it wasn't too hot, then I grabbed it with both hands and tried to get close enough to Ripley, but it was so heavy I could barely move it. Soon Alexander grabbed one of the handles, and together we tossed the water on the animals like we were putting out a fire. The bad news was there was no water in the pot. The good news was it was filled with a bunch of wet ravioli, and when they hit Sally Claws, she hissed and finally let go of poor Ripley. The bad news was the ravioli was what Chef Larue had made for our dinner. So the only thing more slippery than baked Alaska on a tile floor is baked Alaska and ravioli.

Taisy rushed in to grab Ripley, and she slid across

the floor, waving her arms in large circles to keep her balance. She was heading right for me. I stepped forward to break her fall, but she slammed into me and the two of us slid another three feet, crashing into Genvieve's birdcage. It toppled over and clanged to the floor.

"Genvieve! Mais non!" Chef Larue screamed, covering his face in horror.

Then he dived for the birdcage, but it was too late. The birdcage door flew open and Genvieve flew right out, taking off. Who could blame her? It was total chaos in the pastry kitchen.

Suddenly, the kitchen was filled with a really loud clanging noise. Everyone shut up and turned toward the sound. Agent Daniels stood holding the tops of two pans, clanking them together like cymbals.

"Everyone stop and shuuuuut up!"

And we all did. I was lying facedown in a soppy mess of slimy grossness. Taisy was lying across me. Alexander was still holding the pot, which he let go, and it banged to the floor. My mom was still holding Elvis, who was covered in baked Alaska. And Mrs. Chang-Cohen was holding a towel to Ripley's now bloody ear. Big Tate McDonald was back to laughing, and he announced, "Man, that was the craziest thing I've ever seen, and I've seen some crazy things."

I looked around because I didn't see Kimmie. Then I saw her. She had climbed on a counter above all of us. She held up her phone, filming the entire disaster.

No one spoke for a moment. Then my mom and Agent Daniels spoke at once. Then they each stopped and motioned the other to go ahead.

"You go first. This is more your house than it is mine," my mom said to Agent Daniels.

"We're going to handle this mess systematically and efficiently. Now, first things first. How's Ripley?"

"He definitely needs to see a vet. That crazy cat really tore his ear up," said Mrs. Chang-Cohen.

"I'm going to need a vet ASAP, thanks," Agent Daniels said into the microphone hidden in his sleeve. "Did Elvis get hurt?"

My mom squatted down next to Elvis and checked his face. "I don't think so. He's just got so much hair, it's hard to tell. I think all the blood is probably from Ripley. But he does need a bath, because he's got a lot of meringue stuck in his fur." It was kind of a toss-up on whether my mom was so sad because of Elvis or the meringue.

Agent Daniels nodded and radioed in for a dog groomer. "Now, does anyone know where that crazy cat went?"

We all looked at one another and shrugged. Kimmie pointed left.

"I think she went that away. She was all mad because she was wet. Cats really, really don't like to be wet," she said.

"We have a small wet orange cat on the loose in the house. Consider it slightly dangerous. It has really sharp claws and it's not happy. It's probably bloody, but I don't think it's hurt. It's dog blood. Long story," Agent Daniels said into his sleeve again.

Kimmie raised her hand. It was odd, seeing her be so polite, but I'm assuming she was feeling slightly chagrined because she basically started this whole mess with that crazy cat.

"Yes, Kimmie?" Agent Daniels sighed.

"The cat's name is Sally Claws. You know, like Santa Claus, but different."

"Will the cat answer to that name?"

"Probably not, because I just thought of it on the way over."

"Is it your cat?"

"Not exactly."

"What do you mean?"

"Well, you see, I tried to get the black cat that may or may not have been my neighbor's cat, but I couldn't

288

catch it. So I put out a bowl of milk on my back patio and was hoping that would attract it, and then next thing you know Sally Claws showed up. I think she's a stray that lives in my neighborhood."

My mother, Mr. McDonald, and Mrs. Chang-Cohen all stared at Kimmie in shock. Agent Daniels grimaced and spoke into his sleeve again. "Okay, the cat could possibly be feral, so use extreme caution. We don't know if it's had all its shots. Better call in animal control."

Right then another agent came in, and Agent Daniels introduced him as Eddie Quintana.

"Wait, are you Eddie Quintana, the brother of another Secret Service agent who is the girlfriend of Petey who works at the Hay-Adams Hotel?" I asked.

"That's me. Petey texted me to be on the lookout for you guys. Quite the little adventure you all had last night, though this one looks much bigger." Agent Quintana smiled.

"Adventure? What is he talking about?" my mom asked.

Eddie must have seen my eyes go wide, because he looked immediately sorry for spilling the beans.

"He means that we went up to the roof with Petey and made balloon wishes before we came over. The roof has an amazing view of the White House. It was Petey's first time making a balloon wish, so it was quite an adventure," I said.

It's hard to say whether my mom bought the story, but Agent Daniels interrupted. "Can we powwow about all this later? Kimmie, we're going to have to call your mom over."

"Yes, sir. But do you have to tell her about the cat in the suitcase part? She'll be furious with me."

Kimmie looked really nervous, and now I felt bad. I mean, even though it was kind of her fault for bringing a crazy cat into the White House in a rolling pink Barbie suitcase, she wouldn't have done it if I hadn't asked her to in the first place.

Before Agent Daniels could speak again, Chef Larue finally caught his breath. Apparently the more upset he is, the harder it is to understand him.

"Hello, what about my Genvieve? That's certainly the most pressing of all the problems. Well, except for the poor doggie's ear. Number one, I need my canary back immediately. Genvieve is not used to being outside her cage anywhere except in my house. So she will certainly be upset and nervous. Especially with a deranged cat roaming around. And number *deux*, my desserts are totally ruined, and the president himself requested my baked Alaska, and now what am I going to do? Also, I'm not sure what I'm going to eat for dinner now that my ravioli is all over the floor. If I don't eat soon, I will get cranky, so I'm just warning you all that you will very soon be dealing with a most unhappy French pastry chef. Finally, who's going to clean up this mess?"

"All agents be on the lookout for a small canary," Agent Daniels said into his sleeve. Then he stopped and looked up. "What color?"

"Genvieve is yellow, with gray on her chest and a little on her wings. Do you need a picture? She has some flecks of green at the tips of her wings too."

"The canary is yellow and gray and is a VIB, a very important bird. Agent Quintana will be running point on this 'Find the Canary' operation."

"Are you serious?" Eddie asked. "You're assigning me to find a lost canary?"

"Does it look like I'm serious?" There was something in the tone of Agent Daniels's voice that showed he had just reached his limit. "You do realize I'm the agent in charge of the house, and protocol is: what I say goes."

"Yes sir, of course, sir." Now it was Eddie's turn to talk into his sleeve. "All agents please make sure all windows and doors are closed and secure so the bird cannot leave the premises."

Agent Daniels called for a cleaning crew to report to the pastry kitchen stat. "Now, let's discuss the president's dessert. Do you have all the ingredients to make the president another baked Alaska?" he asked.

"Of course I do, but the question is the time. Baked Alaska takes time. The meringue needs to be whipped for a long time. I make the cakes from scratch. Do we think Genvieve is okay?" He turned to Agent Quintana. "I know your sister. She loves my peanut butter pie, doesn't she?"

"I think so, but I'm not sure."

"I never forget a person and their favorite dessert. Find my Genvieve and I'll make you whatever you want."

"I'll do everything I can, Chef Larue."

My mom stepped forward and told Agent Daniels that she could and would absolutely help Chef Larue make a new baked Alaska.

"It's the least I can do, because somehow I feel this may be partly my son's fault." She turned and stared at me. "Could this have anything to do with the kitten you were asking about earlier?"

"Uh, well, you see, funny story, but—"

"Again, we're going to need to shelve all sidebar convos until we have the president's dessert situation taken care of. Now, how much time do we have before the president needs his dessert?" Agent Daniels then talked into his cuff. "Whoever has eyes on the president, can you please tell me the ETD, estimated time of dessert?" He listened for a moment and said, "Okay, we have a few hours."

"Find Genvieve and I'll start making the baked Alaska again, but let's find her first," said Chef Larue. "I don't know if I can really focus on baking at a time like this. Genvieve is the most important bird in my life. What if you can't find her? What if I never see her again? What if she's hurt, or alone, or scared? Poor little Genvieve Fifi Larue!"

And just like that, Pfeiffer Larue started to cry. My mom's mothering instincts kicked into overdrive. The only thing she hates more than seeing a child cry is seeing an adult cry. She walked over to Chef Larue and held out her arms. He fell into them gratefully, sobbing into her shoulder. I grabbed a dish towel off the counter to give to my mother, but she held out her hand.

"Benji, don't move. You're covered in grossness. The last thing we need is for you to slip and fall."

I looked at myself and realized I was covered head to toe in sticky food slime. Taisy wasn't as bad, since she'd landed on top of me. But she definitely needed some new clothes.

"Agent Daniels, is there somewhere we can get cleaned up and get some new clothes?"

"Yes, one of the assistant butlers will be able to help you with that." He spoke into his cuff again. "I'm going to need two assistant butlers to report to kitchen number two immediately. Thanks."

"So, tell us what needs to be done and let's make it happen." Big Tate McDonald raised his hand now.

"Agent Quintana is running point on the canary search-party team. Can you head up the crazy-cat search-party team?" Agent Daniels nodded at Mr. McDonald.

"Heck yeah, it'd be my honor to QB for the crazy cat team. Who's with me?"

"I guess I should go, since it's kind of my cat. But I'm a little scared." Kimmie raised her hand tentatively.

"Don't you worry, little one, I've got your back. Taisy, after you clean up, text me and you can come join us, okay?" Mr. McDonald said, and Taisy nodded.

Mrs. Chang-Cohen said she'd join the canary team, and she said she'd take Alexander Chang-Cohen with her. Agent Daniels said he'd oversee the kitchen and remain the center point man, and he demanded everyone report back in half an hour.

"What about me? After I clean up, what should I do?" I asked.

"Why don't you check in with me, and I'll see who needs the most help? Now, are you going to be okay without a therapy dog? Ripley has to go to the vet, and we can't let Elvis walk around the house looking like he does. He needs a serious hosing down," said Agent Daniels.

My mom said I'd be fine as long as an adult was with me and Taisy was nearby.

Suddenly, the two assistant butlers arrived, one for Taisy and one for me. They blotted us down with towels so we wouldn't drip through the house. We took off our wet shoes and socks, walking through the White House hallways in bare feet. I'm pretty sure not many people have had the privilege of walking around in bare feet in this particular house.

We were taken upstairs to two separate bedroom bathrooms. Another butler arrived with some White House gift shop pajamas, socks, and slippers. They collected our clothes and took them down for washing.

Taisy and I met at the top of the stairs twenty minutes later. We were both scrubbed clean, wearing matching White House pajamas with rolled-up legs. We stared at each other in shock over everything that had happened. Then Taisy gave me a little wave.

"Hey, we're twinsies too now. Like your mom and Chef Larue."

"Yes, we are. So, did what I think just happened actually really happen? Because it's a little nutso," I said.

"No one is ever going to believe this story, that's for sure. I mean, if someone told it to me, I don't know if I'd believe it."

The assistant butlers checked to see where we should go. While we waited, we sat down next to each other on the top step.

"I just showered in the Lincoln bedroom," Taisy whispered. "I bet Mrs. Chang-Cohen will be so excited to hear that. There are tons of famous people who have showered there."

I sighed. While Taisy was showering in the Lincoln bedroom, I was taking my own shower, thinking about how our big plan of Elvis saving a kitten in a tree had turned into a complete and total disaster.

"You know, I'm pretty sure even if we did manage to get that cat up in a tree, nobody would want Elvis to save her. I doubt you get to be a national treasure for saving a crazy cat," I said.

"If anything, we may have had to save Elvis from the crazy cat. I feel really bad for Ripley. Talk about being in the wrong kitchen at the wrong time. I just can't believe Kimmie zipped that poor thing into a Barbie suitcase. I know she cut out a few airholes, but there's no way any animal or person would be thrilled to be zipped in a suitcase." Taisy said, shaking her head.

"Yeah, she clearly didn't think that idea through very carefully. But in a weird way, I'm not totally surprised that she picked the most bizarre way to do something. She sure knows how to make an impression. But I do feel bad because it's my fault."

"Benj, this is not your fault. You didn't let a wild, crazy cat loose in the White House."

"I know it wasn't actually me who brought the crazy cat, or let the crazy cat out of the bag." I chuckled. "Ha ha, she actually, literally let the cat out of the bag. Sorry, anyway, as I was saying, but it was my idea to call her and ask her to find a kitten."

"Actually, Benj, if we're assigning blame, which we're not, it was my idea. I gave you her number, so it's just as much my fault as it is yours. But it's not our fault. You know why? Because that crazy wild orange cat was no kitten. Kittens are cute, kittens are sweet, kittens don't have claws like deadly weapons. I've said it once, but I'll say it again: poor Ripley."

"I know. Do you think he's going to be okay?"

"I'm sure he'll be emotionally fine, eventually, but that ear looked pretty bad. He may be the dog with one shredded ear."

"I know I shouldn't be worrying about this now, but we still have the whole getting Elvis declared a national treasure thing to deal with on top of finding a lost canary and a crazy cat. I guess our plan is done-zo."

We both stopped talking and sat in silence, taking in the grand staircase and the paintings on the walls and the fact that we happened to be sitting on the steps in the White House.

"Hey, Benj, can I talk to you about something?"

There was something in Taisy's voice that made me forget everything, where we were, what had just happened, and even Elvis. Suddenly, she looked sad. She rested her chin in her hands. "Of course, Taisy. What's up?"

"I—well, you see—it's just that—" she stammered, unsure of where to start. "Oh never mind, it's silly."

"Are you sad about losing the tournament?" I asked softly.

She didn't answer right away, which meant I was

right. After a while she finally started to talk. "I'm more sad about not winning it, but I guess that's kind of the same thing. I know I said I didn't care, and I don't really. But . . . I don't know."

"Do you have that yucky feeling when it feels like your chest has been scooped out so it's all empty and echoey?"

Taisy looked at me, her eyes teary. "That's exactly what I'm feeling. Like exactly. How do you do that, Benj?"

"Well, let's just say I've had to deal with way more yucky feelings in my life than you, not that I'm comparing or anything. I'm just saying I know what that feeling is and what it means."

"What does it mean?" Taisy asked.

"It means you're sad that things didn't go your way, but here's the thing, Taisybell, that's going to happen a lot in our lives, I think. And it will never feel good, but I promise you that dull, empty ache will go away. And I know when you talk about it, it goes away faster than when you don't. Trust me, I've tried it both ways."

"Okay, thanks, Benj. I guess I'm just not used to dealing with defeat. I mean, I don't win everything, but when you play team sports, you have others who lose with you. Today, losing in archery was all on me. If that makes sense."

"Well, you did a good job of hiding your feelings."

"I wasn't hiding them as much as I was hiding from them. Does that make sense? I just thought if I pretended like I didn't care, I wouldn't care. Plus my dad's idea of a pep talk is 'Suck it up, T. Sometimes you gotta lose to win.' Which may be true, but doesn't stop losing from hurting. Argghh. I totally hate feeling this way."

I nodded. "Taisy, if it wasn't for you, we wouldn't be here right now at the top of the steps of the White House wearing gift shop pajamas that are too big for us. You got us to DC and you gave me the best gift ever, which is a chance to see Elvis one more time. So in my book, you're the biggest winner ever."

Taisy threw her arms around me right then and gave me a big hug. She smelled like shampoo and vaguely of apricots and lemonade. I hugged her back, and suddenly I got that achy feeling in my chest too, thinking that this might indeed be the last time I would see Elvis. Well, at least there was no way he was ever going to forget this day.

Taisy pulled back and gave me one of her famous happy smiles. She stood up and put her hand out for me. I took it and stood up next to her.

"You know, Benj, this day isn't over yet," she said. "And you know what they say. It's not over till it's over."

"Yeah, it's not over until the yellow canary sings."

"Yep, it's not over till Genvieve Larue sings." Taisy giggled, and I joined in too.

23

A year ago, if you had asked me to predict what I thought my first trip to the White House would be like, I would have said it would be part of a school field trip, and I'm sure it would have been interesting. Well, boy, would I have been wrong, wrong, wrong. This visit wasn't even close to interesting, it was so far beyond

interesting it was on a totally different map altogether. It was on an entirely different planet.

Taisy and I split up after our pajama talk on the stairs. She went to join the crazy cat search party with her dad, while I went back to the kitchen to check on Elvis and get any news on Ripley. When I walked into the kitchen, I couldn't believe how clean it was. There wasn't a trace of mess left. Even Genvieve's broken birdcage was gone. It was hard to believe that what had happened an hour earlier even happened at all. Apparently, the White House janitorial staff performs miracles. If only I could call them when I had to clean my room at home.

Chef Larue was sitting on a stool at the kitchen counter. I heard him sniffling a bit, but overall he looked better. He was busy eating pancakes and drinking hot tea. My mom stood next to him, in her white apron, with a frying pan in her hand. My mom tends to make pancakes in different shapes. She thinks round pancakes are too boring, so she likes to mix it up. She's made all sorts of animals, letters, trees, snowmen, crescent moons, and even snakes. Chef Larue was eating her classic pancake shapes: hearts and Mickey Mouse ears.

"Hey, Mom, is there any news on Genvieve Fifi

Larue yet? And by any chance, are there any pancakes left?"

"No news about Genvieve yet." Chef Larue sighed, and my mom quickly reassured him. "Don't worry, Pfeiffer, I'm sure they will find her."

My mom uncovered a plate for me. She was saving me pancakes shaped like a letter *B*. I was about to grab a second pancake shaped like the letter *E*, but she stopped me. "That one's for Elvis."

"Oh, speaking of Elvis, where is he?"

"He's getting blow-dried in the bathroom. They gave him a bath, but you know how long it takes to get that giant dog's hair dry," she said.

"How's Ripley?"

"Poor Ripley. He's pretty much fine. Luckily most of the wounds were superficial, but Sally Claws certainly did a number on his ear." My mom frowned. "The vet did her best to get him all sewn up. He'll be fine eventually, but he was given a tranquilizer to keep him calm. He just wouldn't stop shaking, poor thing. That crazy cat really upset him."

"Any news on Sally Claws?"

"They've apparently checked out and cleared most of the rooms on the first floor of the main house. Now they're working their way upstairs. What's funny is no one has heard either of them, not the cat or the canary."

"Well, let's hope they find the canary before that crazy cat does."

"Benji!" my mom scolded me, and motioned her head at Chef Larue. He burst into tears again.

"*Mais non!* What if that crazy cat found my beloved Genvieve? My heart, it cracks open with breaks." I mouthed to my mother that I didn't understand what he was saying, and she mouthed the words "He's heartbroken."

"I'm sorry, Chef Larue. I shouldn't have said that. I didn't mean anything by it. I have a tendency to joke in times of high stress. My doctor said it's what people call a coping mechanism. And I really and truly believe the search party will find Genvieve before the crazy cat does. I'm sure of it." Even as I said it, I was thinking it'd just be my dumb luck that Kimmie's crazy cat would find his bird first.

"So, Mom, do you need any help in here? Or can I go check on Elvis?"

"Well, I'm trying to learn how to make the president's baked Alaska dessert, but it's going a little slower than I would like because Pfeiffer was so hungry he couldn't think, and then I made him pancakes so he'd feel better. Now he's having problems concentrating because he's so worried about Genvieve."

"Baker's block! I had it for seven long years. I couldn't make one thing. It was broken when I got Genvieve and took this job. But now, now it's back. I don't think I can bake without her." Pfeiffer blew his nose long and hard as if to punctuate his thought.

My mom walked over and rubbed Chef Larue's back, which is what she does when I'm upset. "Don't you worry, it's all going to be just fine. You'll see."

My mom told me she was making a batch of cupcakes just in case the baked Alaska couldn't get made in time. She did have a little good news. Agent Daniels had reported that the president's last meeting went long, so he was now behind schedule, which bought us a little more time.

"Now you're all caught up, which means it's my turn. So, Benjamin Wendell Barnsworth, can you please tell me what exactly is going on here? Why on earth would that girl Kimmie show up with a crazy cat? Was it supposed to be for Taisy to cheer her up because of the tournament? Because that was hardly a cute white kitten."

"It's a really funny story, Mother, and I can't wait to tell you all about it, but I can't just sit here gabbing with you in the kitchen when I could be helping find

Genvieve. I'm going to get Elvis and we'll join the search. Maybe Elvis can find her using his sense of smell."

"Okay, you can go. But don't think I don't know what you're trying to do. You think I can't tell when you're avoiding telling me the truth?"

"You know, we should really listen to Agent Daniels and sidebar this convo for another time, okay, Mom? And did I tell you today how much I love you?" On my way out to see Elvis, I stopped right next to Chef Larue. "Chef Larue, I want to share with you something that's always helped me when I'm feeling low. Don't give up two minutes before the miracle. And breathe and believe."

"Breathe and believe? Who says this?"

"It's the underdog motto, and it really works."

"What is this underdog you speak of?"

"An underdog is the person you least expect to win, but you cheer for anyway. And sometimes, every now and again, they end up on top."

I found Elvis in a massive laundry room in the basement. Apparently it was one of the only rooms that had a bathtub big enough to fit him. He was almost done getting his blow-dry. I told the groomer how nice Elvis looked. And then I said I was taking him back upstairs. As we walked upstairs, I updated Elvis on everything.

"We have to find that canary, Elvis. Chef Larue can't bake without her, and since the president specifically requested the baked Alaska, I'm pretty sure we need to do everything possible to make sure that happens. The last thing I need is for Chef Larue to get in trouble. I'm pretty sure that if the president doesn't get what he asks for, it's not a good thing."

Elvis agreed that the first order of business was definitely finding Genvieve.

"I'm sorry we're going to have to put our own problems aside for now, and I'm really sorry in advance because our national treasure plan is falling apart. I'm also sorry we didn't have time to come up with a plan B. So . . ." My voice cracked a little.

"Don't worry about me, Benjamin. You are absolutely correct. Helping out the president by finding that canary is our first duty. Do we know if the canary is even still in the house? Or did she get outside?"

"Hey, can't you use your super nose to find the canary?"

"I'm a highly trained and extremely intelligent dog. But I have no special powers beyond just being more awesome than most others of my species. And normally, I could use my so-called super nose, but I can't quite bring up what she smells like, since I was first covered in dessert, and then shampooed and conditioned for the last half hour."

"I know! What if we asked Chef Larue what Genvieve's favorite treats are and we got some and started sprinkling them around the house? We could make a trail of birdseed and lead it right back to the kitchen."

"Well, look who's finally using his brain. Nice thinking, Benjamin. Kudos." Elvis looked at me with something close to admiration.

"Why, thank you, Watson."

"Whoa, whoa, whoa, what makes you think I'd be Watson? I'm definitely more the Sherlock Holmes type."

"Well, too bad, because I called dibs on Sherlock, so now you're stuck with Watson."

"First off, no one is 'stuck' with Watson. He's as important as Sherlock. He just doesn't get as much credit because he's more reserved and not as loud as Sherlock. So normally, I'd be more than happy to be Watson. All I'm asking is when did you call dibs on Sherlock?"

"Dibs on Sherlock. There. It just happened!" I said brightly, trying to not giggle.

"Those pajamas are too big for you, by the way."

"Don't be a sore loser. There was nothing else for me to wear. We can't all just be hosed off, you know."

We bickered all the way back to the kitchen. My

mom was talking to the head butler, and I noticed she looked rather pale.

"Hey, Mom, do you think there's a pipe around here that I can hold? Not to smoke, but just to hold. I'm Sherlock and Elvis is Watson. And I'm thinking if I looked the part, that might help me think better." My mom didn't say anything. "Mom, did you hear me? Hellooooo, Mom. Mom. Mom, Mom, Mommy, Mom, Mom, Mom!"

"What? I'm sorry, were you talking to me?" Finally she snapped out of it.

"What's going on?'

"The president had a big lunch, so he's talking about skipping his appetizer and just having his main course followed by his dessert. Time is running out, and we don't have any baked Alaska. Should I look up a different baked Alaska recipe and make that one instead? What should I do?"

"I thought you were going to give him your famous cupcakes instead."

"I was, as a backup, but if he specifically asked for the baked Alaska, I don't think I can go against a direct order from the president of the United States. You guys have got to find that bird and fast."

"We're trying. Do you have any birdseed around?

We're going to leave a trail for Genvieve. Maybe she's lost and can't find her way back."

Suddenly, I spotted some leftover bagels on the counter. I ran over and grabbed an everything bagel and a paper plate and scraped off all the stuff stuck to the bagel. I had to move fast. I was trying to focus on the president, but it was hard because I couldn't stop thinking about saving Elvis. How could we find the cat and the canary, and since there was no way we could get that cat into a tree, would a small canary stuck in a tree be the same thing? Hmm, probably not. And I don't know that many birds who get stuck in trees.

While I was thinking, the sound of cheering slowly made its way into the kitchen. A moment later, Mr. McDonald, Taisy, and Kimmie all walked in, grinning from ear to ear. They had successfully completed their mission. They'd found the crazy cat on the third floor.

"We got the cat!" Mr. McDonald said.

Apparently, Kimmie thought she heard a noise in one room, but they didn't find Sally Claws anywhere. Then Taisy came up with the idea of using her sound-effect phone apps. She used the one of a barking dog. And just like that, the cat ran out from under the bed and sprinted out the door. They chased her down the hallway to the very last guest bedroom, where they found the crazy cat front and center, clawing its way up some really tall curtains. The problem was that the curtains were silk (and probably extremely expensive), so they started tearing. The more Sally Claws scratched them, the more she tore them up. Soon a big piece of fabric tore loose, and the cat and the piece of curtain landed on the floor. While Sally Claws was tangled up in fabric, Mr. McDonald grabbed a large lampshade off a desk lamp and trapped the cat.

Apparently, Sally Claws did not take kindly to being trapped again. She started making noises that would wake the dead. Kimmie ran to get Agent Daniels, and he called in the animal control guys, who had thick uniforms and long, thick gloves that were impervious (just a little word I learned from Elvis) to angry crazy cat nails. They finally caught Sally Claws and put her in a cat crate.

Mrs. Chang-Cohen and the others heard the celebratory noise and walked back into the kitchen. Agent Quintana did not look happy. They couldn't find Genvieve. And, even more troubling, they hadn't found one trace of her, not even a feather.

"I came up with an idea that I really thought would work," said Alexander. "I found a video on YouTube of canaries singing that I played, hoping Genvieve would hear the other birds and fly back to investigate, and maybe make a new friend. But it didn't work."

"I thought it was a smart idea, myself," Agent Quintana added. "But I have to say I'm sort of at a loss on what to do next. We've systematically searched every room in the entire house." He looked over at Chef Larue, who didn't seem to be paying attention, and he lowered his voice. "Unfortunately, there were a few windows open at the time of the canary's escape, so there is a chance she may have gotten outside."

"But we have to be sure, so we'll just have to go back through every room again," Mrs. Chang-Cohen said. "Maybe we missed her."

"Well, I think it's going to be too late," Agent Daniels suddenly announced. "I just got a radio message that the president had a dinner tray sent to the Oval Office. One of the butlers is on his way now to pick up the baked Alaska that we don't have."

"Cupcakes it is then!" My mom threw up her hands. She put the cupcakes on a plate, sprinkled them with shaved chocolate, and carefully placed a few strawberry slices on the side for decoration. Then she wrote a note explaining to the president why he was getting cupcakes instead of baked Alaska and handed the note to the waiting butler.

"I must resign!" Chef Larue cried, putting his head in his hands. "If I don't have Genvieve, I can never bake again. And I will most certainly never make a baked Alaska. It will only remind me of the day I lost my poor Genvieve!"

No one knew what to say. Everyone just grabbed a stool and sat down. Even though we hadn't eaten dinner yet, my mom handed out cupcakes, and we all ate them in silence. I'm not sure how long we all sat around not really talking, but the mood just got worse and worse.

Agent Daniels and Agent Quintana left to go formulate a new action plan, and I felt bad that because of us their day had gotten much more stressful than they needed it to be. Another few minutes passed, and then we heard a deep voice behind us.

"Well, well, well, what's going on here? I've seen some real sorry sights in my days, but normally they are in Third World countries where they really have something to be glum about."

At the sound of his voice, we all turned around and there, standing right in front of us, was the president of the United States. He was wearing a dark-blue suit with a tiny flag pin on the lapel. He had on a red tie, and there was a white handkerchief sticking out of the top pocket of his jacket. He was actually shorter than he looked on TV, but he also looked much friendlier. There were two Secret Service agents standing right behind him. I thought how weird it must be to need security even when you happen to be walking around your own house.

No one knew what to say, so we just stared at him. Clearly he's used to people being speechless around him, so he just continued talking. "So, who do I owe my thanks to for tonight's delicious cupcakes? I have to admit that I wasn't really all that hungry, so I started with dessert first." Wow, clearly being president came with some spectacular perks. I've always wished I had the option of eating my dessert first.

My mom smiled and introduced herself, shaking his hand and bowing slightly. "It is an honor to bake for you, sir."

"These are the best cupcakes I ever had," the president said.

"That's very kind of you to say, sir," my mom said. She looked like she was calm, cool, and collected on the outside, but I knew on the inside she was jumping up and down with joy. It's one thing to have a normal person tell her she's the best cupcake maker ever, but it's out of this world to have the president of the country tell her. It was a moment she would never ever forget.

"I don't know what it is about reading over trade treaties, but they sure do make me crave sweets. Do any of you find that to be true?"

None of us said anything, because we weren't sure what to say. I was the first to laugh. "You guys, I think he's making a joke." The president nodded, and then everyone laughed. Whenever you think about the president of the United States, no one ever really talks about whether they have a good sense of humor.

"So, I hear we have a lost canary situation going on?"

"Mr. President, it's not just any canary who is lost, it's my Genvieve. She is gone, and now I am afraid I must resign. I cannot bake without my Genvieve."

"Well, I understand how you feel, Chef Larue. But let's not give up hope yet. From what I've heard, she hasn't been lost for a very long time. I'm still thinking we'll find her. Don't underestimate the smarts of my Secret Service guys. If anyone can find a lost canary, I'm sure it will be them. And if not, we can make sure you get another one."

"She is irreplaceable, I am afraid."

Chef Larue put his head in his hands again, and his white hat fell off. My mom caught it just in time. She stuck it back on his head.

24

The night that couldn't get any weirder kept getting weirder. After we were all properly introduced to the president, he asked for a glass of milk and another cupcake. Then he sat down with us like he was a regular person. I mean, sure, of course he's a regular person, but in a way he's just not the same as you or me.

It was even funnier how excited he was to meet Taisy's dad. Taisy's dad told him it was an honor to meet him.

"Well, the feeling is completely mutual, because it's an honor to meet you too. I want you to know I was a senator when you played in your last Super Bowl, and I called in sick to work and went to see you play instead."

"Really?" Taisy asked, "That's so cool you pretended to be sick. Whenever I try that, my mom always takes my temperature and if I don't have a fever, she sends me anyway." The president and Taisy's dad laughed, and she flushed a little with embarrassment. "Not that I pretend to be sick very often."

"I think everyone needs a day off from their lives every now and again. And seeing you catch that game-winning touchdown pass was definitely a moment I'll always remember," said the president. Now it was Mr. McDonald's turn to act like my mom—cool on the outside, but definitely freaking out on the inside, so much so that he didn't even know what to say back. So instead he just patted the president on the back.

When the president met Alexander Chang-Cohen and his mom, he told Alexander that one of his closest friends was also named Alexander, and he was a very good Scrabble player. Mrs. Chang-Cohen couldn't help but brag to the president that Alexander Chang-Cohen happened to be a pretty good Scrabble player himself. She said he was ranked second in the state of Pennsylvania for his age group. When she said it, I looked at

Taisy. Clearly, she didn't know about this either. Who knew Alexander Chang-Cohen still had a few tricks up his sleeve?

The president asked Alexander if he ever played Words with Friends on his phone, and Alexander said yes, he did, but he wasn't allowed to play with strangers. Only people he knew.

"Well, you know me now. Perhaps we could play sometime, if that's okay with your parents," the president said. Alexander Chang-Cohen looked at his mom, who grinned at him and nodded.

"I serve at the pleasure of the president, and I'll even let you win," said Alexander. Everyone laughed, but I knew he wasn't making a joke.

By the time we got to me, Agent Daniels was back with Agent Quintana. Agent Daniels told the president that I was the boy who'd first received Elvis when there was a mix-up. He even told him about the letters I wrote to Elvis. The president looked at me.

"Elvis is one of the best dogs I've ever known. He always makes quite an impression on people. Most recently the prime minister of Japan was here visiting, and he fell in love with him. He had a pretty amazing Newfie story himself," he said.

"Yes, I heard about that," I said.

"You did, and how is that?"

Uh-oh. Now I'd gone and done it. I needed to say something and fast. "It turns out our room service person at the hotel is dating one of your Secret Service agents, sir." There, that wasn't exactly a lie, because what I said was totally true, and it's not like I'm saying he's the one who told me that. I felt it was best to power through. "But I couldn't agree with you more, Elvis is really one amazingly awesome dog. You should put him on a stamp."

"I will look into that, Benji," the president said with a laugh.

"Did you hear that, Elvis?" I asked, turning to him. "Wouldn't it be amazing if you were on a stamp? It'd be pretty cool. That's something I've always wanted to be on too."

As I petted Elvis, he gave me a funny look, so I leaned in.

"What's up? Do you need to go outside?"

"Yes, but it's not for the usual reason. I have a hunch I know where Genvieve is." Then Elvis started barking.

"Don't worry, that's not his 'something's wrong' bark," I explained to everyone. "That's his excited bark. I think he might know where to find Genvieve." Elvis barked and thumped his tail once, which definitely

320

meant I was right.

"Well then, what are we waiting for? Let's go see," said the president. When the president speaks, who are we not to listen to him?

Elvis took off toward the side door, and we all followed. I heard the Secret Service agents tell the president to wait, but he refused.

"This I've got to see," he said.

Elvis was walking toward the back of the White House, where there was a large cage that had a huge Dumpster inside it. Elvis stood by the locked gate and barked and barked.

"I think he wants you to open the gate," I said.

Apparently, White House trash isn't picked up by regular garbagemen. It's burned so no one can go through it. One of the assistant butlers appeared with a key in seconds. I guess when the president is involved, everyone moves fast. The president is a busy guy, and no one wants to be the person who slows him down. It was getting pretty dark out, so I flipped on the flashlight on my phone, giving us a little bit of light.

Elvis walked through the open gate to the back of the Dumpster area. He barked again. I entered the cage and walked over to see what Elvis was barking at. Then I saw it. Genvieve's broken birdcage. A few of the bars were bent, but the door was still open. Suddenly, there was a tiny flash of yellow. Could it be? Was it really? I couldn't believe it.

"You guys! You're never going to believe this. Elvis found Genvieve. She's back here in her broken cage. When she got loose, she must have somehow gotten outside, and then somehow she managed to find her home again."

Agent Daniels and Agent Quintana picked up the broken birdcage with Genvieve in it, closed the broken door, and brought it back outside for everyone to see.

"I cannot believe a dog is smarter than me," Agent Quintana muttered.

"Trust me, Elvis is smarter than lots of people, but he thinks he's smarter than everyone," I said. It was pretty amazing to see Genvieve sitting on her perch in her broken birdcage. "Don't you worry, you pretty little thing. I'm sure you'll get a brand-new cage before you can whistle Dixie."

Even though it was Elvis who found her, everyone thought I should be the one to tell Chef Larue the good news. He was exactly where we'd left him, sitting at the counter with his head in his hands. Just as I was about to say something, Genvieve beat me to the punch and whistled a few notes. Chef Larue's head shot up so fast,

I'm surprised it stayed on his neck. He took one look at the cage and started to cry again. But this time, I knew he was crying because he was happy. When he heard that Elvis had found Genvieve, he knelt on the ground and kissed Elvis from cheek to cheek again and again and again. "I'm going to make you the biggest steak in the freezer!"

There was quite a celebration in the pastry kitchen. Chef Larue insisted on making crepes for everyone. My mom and Mr. McDonald helped him, while Mrs. Chang-Cohen worked on repairing Genvieve's cage door so it would close. The president stayed for just a few more minutes, and then he said his good-byes. He remembered all our names and told us each individually how happy he was to meet us. He even said we were welcome to come back anytime.

"You have certainly given me a much-needed reprieve from running the world. This is a night I won't soon forget."

We all nodded, because I'm pretty sure it was a night that none of us would ever forget either. Before he left, we got to take a group picture with him, and in the very center of the picture was Elvis next to Genvieve Larue's birdcage. The president waved good-bye again, but before he walked out the door, I couldn't help myself.

"Excuse me, sir, Mr. President?"

"Yes, Benji?" He turned around.

"I hope you forgive me if this is a little too forward, but I was thinking since Elvis is the one who found Genvieve, and now your pastry chef is staying on his job so you'll have your baked Alaska desserts, well, doesn't that make Elvis an extremely important asset to our country?"

"Yes, Benjamin, I do believe it does make Elvis extremely valuable to the country."

"So valuable that you would consider declaring him a national treasure and maybe putting him on a stamp one day?"

I figured there was no way I was ever getting on a stamp in my lifetime, but Elvis at least had a chance, and it's not like he could ask that for himself.

"The national treasure part I can absolutely do. The stamp he may have to wait on, because I'm getting on a stamp before my dog does." The President smiled and laughed at his own joke.

"And can we quote you on that, sir?"

"Yes, you can."

And then the president of the United States turned and walked away.

I threw my arms around Elvis's neck.

"See, you're a national treasure now. There's no way he can give you away."

Taisy and Alexander Chang-Cohen came running over and joined in on the group hug. We even invited Kimmie to join in, because in her own way, she'd helped make this all possible. When Kimmie left with her mom a little while later, I told her I'd miss her, which was weird because I hadn't known her for very long.

"Benji, it's been real," she said back, and then she patted my head like I was a dog.

"Real what?" I asked.

"It's been really fun meeting you and your cool friends. You're lucky to have them." And then she couldn't help it—she gave me a big hug, and not surprisingly she squeezed so tight it made me gasp a little.

"Kimmie!"

"Oops, sorry." She pulled back, and then she took off her lightbulb sunglasses and put them on me. "Here's a bright idea . . . never forget me."

Boy, you have to hand it to her, she really knew how to make every moment dramatic. I laughed. "Kimmie, I don't think I could forget you even if I tried."

By the time we left the White House that night after eating crepes and my mom's cupcakes, it was really late and most of us were falling asleep at the table. Mr. McDonald carried Taisy. My mom gently woke me, telling me to say good-bye to Elvis. Elvis clearly understood, and he licked my face good-bye. Neither one of us wanted to say the actual word "good-bye," so we didn't.

There were lots of hugs all around by the adults and promises that we'd come visit again in the summertime.

Chef Larue said if we gave him notice, he'd try again to make his famous baked Alaska. Or maybe he'd try out a new and exciting dessert.

"You know what? I never thought I'd ever say this, but perhaps we should skip dessert next time." My mom smiled. "Or at least skip the exciting dessert. I'm thinking for our next visit, boring might be the way to go."

25

When I woke up the next morning, I could have sworn the whole crazy day was just a dream, but then I rolled over and saw Ripley and the bandage on his mangled ear. I reached down and petted his back. He thumped his tail good morning, and I knew he'd be himself again soon. He had some scratches on his face, but he seemed better than I would be if I had been attacked by a crazy cat.

"Hey, Ripley, boy. I'm sorry about your war wound from Sally Claws. But you were brave to protect everyone from her. If your floppy soft ears didn't keep her busy, who knows what other damage she would have caused? You really took one for the team." I got out of bed and sat on the floor next to him and gave him an extra-long belly rub, which he enjoyed because he made happy noises deep in his throat.

We all packed up our room quickly and met Taisy and her dad down in the lobby. Taisy was carrying her big bouquet of balloons, so she was easy to spot. Our parents decided it was probably best to eat breakfast on the road, even though Taisy, Alexander Chang-Cohen, and I voted for one last room service meal (apparently three kids' votes do not equal three adult votes).

"No way, we're already getting on the road an hour later than we planned. I felt like everyone needed a little extra sleep after our late night at the White House." My mom grinned. "I don't think I'll ever get tired of saying that sentence. Oh, and by the way, Agent Daniels called to wish us a very safe drive home, and to let us know the president told him when we come and visit again, he wants us all to be his guests and stay in the White House."

Mrs. Chang-Cohen and my mom both grinned like

schoolgirls at the thought of it. Taisy's dad said next time he plans to bring a football, because he'd love to be able to say he tossed the ball around with the leader of the free world.

"That might be the only thing cooler than winning a Super Bowl," he said.

While the parents packed up the car, Taisy, Alexander Chang-Cohen, and I sat on the curb in front of the hotel and watched. We were all pretty quiet. Taisy spoke first.

"Hey, Benj, you okay?" I nodded, not sure if I could speak, because I really didn't want to cry.

I had done exactly what I came to do. Elvis needed my help, and I came here and gave it to him. Mission accomplished. Sure, it wasn't exactly how we planned it, but it all worked out just the same. Kimmie had promised she'd make sure her mother would follow up with the president and get it on record that he officially declared Elvis a national treasure. And I promised to keep in touch with her too. She also said she'd keep an eye on Elvis for me.

I swallowed hard, took a deep breath, and finally found my words. I thanked Taisy and Alexander Chang-Cohen for all their help and told them there was no way I could have done it without them.

"We are a team, Team Underdogs!" I smiled. "Now and forever."

It was Alexander who noticed the motorcade. He elbowed me and stood up to get a better look. When the president travels, there are lots of cars and police traveling with him. Let's just say it's an impressive sight. The motorcade turned up the street, and it looked like they would drive right past our hotel. We walked out farther to get a better look. Then, instead of passing the hotel, the entire motorcade slowed down and stopped.

The three of us just stood, completely silent. A moment later, the limo door opened and the president got out. He was flanked on all sides by some really scary-looking Secret Service guys. I guess he needed two when he walked around his house, but outside he needed at least six. Anyway, the president appeared to be holding something in his hands. I couldn't tell what it was. As he walked closer, I saw he was holding a balloon. It was all crumpled and almost out of helium, but I read the words CONGRATS. Tied to the long red ribbon was a note. I couldn't believe it. The president of the United States was holding the very balloon I'd let off the hotel roof with my wish tied to the end.

The president's a busy guy, so he didn't have time for greetings. He just got right to the point.

"Every morning I wake up early, and I like to walk around the Rose Garden alone, just because it's so quiet and it gives me a little time to myself. And this morning, stuck among the tulips, I found this balloon with a note tied to the end of it. Well, it wasn't just a note. It was actually a wish. And do you know what it says?"

Taisy and Alexander Chang-Cohen silently shook their heads no. They didn't know what it said because I had never told them.

"Benjamin, do you want to say it or should I read it?"

I opened my mouth to speak, but no words came out.

"'This is my balloon wish, and even though I know I'm supposed to make a general wish that would work for anyone who may find this, I can't, not today,'" the president read from the paper. "'Because my one wish, my only wish, is that my first dog, Elvis, who I love with all my heart, would come home to me. Signed, Benjamin Wendell Barnsworth of Wyncote, PA (but who is currently staying at the Hay-Adams Hotel in DC, which I highly recommend because they have the best room service in the country).'" The president paused for a moment and then continued, "It's my understanding that the way these balloon wishes work is if a person finds it, they get the other person's wish, but if an angel finds it, then they grant the person who made the wish their wish. Is that correct?"

I nodded and tried not to cry. The president was right. He got my wish, so he should be the one to keep Elvis after all. "Yes, sir, you are correct. That is the way balloon wishes work, according to Alexander Chang-Cohen. He's really smart, so I'm sure it's true."

"Benjamin, as the president of the United States I have a lot of powers, and one of them is that I can break the balloon wish rules if I choose to do so. It may even be in the Constitution in the small print that no one bothers to read. Anyway, it's just one of the many perks of the job. And frankly, I'm not sure I'm really breaking the rules, because when you think about it, it's pretty unbelievable that I would be the one to find your balloon wish at all. The chances are probably one in a billion. So what I'm thinking is that an angel did find your balloon and just chose me to be the one to deliver your wish. And I want you to know, it's my honor to do so."

The president whistled, and Elvis jumped out of the car and trotted over and stood by him. He held his chin up high and looked right at me. I think if dogs could smile and wink, he absolutely would have done it now. Instead, he just opened his mouth a little and a big drool strand dropped out, and I wondered if he was drooling with excitement not for food, but for me.

"But sir, Elvis is such an extraordinary dog. He deserves to be with you, in someplace extraordinary, like the White House."

"Yes, he is an extraordinary dog, a national treasure, in fact, but I'm pretty sure that the someplace extraordinary he should be living is at home with you. Isn't that right, Elvis?"

Elvis barked once, held out his paw for the president to shake, and then trotted over and gave me a big face lick, and the strand of drool stuck to my shirt.

"Elvis, are you sure about this?" I leaned in and whispered to him.

"Positive. But I get dibs on Sherlock."

"Deal."

"So I guess that leaves me with Ripley the one-eared Labrador?" the president said. "Come here, Ripley. We'll get you a nice new collar and no one will even notice your weird ear."

Ripley looked at me, and I nodded, squatted down, and gave him a big hug, carefully avoiding touching any of his scratches. "Go on, Ripley. Thanks for everything. You really are a great dog. I love you, and be sure to take care of the president." And just like that Ripley walked over to the president of the United States. The president leaned down and petted Ripley, whispering in his ear. We watched them both get in his limo, waving good-bye as the motorcade pulled away.

And that's how I got my dog Elvis back. I know, it's a crazy story. But like they say, it's so crazy it has to be true.

Jenny Lee is a writer and producer on the TBS sitcom *Ground Floor*. She was also a writer and producer of the Disney Channel's number-one-rated kids' show *Shake It Up* for all three seasons and is the author of four humor essay books. *Elvis and the Underdogs* was Jenny's first book for children. She lives in Los Angeles with her 110-pound Newfoundland, Doozy (and yes, it's a toss-up as to who's walking whom every day).